IT TAKES A CORPORATION
TO RAISE A CHILD

SARINA M. SINGHI

PublishAmerica

Baltimore

First printing

ISBN: 1-4137-3287-9
PUBLISHED BY PUBLISHAMERICA, LLLP
www.publishamerica.com
Baltimore

Printed in the United States of America

For all those who read...and dream....

TABLE OF CONTENTS

Chapter 1:   An Uneasy Beginning   7

Chapter 2:   A Rumble in the Strip   18

Chapter 3:   Mr. Mysterious—A Too-Perfect Blond   27

Chapter 4:   Keep My Nose Where?   37

Chapter 5:   Not a *Little* Q & A   41

Chapter 6:   *I* Have That Effect on *Him*…Right?   52

Chapter 7:   A Tearful Trip to The Galaxy   66

Chapter 8:   Mother Knows…Business   81

Chapter 9:   The Happy (?) Couple   86

Chapter 10:   Smooth Transit, Rough Transition   90

Chapter 11:   Out of the Mouths of Babes   107

Chapter 12:   Some Kinda Soccer   122

Chapter 13:   The Lay of the Land, and, What *is* in a Name   133

Chapter 14:   Out of the Mouths of Old Fogies   143

Chapter 15:   My Secret Desire   156

Chapter 16:   A Return to Product Life   164

Chapter 17:   Daughter-Enforced Mother-Daughter Chat   178

Chapter 18:   The "Doctor" Is *In*   183

Chapter 19:   The Gathering Cast   188

Chapter 20:   New Beginnings   211
                         (What Else, in the Last Chapter?)

CHAPTER 1
AN UNEASY BEGINNING

As they caught the jetliner back to their other lives, Liz wondered what would become of her. She was different now; she even had a name. "Liz." A name she would have to conceal. A lot she would have to conceal.

But conceal from whom? Who in corporate America even cared what went on inside her head? In Flagstaff, she was a person. In New York, she was a product.

When they were securely 3,000 miles above the ground, she took George's hand in hers, felt the nascent callouses on his palm. She wanted to kiss him again, not because she wanted to kiss him, but because it was the only thing that would calm her down right now, that could occupy her so completely that her thoughts and worries wouldn't stand a chance against it. He smiled at her distractedly and looked back out the window. Liz sighed internally but didn't dare let it be heard.

"Mommy, what's that?" A high-pitched voice drew her away from her companion's profile. A boy, about five or six, tapped on the window beside him three aisles behind to the left. He wore a navy blue pinstripe suit with "Vindyne—talk for life" emblazoned on it, surrounded by images of manicured hands of all sizes holding cell phones and disembodied smiling lips at the receivers. He divided his time between the window and the woman to the other side of him, dressed similarly, who must have been "Mommy." She clacked quickly at her laptop keyboard, pausing every few seconds for some new piece of data on the monitor to direct her next strokes. "Mommy, what's that?" he repeated. "What city is that? Is that a river?" After a few minutes of this, the boy's gaze laid longer and longer on Mommy every time she didn't respond, until he was staring at her, his mouth open and eyes down at the edges. Liz turned back from the scene, her heart in a vise. She saw everything she hated there, everything she had earned a right to despise. As she slipped her hand free, a plan began to emerge.

*****

"Woo-hoo!" The sound undulated through the auditorium in waves, silver and black pom-poms shaking beside pretty young faces at the foot of the stadium seating. Speakers shook with the beat of the music. The young dancers before the crowd spun with precision, deftly transitioned into high kicks and pyramid formations without losing a measure of their ordained cheer. Though their short pleated skirts and tight tank-tops displayed the Gatelink Computing and Software, Inc. logo, everyone knew they were hired from an agency. Though they obviously found it an effective complement to the speakers, the company would never have its own students waste their time on cheerdancing.

"Thank you, thank you." Cheers from the thousand or so students ages five through eighteen who filled the large room always peaked when the speaker arrived. Usually it was a mid-level executive of the company, sometimes a hired motivational speaker, if the company was implementing a difficult change, and once in a while, an upper-level exec. In those days, you came to school even if you were sick.

A woman who looked to be in her thirties strode up to the podium in a power suit, red with the words "Socrates: Clarification Specialists" imprinted tastefully in small print in several places. As she began to speak, Gatelink Jones's friend, Easycalc, leaned over to her in the tenth row, reserved for their class.

"She must be here to help us with the new grading policy," he tilted his head towards Gatelink and whispered. He was close enough that she could smell a scent wafting out from him.

"Yeah, hopefully she'll say something about the new salary policies too, because I'm curious about that," she whispered back. "Hey, are you wearing cologne?"

Their other friend, Tablesoft, leaned towards Gatelink, pressing slightly against Easycalc with her shoulder to move in closer. "It's aftershave," she declared with a knowing glance. Gatelink raised her eyebrows and nodded in mock approval. She turned forward again to the speaker, now holding up a graph of some sort. *Why does she always know this stuff before I do?* she thought.

"As you can see, grading was in the past based on project results and the time in which they are completed. Under the new grading system, project complexity will also be taken into account...."

"She kinda sucks," Easycalc said in low voice.

"Yeah," Tablesoft agreed. "I like her suit, but that guy last week was a lot better." The exec who led the motivational assembly the week before hadn't used graphs or strode around like this speaker, but had spoke with a boldness that made the students catch their breath.

"All of you are symbols of this fine corporation," he had announced. "You are our ambassadors. You enjoy a privilege that none before you have had the fortune to know. Because you were chosen by Gatelink Computing and Software, Incorporated for this competitive position, you have lifetime job security. Should you choose to leave us, of course, you may...but you know that as long as you work as hard for us as we do for you, you have a lifetime to look forward to here." At this, he shook his head with envy at the young crowd and declared, "I tell you, you don't know how *good* you *have* it!"

As the assembly wore on, Gatelink gazed around at the rows in front of her. Most of the students wore dark colors in approved Gatelink-logo clothing with matching images of computer monitors or software initial screens, depending on the product goals. She knew that if she saw any of her schoolmates after the end of the workday, the clothes might be more casual but would always be Gatelink; that was a policy. The first rows of the seating were reserved for the top students in each class. They presented a spectrum of functioning: the first three were the pre-productive years—mastering the alphabet, reading, numbers, math; then, in the productive years, data entry and formatting gave way to market analysis and, finally, all the different levels of programming. The first in her class to be put on programming, Gatelink knew that if she turned around, she would see kids in her year still on data entry. They were the ones the company was probably not going to try too hard to keep.

"—now the grading system was much different in my day, of course, and we didn't think to question it then, but now you all can reap the benefits of the enlightened educators we have today. So best of luck with the new system, and enjoy!" At this, the students rose in ceremonial closure applause.

"What did she mean, that the grading system was different in her day?" Tablesoft asked Easycalc and Gatelink. "They still got paid for performance, right? How different could it have been?"

"Yeah, that is interesting," Gatelink agreed. "That makes me a little curious, too. I think I'm going to ask her."

"That's cool. Let us know what she says, hey?"

"No prob." Gatelink made her way against the crowd down towards the podium and the speaker whose suit was more exciting than her talk for the answer to a question that vaguely itched her now. When she got there, she found she had to wait; Achievelink Cho, a boy a year behind her and very smart, was already engaged in a personal conference with the speaker as he did with most of them. She stood back a few feet and pulled her Palm Assistant out of her bag while she waited. When she saw him leave through the corner of her eye, she moved forward a little. She could tell she'd have to wait a few more moments, though; she had been so discreet that the speaker was now conversing with a company exec to the left of the podium.

"Poor kids," Gatelink heard her saying. "Ya know, I think it's great that they're starting productivity so much earlier, don't get me wrong, but god, sometimes I think it's a little too much. Especially when you see a kid like that—what, fourteen, fifteen years old? And good-looking, too. He should be thinking about girls, or how to get his hands on some beer, or something," the speaker laughed, "not how to work promotions. I mean, 'cos I do this all the time, ya understand, sometimes I look at these kids and it just kinda breaks my heart. I mean, they don't even have na—" Gatelink could see why the speaker had stopped short. The executive she was talking to was looking hard past her shoulder at Gatelink now, who kept her head buried in her Palm Assistant, scribbling on it with her digital pen.

"Oh, yes, um." The speaker cleared her throat. "I'm sorry, there. Did you have a question, too?" Gatelink was surprised she could remember her intended question and stammered it, the exec eyeing her with guarded suspicion. "Oh, no," the speaker answered blithely. "No, I didn't mean very different at all. No, it was just about the same, actually. Just that the criteria for performance was different. And of course, I went to a speaker school, so we were graded more on, uh, speaking abilities and such." A smile too tight at the edges punctuated this sentence and indicated it would be the last in the conversation. "So I'm sorry if I caused you any confusion about that. Was there anything else you were wondering?"

"No, thank you." Gatelink turned and left. She didn't doubt she wouldn't be seeing this speaker at the school again.

Word snippets echoed in her ears as if they were spoken in the empty hallways as she made her way late to her classroom. "Poor kids." "It's a little too much." "Not how to work promotions." "Kinda breaks my heart." "They don't even have na—" *What was she going to say?* Gatelink wanted to know. *Don't even have names?* What could she mean by that? Of course they had names, and important ones, too. Gatelink's revealed her status at the top of the hierarchy, in a way— she knew her parents had been chosen to have their child be the one to represent the whole corporation, not just a software application or some other product goal. It's true that her parents had "old" names that didn't represent anything, but that wasn't because they wanted it that way, it's just that naming had started only twenty years before, and it was more efficient to name children for longer project life. "Not how to work promotions": did people not used to think this way? "Breaks my heart"? Why would she say that? The digital plaque along a wall marking room 402 interrupted the slow congregation of Gatelink's thoughts, and it was not unwelcome.

The classroom was quiet. Had anyone looked up, they would have seen her enter with a frown, but no one did. Heads were bowed over keyboards, fingers clicking quickly against them. The teacher, Ms.

McUthrie, motioned for Gatelink to go to her station. Gatelink guessed that there was a surprise exam, the biggest fear for the kids in Gatelink-Manhattan's tenth grade. Classes were tough, and kids were expected to do well. That's what they got paid for.

As Gatelink slid into her seat and eased onto her mouse, she glanced over at Easycalc, a few rows away. He raised his head in her direction, his curly brown hair bouncing up with the suddenness of the movement, his green eyes afire with caffeine and adrenaline. He smiled fast and returned to his typing. Gatelink glanced next to her at Tablesoft's still-lowered dirty blonde hair. *She's so engrossed in the exam, she didn't see me come in,* Gatelink guessed.

The quiz was on Linear Algebra. There were straight numerical problems, and some word problems: "If you bought so much of such-and-such, then a new and better product came out which offered such-and-such level of increased value, but cost more, what ratio of the two goods would give you an increased utility-to-cost ratio?" and so on. Gatelink found the word problems tedious, but didn't mind the numerical problems too much.

"Time's up, people," Ms. McUthrie said after about ten minutes. The class all appreciated that she called them "people" instead of "children." They didn't know that it was Gatelink C & S, Inc. policy that teachers' interactions with the students were structured, down to the approved salutations for each class year. Gatelink C & S, Inc. had hired educational and child psychology experts to design the school. Gatelink had a plan, and knew how best to accomplish it, just like the other corporations with their own progeny. Knowing how to achieve their goals was how these companies got to the top and stayed there.

"Aaaarh!" came the collective groan, inevitably. It was policy to never give students enough time to finish a test comfortably. But the computers clicked off. Gatelink Computing and Software, Incorporated kids were very obedient.

The school day progressed through a Corporate History lesson, physics, more math, programming, and, at last, lunch. Gatelink sat as usual with her friends Tablesoft and Easycalc.

"I like your shirt, Tablesoft," Gatelink started.

"Oh, you do? Thanks," Tablesoft responded slickly. Her eyes darted almost imperceptibly down to the bright blue fitted top with muscular, mostly-naked men and the Gatelink C & S, Inc. logo on it strategically placed to emphasize the smallness of her breasts. Though she'd never asked, Gatelink knew and envied that Tablesoft's parents had funded the reduction. "I knew everybody else would like it. The kind of shirt you wish you'd seen first, isn't it?"

Gatelink and Easycalc traded a wide-eyed glance as Tablesoft turned her attention to opening her lunch case and to flipping back her long, wavy hair. As long as they'd known and been friends with Tablesoft, the arrogant answers she sometimes gave still surprised them. They seemed to be happening more frequently lately, too. "She doesn't do it on purpose; she's just…clueless," Easycalc and Gatelink had agreed once. Satisfied with this explanation, they were content to diffuse these situations with knowing looks at each other, unspoken understanding. In a way, Gatelink was glad for Tablesoft's uncomfortable trait since it gave her and Easycalc something just their own, like a secret. It made them complicit.

"So, did you guys see that episode of *White Star* last night?" Easycalc asked. The conversation turned there for a while. When that topic had been exhausted, Gatelink hesitatingly brought up something they were all wishing she wouldn't.

"So, what do you guys think about my idea about us petitioning to make them let us do a school play?" She waited for a response. "I read about one in this book—they sound like everybody has a lot of fun. It's just like a TV show, except we do all the acting and everything ourselves. I've got some great ideas for a script."

"Gatelink, you already asked, and they said no, don't you remember?" Tablesoft spoke. "Why would they change their mind? And besides, we have TV. What would be the point of a 'play'? Sounds kinda lame to me."

"Yeah, and you know, I gotta say," Easycalc did say, "their reasoning did make a lot of sense. I mean, how's 'playing' gonna help us to learn how to make money when we're done with school—there's no money in 'art,' that's why nobody does it anymore. It's not gonna contribute to product development and improve our lives or anything like that. It's useless. It's because of backward stuff like that that it took us so long to advance as a society, to have things like "The Shield" and "Hair-Makers," and better clothes than people used to have. There's a good reason no one wastes time on that kind of stuff anymore."

Blood rushed to Gatelink's face as if coming to her defense. It wasn't that she disagreed with Easycalc, but she had wanted him to agree with her. His opinion had come to mean more to her lately. She considered Easycalc to be the smartest, coolest boy she knew. Lately she had been catching his eyes on her in random moments during class, and her stomach would knot in on itself. She would start to feel her heart beating in her head and she'd have to stare down at her desk and bite the inside of her mouth to get herself focused on the lecture again. She told herself she was being stupid, that he would never think of her like that, but her brain never seemed to get those messages to her other organs.

"Maybe," she said quietly, and took another bite of her anchovy sandwich.

"Gatelink, I know how you can be when you get your...ideas, and I'm telling you for your own good," Tablesoft said. "You should really just forget about this. I don't know why you keep reading those *books*, anyway," she added in a low voice that was almost a hiss through her whitened teeth. "I'm sure it's not good for you, Gatelink; it's not normal—we keep telling you."

Gatelink looked into her sandwich, counted the anchovies. She delivered a quick, tight smile in Tablesoft's general direction.

"Speaking of ideas, what do you think of my new haircut?" Easycalc said lightly in his what-a-bad-transition-isn't-it-funny-aren't-I-clever tone of voice. "My dad said I look just like him now, and then my mom came in a few minutes later and she said it looked awful!" He laughed infectiously.

When class resumed after lunch, Gatelink was still mulling over the roots of that lunchtime discussion. She had put in a request a few weeks ago, via memorandum to the School Board, and been told that even the request for permission to put on a play was inappropriate.

"We pay for your education because you represent our fine corporation. You should be focused on how best to fulfill this privileged role, Gatelink Computing and Software, Incorporated Jones, rather than conjuring up ways to squander your and your classmates' time." Hurt and confused when she received the reply memo, Gatelink was able to convince herself that what she had suggested was somehow wrong, bad. But when she thought about it, logically, she couldn't see why it would be. She simply had a suggestion regarding something students could do for fun in their spare time—she wasn't asking to detract from class time. The Board's reaction didn't make sense to her. *They didn't even give me an explanation,* she thought, *which isn't like the Board. They're logical—they're supposed to explain.* Finally she resolved the matter with a shrug. *It's no big deal. I was just curious. There are more important things to think about. Like the programming test I have next week.*

The school day ended at 5:00 p.m., as usual, and the students lined up single file at the back of the room to punch out their timecards. None of the children had after-school jobs—it was forbidden by the firm: it would cast a negative light on the company, the students were told. Besides, none of them needed to earn extra money.

Officeworks Hayes bounded up to Gatelink, Tablesoft and Easycalc, who had regrouped after the punching-out ritual. "A bunch of us are going to shop—do you guys wanna come?" she bubbled. Gatelink narrowed her eyes at her classmate's unprecedented effervescence toward them. Officeworks was blonde, beautiful, and always expensively dressed. Though she was hardly the highest-paid student, it was well-known that her parents had advanced far beyond any of her classmates' parents; great things were expected of her despite her poor grades. She'd been heard to remark famously that with what her parents had taught her about how to get ahead in the company, she didn't need good grades. She also didn't need good manners, it seemed, because the possibility of this secret knowledge rubbing off kept people vying for her attention through all manner of slights and insults. Officeworks was the most scandalous, and envied, girl in school; she was the one everyone hated to admit they secretly wanted to be.

"Yeah, sure," Tablesoft stepped forward and smiled broadly back at Officeworks, without consulting or even looking at her friends. "Should we meet you somewhere?"

"We're going to The Strip. Why don't you guys meet us there? We'll be in Lambert's," Officeworks told them.

"Cool," Tablesoft said, shrugging her shoulders and obviously trying hard to sound offhand. Officeworks smiled and turned and walked away. Tablesoft stood, watching Officeworks' retreat, still smiling. Gatelink and Easycalc, behind their pal, felt free to raise their eyebrows to each other in surprise and a little frustration.

"Umm, Tablesoft..." Easycalc began.

"Mmm...what?" she snapped.

"I don't know if we should be doing this," Gatelink said. "If it's such a good idea."

"What are you talking about?" Tablesoft replied. "It's just shopping; what's wrong with shopping? What *could* be wrong with shopping? Shopping's great."

"Of course nothing's wrong with shopping. It's just that—" Easycalc paused. "Well, you know how the company feels about students 'going out' on school nights."

Tablesoft nodded. "'It's an affront to your educational experience, and may be taken as a negative image for the firm,'" she quoted verbatim from the handbook.

"Most impressive, Tablesoft," Easycalc said, both he and Gatelink nodding their approval.

"Yeah, but this is just one time," Tablesoft retorted. "That policy refers to *frequent* going out on school nights. There is *no* policy about going out just once." Tablesoft flashed her most endearing, charming smile at Gatelink and Easycalc. "And so we, my good friends, my *great* friends, my *best* friends, have no reason not to go out and have a great time shopping with our fellow classmates tonight."

Gatelink felt she had to smile back—Tablesoft could have that effect on people when she wanted to—but she did let escape a small sigh of exasperation before saying, "Okay, okay," with a slight shake of her head and a roll of her eyes. "You win."

16

"Same here," Easycalc said.

"When I win, we're *all* winners," Tablesoft replied. "And I wouldn't have it any other way."

They headed to The Strip.

CHAPTER 2
A RUMBLE IN THE STRIP

The Strip was crowded, as usual. Internet, TV, catalogs—so many other ways to shop and people still packed into The Strip, day after day, looking for a better watch, or blouse, or belt, at a better price. Science had proved years ago that you had to replace your wardrobe every two months; after that amount of time, clothing and jewelry began to emit harmful rays, or catch some dangerous viruses, or something like that—everyone knew the danger but no one could remember the specifics. The fact that clothing shopping was a necessity made it no less of a sport, however.

Everyone at The Strip was wealthy, it seemed, if you looked around. Everybody wore expensive dark-colored pants with designer names and logos patched all around them, and shirts with the same names and photographs of beautiful, high-class models. No one wore the cheaper brand names, with pictures of plain or mousy models, unairbrushed and unperfected. The Strip was a place to achieve shopping mastery, but that was only one of its allures. As the almost painfully erect torsos and jutting hips attested to nightly, The Strip was also a place to be seen for who you were, or wanted to be—a success.

Likewise, Gatelink, Easycalc and Tablesoft had returned home to change into their most expensive attire, upon Tablesoft's insistence. When they stepped into The Strip, the other two friends were grateful for her request.

The Strip was not a place kids often went without their parents. Built of marble and fourteen-karat gold, with occasional patterns of inlaid diamonds in the walls, it was an arena for serious-minded shoppers, big spenders. The threesome had an idea that they might buy a few accessories, a nice belt, or scarf. Beyond that would be beyond their personal means. Nonetheless, it was fun to look, and they believed this to be the main purpose of this extra-curricular gathering.

"Lambert's," Tablesoft declared when their feet had barely cleared the threshold of the mall.

"Right," said Gatelink, and the three made their way past stores of leather goods, jewelry and apparel with the determination of returned explorers on the way to meet their queen.

Officeworks was already there, with four friends. Two of them were from Gatelink Computing & Software, Inc.: a plump red-headed girl, Papersaver Wells, and a scrawny olive-skinned boy with tight hips named Gatelink-Pentium Perkins. The two blonde, small-breasted girls with them were not familiar, but looked remarkably like each other. The five were looking together at a dark brown leather jacket near the front of the store.

"Hey guys, glad you could make it!" Officeworks called out, waving to them, smiling. "I was starting to think you might have...*chickened out*."

"What do you mean?" Tablesoft asked, her face squinting, though they were getting closer to the five, not farther away.

"You know," Gatelink-Pentium quipped. "Scared. Chicken. Chickened out. Haven't you ever heard that old expression?"

"What Tablesoft *meant* is why would we have any reason to be 'scared'?" replied Easycalc.

"And why do you think I said 'chicken' instead of 'scared'?" Officeworks retorted. "Why do you think I invited you three here?" They were all face-to-face by now. "You're not exactly in my social class, you know. But I thought you could help me and my friends to break the boredom." She paused. "It can be so monotonous having it all." She turned toward her friends and stretched her arms out and yawned, for effect. She got the laughs she was so obviously pawing for.

"What the hell are you talking about, Officeworks?" Gatelink said.

"There's no need to get nasty, Gatelink," Officeworks said. "You and Easycalc and Tablesoft there are usually such quiet, *dull* creatures.

I'd hate to see you all worked up. You might actually be *interesting* or something, and that would just be too weird!" The groupies snickered. The threesome's mouths fell open just enough to be noticeable.

"Oh, can't think of a clever response?" she mocked them. "*Why* am I *not* surprised?" she looked back at her group again. They didn't miss their cue to cackle.

"C'mon, guys, let's go," Gatelink said to her friends. They started to turn around, to leave.

"I don't think you guys should do that," Officeworks said to them.

"Oh really. And why's that?" Easycalc said.

"Well, for one thing, the rest of *our* evening might be pretty boring." The Officeworks group nodded in mock sobriety, their eyebrows cocked for effect. "And for another, I happen to know that you three were discussing that stupid idea of 'having a play' at lunch today, even though the Board told you not to waste their educating you on such a stupid thing. I would think that they'd be *pretty* unhappy to know that you three are still obsessing about something they told you *off* for, and told you to *forget* about." The tormentor began to circle her prey slowly, her arms crossed authoritatively across her chest, heels clacking methodically against the cool marble floor. "I would think they would be so unhappy that they might even decide it's not worth educating you anymore at *all*! I expect the only reason they haven't tossed you out *yet* for that *bizarre* request, Gatelink, is that you're so damn *smart*." She paused. "But that will take you only so far. If you don't keep me and my friends occupied today, well, we might just wander over back to Headquarters, to the Board's office, and find some *other* way to keep ourselves amused."

Three jaws went slack again, while those of their adversaries lifted in whooping laughter, along with high-fives. A full minute passed in this way.

At last, Gatelink asked Officeworks, "What exactly do you want from us?"

"I had *asked* you why I used the word 'chicken.'" She paused again, arms crossed, eyebrows raised. "No? Well, I'm sure you've heard about that really old game called 'chicken,' where two cars race toward a cliff, or each other, and the first to stop is the chicken, and loses. The winner is the side that goes all the way." Another pause.

"What I want from *you* is to play you in chicken."

"Here?" asked Tablesoft, the first she had spoken since Officeworks dropped her mask.

"Of course, *here*," was Officeworks' retort. And surprisingly, that was all she needed to say. Gatelink, Tablesoft and Easycalc picked up on her meaning right away. She wasn't talking about playing with cars; she was talking about playing with cards—credit cards. The three looked at each other uncertainly. Their rivals began to whoop again.

"Or, of course, we can all just head back to Headquarters," Officeworks said, when she had calmed down enough to speak.

Gatelink turned to Tablesoft and Easycalc, and motioned for them to come with her, several yards away from Officeworks and her hyenas. They did.

"You guys don't have to do this," Gatelink said to them. "I'm the one who made that request. I'm the one who brought it up at lunch today. You guys just shot it down, that's all; there's nothing wrong with that. I'm the only one who stands to get into trouble, and so, I'm the only one who should have to play Officeworks' stupid game."

"Are you on crack?" Easycalc almost cut her off. "We're your friends. We're not gonna just leave you here with that…creep."

"Yeah," said Tablesoft. "What one of us is in, all of us are in, together," she quoted one of the company's internal mottoes with an emphatic nod of the head.

Gatelink smiled. Tablesoft had a way of applying the firm proverbs at just the right moments. "I still think you guys should leave, but…thank you so much for staying!" She hugged them both, one with each arm.

"Well?" Officeworks bellowed.

"Okay, *Hayes,*" Easycalc sneered back. "You've got a game." The three walked back to face their foes.

"Are there some kind of…rules?" Gatelink asked. Surprisingly, the Officeworkers did not laugh. They seemed to have become very serious all of a sudden, now that the game was to begin. Gatelink wondered if they might be starting to repent their rudeness.

"Yeah," spoke up one of Officeworks' unfamiliar cronies, never introduced. This was okay, however, since Gatelink and her friends had no desire to be better acquainted with any of that bunch. They listened with hard faces. "The first team spends a certain amount, a *high* amount, and the second has to spend the same amount or higher. Then we go to the next store, and the same thing, except the minimum amount in the second store is the highest amount from the last store. And the game goes on until one side, um—she cleared her throat— BAWCK, BAWCK, BA-A-AWCK, BAWCK, B-BAWCK, BAAWCK, BAAAAWCK!" Now the fivesome hooted again, to Gatelink's chagrin. The threesome narrowed their eyes. It was assumed they would chicken out, and they didn't like it.

"And," said Officeworks, "each side burns the other side's receipts as soon as we leave the store, so you can't wimp out and go return the stuff the next day." She looked proud of herself for coming up with this by-law. Else, she was drawing pleasure from the growing discomfort of her opponents, so visible that it had begun to draw stares from the painfully erect passers-by.

"So, where do we start?" Easycalc asked, aware that they were asking too many questions, giving Officeworks and her followers all the power. But then again, it was such a stupid thing they were about to do, maybe it was better not to have made any of the decisions in the situation, for their own self-respect.

"Oh…here," was Officeworks' reply, riddled with condescension.

"And I suppose you guys go first?" said Tablesoft.

"And have five people when we only have three?" added Easycalc.

Officeworks smiled cunningly. "It wouldn't be much fun if it were completely fair, now would it?" She paused, yet again. Gatelink was starting to get annoyed at the girl's drama. "Of course *we'll* go first. But no, we won't go five on three—in each store, two of us will abstain."

Gatelink and her friends realized that this was still not even, since the two abstainers could alternate. However, it was more acceptable than the alternative.

"And if we play this game with you," Easycalc said, "what guarantee do we have that you won't go to the Board tomorrow, or whenever else, with what you heard today?"

Gatelink smiled secretly. She knew Tablesoft was helping her too, and she should feel equally appreciative to both her friends, but she felt like Easycalc was not just helping but *protecting* her. She liked the feeling, even in this unpleasant situation.

"'*If*?'" Officeworks retorted. "Well, '*if*' you play this game, *our* game, I guarantee that none of us will ever go to the Board with what I heard after today. I promise."

Easycalc looked suspiciously at the five hyenas. "You all promise?" he asked.

"Yeah. Sure, man," they replied, shuffling their feet or looking at their watches. "Can we just get on with the game?" Officeworks' entourage exaggerated all their statements with body language, as if afraid that their words wouldn't suffice and loathe to let down their leader.

"What do you think?" Easycalc asked quietly aside to Gatelink and Tablesoft.

"We say," Tablesoft said, after conferring with Gatelink via glance, "let the games begin!"

The game began. In Lambert's, Officeworks' team spent $1800 on a dress suit for Officeworks and a silk shirt for Papersaver. They spent only fifteen minutes shopping.

Gatelink and her friends huddled while Officeworks and Papersaver stood in line to purchase their items.

"What are we going to do?" Tablesoft moaned. "I mean, $1800! Headquarters only pays us $300 a week!" Gatelink didn't mention that she got $500 since her raise when they put her on programming.

"My credit line goes up to $2500," she said gravely. "And I think I should be the one going into debt here, not you guys."

"My credit line's $3,000, and didn't you hear what I said before?" Easycalc said. "We're in this together."

"My line's $2800," Tablesoft said. "And yeah, Gatelink, pay *attention*! Get with the *program*!" They all chuckled a little at the intentional gaucheness of the remark. But not much.

"Hey, it's almost 6:30 now, and Headquarters closes at 9:00. The important thing is just to keep these goons occupied until then. We get through today, and they promised not to say anything after tonight. Let's not forget that," Easycalc said.

"But they took only fifteen *minutes* to pick out their stuff," Tablesoft shook her head. "Like they already knew what they were going to buy or something."

"Yeah, but they forgot to put something in the rules about how much time *we* can take," Gatelink said. "They didn't say we had to shop as fast as they did, just that we had to spend as much money."

"Hey, you're right, Gatelink!" Tablesoft exclaimed.

"Hey, I'm glad you're on our team, Gatelink!" Easycalc said comically, poking her lightly with his elbow. Gatelink laughed nervously at the joke, knowing she was the only reason they all couldn't just walk away from this potentially dangerous game.

"So, we can take a long time, just not so long that these guys get bored," Tablesoft whispered.

Gatelink opened her mouth to agree but was interrupted by one of Officeworks' unidentified followers, pointing at them and calling from about twenty feet away. "Hey, look guys," she sneered from her head turned sideways to her cronies. "It looks like they're scared already and they haven't even started the first round yet. Bawck, bawck, bawck, baaawck!" the five cackled predictably.

The recurrent raucousness was getting on Gatelink's nerves. Their 'jokes' were not that funny. Were these people so immature? Or did they just have a low threshold in humor when bullying was mixed into the situation? In any case, Gatelink decided, it was time to start shopping.

And shop they did. Gatelink, Tablesoft and Easycalc spent an hour and a half in Lambert's, spending their $1800 allotment on only the very best-fitting clothes that best went with their complexions and lifestyles. They took turns explaining this to their challengers, and that anyone who didn't consider all these factors when shopping was a peon. The Officeworkers luckily seemed content enough to be playing their game and did not sense the stall tactics going on right before

24

them. They mistook the three's apparent excessive vanity for actual excessive vanity, and nodded in agreement to the crafty excuses.

It was nearly 8:30 when Tablesoft, Gatelink and Easycalc walked out of Bambergers with eight pairs of pants, eleven shirts, two ties, one scarf and a pair of pearl earrings between them, and handed over their receipts to Officeworks' side. They had shopped strategically for themselves, however, as well as for the purposes of this situation; they bought some of the clothes in a size bigger, to hold on to until they needed it. They would be in some credit card debt for a while, but the higher-sized clothes might convince their parents to forward them some of their clothing allowance for next year. What Officeworks and Papersaver would do, they could only imagine.

In the next store, "Power," Officeworks and her buddies seemed to have a little more trouble deciding on what they wanted to buy. *Maybe they didn't pre-shop anywhere else because they didn't expect us to last through Round One,* Gatelink thought bitterly. But considering what would have happened to Gatelink if she didn't agree to their game—well, she'd have had to be a fool to refuse. *Officeworks may think I'm boring,* she thought, *but she knows I'm not stupid—she even said so. So...they must have known, or at least strongly suspected, that we'd have to play, and at least until 9:00, and they're just not prepared enough!* Gatelink smiled at this realization. It consoled her though she didn't see exactly why it should. Maybe because she believed that she and her friends would have done a better job than Officeworks, *that even in a game of cruelty, I could have been better than her if I'd wanted to,* Gatelink thought. And this did make her feel good.

At 9:00, Officeworks and her friends were still shopping, trying desperately to spend more than $1800. They were focused and intent, and quite likely did not realize that their hold on their opponents had worn off, that they had lost their powers like Cinderella at midnight.

"They look so determined, shopping like that," Tablesoft said, pronouncedly patronizing as they watched from a comfortable distance of a hundred feet.

"Yeah," Gatelink agreed with mock sincerity. "I'd hate to disturb them and tell them that we, um, have to leave."

"Well, you know what," Easycalc said, "how 'bout let's *not* tell them." He smiled. "That way we don't *hurt* their *feelings!*"

"And they get to keep on shopping," Gatelink leaned forward and declared in hushed tones, "until they've spent as much as they possibly *can!*"

"Which is, really...what they want," Easycalc replied, smiling again. This time, Gatelink and Tablesoft joined him. The three walked subtly out of the store, stopping to analyze items on their way, so as to not draw attention to their exit.

They were all tense and didn't talk until they got out of The Strip; they were all too focused on just getting out first and starting to put this event behind them. As the cool, fresh night air met them outside the doors, however, they began to laugh—shocked, nervous laughter.

"That was the craziest thing...." Easycalc said.

"All that 'bawk'-ing!" Tablesoft smirked. "They sounded like such idiots."

"Yeah," Gatelink said. "'Chicken,'" she snorted. "I thought we were supposed to be so much smarter now than people used to be, back when they used to play that game. Looks like Officeworks and her buds haven't caught up to the rest of us yet!"

They laughed harder, relieved at the opportunity to start sharing their anger, and put aside the fear part of the experience.

"Yeah," Easycalc said. "I bet they've got a poor genetic make-up!"

"I bet that Officeworks," Tablesoft gasped between laughs, "I bet her whole family doesn't even know how to use a Shield, or a Hair-Maker. I bet they don't even open them, and use them *rolling* pins!"

"Yeah, I bet they think a Time-Saver is a clock!" Easycalc elaborated. The two laughed even harder—they started to lean over and clutch their stomachs from laughing so hard. Gatelink smiled tightly. *What's wrong with them?* she thought. *They're being almost as lame and superficial as those idiots. Is this supposed to be funny?*

"What do you guys say we get outta here?" she said, barely waiting for their agreement before she began to make their way to the trains.

CHAPTER 3
MR. MYSTERIOUS—A TOO-PERFECT BLOND

Gatelink awoke to the sound of trumpets the next morning. The song on the company-approved CD in her alarm clock was *Ambition*. Or maybe it was *Motivation*. She couldn't remember exactly. She liked the tune, though. It did get her out of bed and setting about getting ready for work.

"The Facemaker" applied the usual cake of foundation and blush that morning that her mother had selected long ago for Gatelink's low, pale cheekbones and unfashionably full lips. The lip color applicator misapplied its thick cream as it did every day; Mrs. Jones had never accepted that Gatelink did not inherit either of her parent's symmetrical features, and she steadfastly refused to purchase a Facemaker with the right settings for her daughter's face. Gatelink sighed and wiped the left side of her top lip clean of "Corporate Power Pink." She looked at her disgusting pug nose in the mirror, her limbs too skinny to be sexy and overwhelming breasts that she wished her parents would pay to get reduced so she could look even a little bit like the models and actresses she looked at all day long, and thought to herself, *Good thing you're smart.*

Mother and daughter drove to work after a cursory breakfast in a car, blue with "Danube Life—There When You Need Us" emblazoned in gold on each side of it, next to a picture of a three-generationed family looking happy and safe. The New York City streets that took them to work bore pictures and company logos on their every inch of asphalt save the yellow lines in the middle of the road—plain-colored by state mandate for safety reasons. "Why waste space?" the mayor had agreed with the wisdom of corporations when agreeing to the proposal publicly years back. The sidewalks were peopled with pants and skirts below dark opaque plastic half-tubes from the waist up. In the city, it was rare to see a person above the waist walking about; everyone wore their "Shields," to keep from being mugged or attracting a psycho. Gatelink thought she remembered a time, when she was very young, when people didn't use "Shields." The advertisements never let you forget how dangerous it was to walk on the streets back then, how much higher crime rates were then, but Gatelink didn't remember feeling scared. She asked in school once when people had starting using "Shields," and what they did before to keep themselves safe, and what was it like to be able to look around and see the faces of all the people. The teacher had told her that such questions had no purpose; the "Shield" was here now, and it was a wonderful advancement. "Look at how many good things we are always hearing about it," she had said. "With such a wonderful product, why would we even want to consider what it was like to live without it?" Gatelink didn't know if she was the only one confused by the teacher's response. No one else in her second grade class had said anything, so she figured she probably was.

The door slammed shut across from Gatelink, bringing her violently to the present. "Gatelink, why are you always daydreaming?" Mrs. Jones reprimanded. "Honestly!" Gatelink didn't need to look to know that her mother was shaking her head and rolling her eyes, livid with a disappointment that morning after morning of the same routine didn't seem to quell. Gatelink left off biting her nails, and her mother gave up shooting her dirty looks. They crossed the parking lot, colorful with ads for various Gatelink products, and gave themselves to the company for another day.

When she got to school, though, she could see that this day was not going to be like the rest. Something was very different about the classroom. There was someone in it who had never been in it before, at least not in her sight. A young man in a navy jacket with a "Sundaram Blarney" logo on it and tan khakis with the same logo stood before the class. He had wavy blond hair, tanned skin, and bright blue eyes. He looked almost as handsome as one of the models on her matching shirt and pants, except that his nose was a little too long. He was standing at the front of the classroom next to Ms. McUthrie, easily a foot taller than her but standing in such a way that he seemed to be in deference to her as they talked. She was pointing something out to him on a piece of paper she held in one hand, and seemed to be explaining something. He looked just a little too old to be a student, Gatelink concluded quickly, but much younger than Ms. McUthrie or any of the other teachers.

Gatelink slid into her seat next to Tablesoft. There were still ten minutes before the start of the workday, so there was plenty of time for them to compare theories on this handsome stranger. The buzz level among the other students was considerably higher than usual.

Tablesoft turned in her seat to face Gatelink, and didn't waste any time, "I think he's the new school masseuse!"

Gatelink laughed. "Tablesoft! Come on!"

"I'm serious," Tablesoft pretended to be mad. "I've always said that they work us too hard here. I mean, Programming, Softwares, Matrix Algebra—we're all so stressed out and tense, well, it's just not good for our health!"

Gatelink laughed some more.

"Why are you laughing," Tablesoft continued pretending to be cross, though she emitted a laugh or two whenever she paused. "It's basic product maintenance. If they want to maintain us, they have to take care of us. Just like I've always thought, and Management has finally caught my…"

"What?" Gatelink broke in. "Your mental illness? Your warped sense of humor?"

"You should only *be* so lucky," Tablesoft narrowed her eyes in comic seriousness, "to have so many more of *me*! No, I meant they've caught my *vibe*."

"Oh, your vibe, okay."

"Yeah. Maybe. Or maybe he's Ms. McUthrie's lover, and she brought him here because she couldn't stand to leave him at home for fear of some other old married woman snatching him up!"

Gatelink smiled and shook her head. She hadn't seen Tablesoft act like this, so *natural*, for a long time. She used to be creative like this, making up wacky, entertaining stories, until one day in eighth grade when the teacher, Mr. Bassel, intercepted a note Tablesoft was passing to Gatelink, with one of her crazy stories on it. Mr. Bassel had been very upset, even though the story wasn't about him in particular but a crazy story about the school—he had sent copies of the note to the Board and to Tablesoft's parents. Tablesoft didn't say too much to Gatelink and Easycalc about what happened except that it had cost her parents a lot of money and that they yelled at her for hours about how disappointed they were that she was goofing off and being so ungrateful to the company and jeopardizing things for all of them. They had said that if she was ever caught goofing off like that again that they would take away all her electronics, and she'd never get a paycheck or allowance again. Gatelink knew that Tablesoft had always worshiped her parents, from afar, as they all had until they got old enough to return the indifference with indifference; she knew that at that point in her friend's life just the censure of her parents, let alone the threats, was enough to stop her from doing anything—even just being herself. After that, Tablesoft had always seemed reserved, a little aloof, and rarely made jokes let alone stories.

Gatelink was happy to see her friend being her old self again, and almost said so, before she realized that doing so would surely break the spell and the aloof Tablesoft would return. So she said instead, "He is pretty delicious, isn't he?"

Tablesoft raised her eyebrows, smiled and nodded just as the nine o'clock bell rang. They both whipped around in their seats to face forward and pretend they hadn't just been lusting after the mystery man they now looked openly and curiously at, along with the rest of their class.

"Okay, people. I'd like you all to welcome our new teaching assistant, Mr. Robinson. He's a student at New York University, working on his master's degree in Secondary Education. He's here to observe and to help me out."

"Beauty and brains," Tablesoft whispered. Gatelink smiled, stifled a laugh.

"Welcome, Mr. Robinson," the class called out in a coy and overwhelmingly feminine collective voice.

"Thank you very much," he responded. "It's a pleasure to be here." His voice sounded a little different from everyone else's, Gatelink noted, like he had an accent that was not completely gone yet. She wondered where he was from.

The day began with Physics lecture, and progressed slowly through the other subjects. Mr. Robinson sat at a station that had been rolled in for him, at the side of the room. Class participation was at an all-time high that day, Gatelink observed, especially from her female classmates. To be fair, she noted that she too was in this category of sudden overachievers.

By lunch, the excitement had died down a bit. The lunchtime chatter was at an average volume, and Tablesoft wasn't funny anymore. Things were back to normal.

"Did you guys see TaxHelp's hair?" Tablesoft asked. "I like that color. I wonder if she has the new edition of the Hair-Maker—you know, the kind that colors?"

"Well, considering how much programming work they're making us do lately, I would guess that she doesn't have time to go out to get it done, so she must *have* the new Hair-Maker," Easycalc said.

Gatelink was only half-listening to the conversation. She was surreptitiously watching Mr. Robinson as he sat at the teachers' table several yards away. Though his behavior was completely appropriate, there was something about him that seemed out of place. He seemed...surprised at everything—Gatelink didn't know what had given this strange impression of her new assistant teacher, but she had it. Maybe his eyes were a little too wide-open, or his eyebrows arched—she didn't know. But she felt that anyone looking closely enough would have seen it, too.

"Gatelink...Gatelink!" Tablesoft was saying as she leaned over the table and tapped Gatelink on the forearm. "Wake up, sweetie!"

"Oh, sorry, what?" Gatelink responded.

"Do you like Easycalc's new sneakers?" Tablesoft asked. Easycalc raised one sneakered foot off the ground to give Gatelink a better look.

"I saw them in black in Smith's and thought they looked much better in black, though Easycalc insists on white. So, which would you like better?"

"Black," she said. "Definitely black."

Through the rest of the day, Mr. Robinson sat quietly at his station. He crossed his legs as all the teachers did and took notes through all the classes. Gatelink noticed, however, that he would often turn from Ms. McUthrie to the class, and watch them instead. When his eyes would meet Gatelink's, he would smile unabashedly and let his eyes drift slowly back to Ms. McUthrie, as if he were just doing a lap of the room. Gatelink didn't think any of her classmates noticed Mr. Robinson watching them, only her. She thought about nudging Tablesoft and alerting her too, the next time they were being watched, but decided against it. Mr. Robinson's way of watching the class was not really scrutinizing; it seemed to Gatelink to be with a kind of wonder, like one watching strange animals at the zoo. Gatelink found it curious, and thought to herself that she should wait until she could find out more about Mr. Robinson before saying anything to anyone, even her friends. She didn't want to concern them for nothing, she told herself, but didn't quite believe that was her reason.

Gatelink continued to observe Mr. Robinson observe the class for the next week and a half. She had also, just out of curiosity, she told herself, checked the roster at the Graduate School of Education at NYU and had indeed found Mr. Robinson listed as a Master's candidate. Gatelink wanted to find out more about him, and searched the internet for his name, but to no avail. This too struck her as odd, since everyone she knew was on their company's web site, under the 'progeny' section that every corporation now had; she wondered who his parent firm was. She had assumed it was Sundaram Blarney, since he wore their logo on the first day, but their web site didn't contain his name. He looked young enough to have not been from "the Dark Ages of pre-progeny" like Gatelink's parents; but she figured that maybe he wasn't that young, or else she would have found his name on some corporate web site.

Questions about this man started to occupy Gatelink's mind, though she logically knew she shouldn't care. It didn't concern her. Yet somehow, she thought it might.

During the second week of Mr. Robinson's assistantship, something interesting happened. It was during Corporate History class. They were discussing the history of the Progeny Program throughout the world, and how substandard the public and non-corporate private educational systems had been before the great businessman and humanitarian Justin A. Fairchild had the breakthrough vision of corporate sponsorship. He didn't even have any background in education, but his tremendous love of learning and concern for young minds led him to fight for this system to be implemented worldwide. "Now," Ms. McUthrie said, "this educational advancement enables us all to work harder, smarter, so we can all afford the wonderful products available today, as well as to help us continue the production of existing products and contribute to the creation of new products, through our various talents in production engineering, advertising, and so forth."

Gatelink glanced in Mr. Robinson's direction through the corner of her eye and saw that his eyes were wider than they'd been since his first day there, and his mouth was slightly opened. He seemed to be trying hard to suppress a look of surprise, shock, or something else. Gatelink couldn't imagine why. The class had certainly already learned about the educational aspects of Corporate History; this was review for them.

Ms. McUthrie continued, "Now education is *only* held in the highly efficient and effective corporate system. Companies all over the world share a similar system, but with slight differences, adaptations. For example, it wouldn't make much sense for Fizz Cola's schools to focus as much on programming as we do here, now would it? Or for Hair-Maker, Inc.? They probably focus much more on Mechanical Engineering, or Food Science. Mr. Robinson, what's your parent company?"

Mr. Robinson looked like a deer in the headlights.

"I'm sorry?"

The girls of the class giggled, except Gatelink; the boys snickered. They all assumed Mr. Robinson hadn't been paying attention and that's why he was taken aback. But Gatelink knew he had been. She'd been watching. Her brow furrowed.

Ms. McUthrie repeated herself, a little impatiently. She crossed her arms at the waist. "I *said*, Mr. Robinson, what's your parent company." She had assumed what the rest of the class had, it appeared.

"Oh, I'm sorry, Ms. McUthrie. It's...uh..." Gatelink noticed Robinson's eyes lower, subtly, just enough to read the name on his pants it looked like. "...Sundaram Blarney."

"And what was *their* educational focus?" she asked, determined not to lose the example portion of her lecture.

"It was...um...." he stammered.

"Oh financial analysis, I presume?" she stated in the form of a question, unquestionably exasperated by now.

"Yes, yes, of course!" Mr. Robinson exclaimed, sounding more relieved than he should, Gatelink thought. A few girls in the class giggled again.

"So class," Ms. McUthrie resumed, "some key words to take away from this discussion are: Justin A. Fairchild, founder of modern education; global educational system; and educational focus. You should be able to write intelligently on any or all of these topics for the midterm."

The bell rang for lunch and as Gatelink looked over, Mr. Robinson seemed to be regaining his poise. Gatelink was perplexed by what she had observed, and must have wearing that on her face because at lunch Easycalc asked her if something was wrong.

"Well," Gatelink began, uncertain of how much she should, or wanted to, tell her friends about her growing suspicion. "Have you guys noticed anything a little, well, *off*, about Mr. Robinson?"

"The new teacher guy?" Easycalc said, surprised at the topic. "Well, I think his fashion sense might be a little bit off—I mean, those shoes don't really go with his suit."

"I agree," said Tablesoft. "And he needs to get new batteries for his Hair-Maker or something—it does *not* appear to be doing the *job*. Is that what's bothering you, honey?"

Gatelink smiled. *I think too much,* she thought playfully. "Yeah," she said. "Something like that."

*****

After a few more days, Gatelink's continued web searches had yielded no more information about Mr. Robinson and she decided to take matters into her own hands. But she had no idea how to do that. She really wasn't even sure why she was so determined to find out about him, which didn't make it any easier trying to figure out what to say to Mr. Robinson and when.

She decided to tackle the "when" question first, since it was the easier of the two. Before class was a possibility: If they were both there at least fifteen minutes early, she could catch him alone. But the risk of getting caught asking the assistant teacher…what?…was too high. Gatelink ruled out morning. Lunchtime also held too great a chance that someone like Hayes would overhear her question and report her to the Board for "wasting their education on her." It would have to be after the workday ended, after punch-out. Of course, after punch-out, which would also be the time when classmates will have gone, would also be the time when Mr. Robinson would have no requirement to say and answer any question to Gatelink, especially if he didn't like what she was asking.

And what would she ask, Gatelink considered. What if she was wrong? His name didn't come up on Sundaram Blarney's webpage, but what if there was some explanation for that, and he really was a Sundaram Blarney progeny? *Then he might get angry and get me in trouble,* Gatelink thought. He seemed like a nice man, like someone who wouldn't do that, she thought, but she couldn't be sure. So, she considered the possibility that asking directly about his parent firm could backfire, and tried to come up with a subtler way to get his story.

She frowned and furrowed her brow and pondered this question for some time as she lay in bed at night, where and when she did all her thinking. "Of course!" she said out loud finally. "I get his *story*!" Realizing she was talking out loud and might wake her parents, Gatelink sat up and began to whisper excitedly to herself. "I get his story! I interview him, like for a school paper! Only, we don't have a school paper. So…I say I'm writing for a community paper, for the Upper West Side. Except…that could get me in trouble too; Headquarters doesn't let us work outside the firm, even for volunteering. I'll have to say I'm trying to start up a student paper. I might get in a little trouble for that, but it can't be considered as delinquent as my idea of a play. I mean, journalism *is* considered a profession, and I'll bet the New York Gazette school has a student paper, so it's not something that companies don't *do*. So even if I get in some trouble for this, it can't be too much," she concluded resolutely. "Hopefully," she then added, a little less so. "This is the plan," she whispered firmly to herself. "Now go to sleep, Gatelink." And she tried.

CHAPTER 4
KEEP MY NOSE WHERE?

The next morning, Gatelink woke before her alarm for the first time in years. She showered and put on her favorite outfit. When she went into the kitchen for breakfast, however, an unexpected sight greeted her. Mr. Jones sat at the breakfast table with a sheet of paper in his hand that looked like a letter. Gatelink had never seen her father at home in the morning; he usually left for Headquarters before she and her mother even woke up. He was fully dressed this morning, in a dark gray Hibachi suit with the Hibachi logo and pictures of handsome muscular men in Hibachi suits on it and black shoes with the Kristovsky logo and gorgeous small-breasted women on them.

"Hi, Dad," Gatelink said, attempting casual. She walked past him to open the fridge.

He looked up. "Hello, Gatelink."

"Gatelink!" a voice stated sharply. Gatelink turned, more out of surprise than obedience. Her mother had entered the kitchen and was standing next to her husband. "Sit down. We need to talk to you about something."

Gatelink closed the fridge. "Yes?" she said.

"How are things going at school, Gatelink? Are things okay? Any problems there?" Mr. Jones asked.

Gatelink was puzzled. Her dad was going late to work so he could ask her how school was going?

"Everything's fine, Dad," Gatelink said. But then she had a thought. "Why? What is that letter about...?"

"This?" Mr. Jones held up the letter, the clean back of it to Gatelink, and looked embarrassed. "Oh, this is nothing." He folded the letter and put it inside his suit jacket. "I'm glad that school's going well, Gatelink. We need you to just keep working hard," he balled his fingers into a fist and shook it, for emphasis, "and keep your nose to the grindstone. And…keep out of trouble."

Gatelink didn't hide her bafflement. She said nothing, but her face scrunched up in a very scrutable question, "What the…?"

"Oh, honestly, Michael!" Mrs. Jones intervened. "Gatelink, your father is up for a big promotion, and if you get into any trouble at school, or if your grades drop—"

"Matilda, can I see you out in the hallway?" Mr. Jones spoke in a forceful voice, standing up.

"Michael," Mrs. Jones said, also rising, but clearly disagreeing, by the tone of her voice.

"In the hall, please!" Mr. Jones took hold of his wife's arm and almost pulled her out of the room.

Gatelink meanwhile, had dropped hold of her lower jaw, at about the point where her role in her father's promotion was explained. She strained to hear what they were hissing to each other out in the hall, knowing that they could see her from where they stood so she couldn't get up to move closer.

"—catch more flies with honey than with vinegar—" she heard her father saying.

"—she's old enough to understand—" her mother said.

"—might screw it up to spite us…know how she *is*—" her father said.

"—she knows where the money comes from—" her mother said.

"—don't like your way of doing things—" her father said.

"—to leave things as they are—" her mother said.

And then her parents returned to the kitchen. Mr. Jones kissed his smiling wife and his still open-mouthed daughter on their cheeks, said, "I'm off to work," and left. Mrs. Jones said, "I'm going to finish getting ready," and left the kitchen also. Gatelink, alone and amazed, poured herself a glass of orange juice.

*****

"Of course I knew," Tablesoft said, pouring ketchup on her fries at lunch that day. "How could you not know that? Gatelink is one big family, after all." She started eating her fries.

Gatelink looked down to hide her disgust.

"Yeah," said Easycalc. "My dad told me about three years back that if I was real good at school for the next few months that he'd buy me a Pilot-bot at the end of it. I just figured he was up for a raise and needed my help. Easiest Pilot-bot I ever made, too." He grinned.

"Pilot-bot?" said Tablesoft in mock distaste.

"Hey, I was 13!" Easycalc replied.

"Why are you so upset about this, Gatelink? I mean, what's the big deal?" asked Tablesoft.

"I don't know," Gatelink said quietly.

"Hmmm," Tablesoft murmured, lowering her eyes to her fries. There was an awkward silence for several seconds.

Then Easycalc said, "Did you see Dan's jeans? I've been looking for a pair just like them," and Gatelink went back to her thoughts.

*****

Through the rest of the day, Gatelink held court inside her head on the various issues pressing her at the moment. She didn't raise her hand once all day, which was very unusual for her. She was starting a pattern that, she thought bitterly, *could cost my father his precious promotion.*

Gatelink still wasn't sure how she felt about her parents asking her to do well in school so her dad's raise wouldn't be at risk. On one hand, maybe Tablesoft was right and she should have realized this all long ago—*Maybe I'm dumb,* Gatelink thought. *I've got my head in those literary books too much, like Tablesoft said.* But on the other hand, her parents were using her, weren't they? Weren't all parents using their kids? That's wrong, isn't it? It felt that way. Though, logically, Gatelink had to admit that she couldn't formulate any concrete *reasons* why that would be wrong.

And Tablesoft and Easycalc—looking so placid, so *content*, while confirming to Gatelink something that made her feel icky inside.

But Gatelink knew these were things she could do nothing about. The only thing she *could* do was talk to Mr. Robinson. With everything else on her mind now, she wasn't sure she cared to anymore, or that she had the calm to withstand his refusing or giving her answers that angered her. Gatelink also knew that if Mr. Robinson wasn't as nice and understanding as he seemed, that he could get her in trouble for asking him waste-of-education type questions—and that thought gave her a certain satisfaction. No, she wouldn't actively seek out trouble, as her dad had implied; she would simply go through with a plan she had made before news of her father's pending promotion. She would simply not let it change her plans. She liked the sound of that also.

CHAPTER 5
NOT A *LITTLE* Q & A

That day, after punch-out, as the rest of her class headed for the door, Gatelink moved in the opposite direction. She approached Mr. Robinson with a pad of paper and a pen in hand. She saw Tablesoft and Easycalc from the corner of her eye staring at her and Mr. Robinson, puzzled, then shrugging as they turned to leave.

"Uh, yes, Gatelink?" Mr. Robinson said, a little nervously.

"Mr. Robinson, I'm trying to start up a school newspaper, and I was wondering if I could interview you on your background and what brought you to our school."

Mr. Robinson smiled a surprised, almost delighted smile. "You're trying to start a school newspaper here." He sounded incredulous. Gatelink hadn't counted on this.

"Yes," she replied, hoping the uncertainty she felt didn't leak out in that single syllable.

After a silence long enough to order a watch from the Home Shopping Network, Mr. Robinson finally spoke. "Well, that's great." He began to nod his head rhythmically like a bobble-doll. "That's super. And I'd be happy to talk with you." The head-bobbing stopped. "But we need to clear out of here, because they'll be coming in to clean soon, and I don't have an office, as you might have guessed." He grinned. "So, is there anywhere else we could go to talk? A park maybe?"

Gatelink's brow furrowed. "A what?" she said.

Mr. Robinson looked startled for a second, then responded, "Uh, nothing. Um, a coffee shop?"

"Oh, yeah. There's one a few blocks away."

"Great. Shall we walk there? It's a nice day out."

"Um, okay." People usually took the subway everywhere, but Gatelink didn't see why they shouldn't walk. She'd just never thought of it before. She pulled out her instant messenger and keyed, "Mom—home late—school project," just in case her absence was noticed.

They didn't talk much on the way to the coffee shop. Gatelink felt very strange walking to get somewhere at first, but then she began to relax and even to enjoy it. Mr. Robinson seemed to be enjoying the walk the whole time, which Gatelink found an interesting fact. He didn't seem to feel odd in the least about walking somewhere when everyone knew you take the subway to get there faster. Gatelink decided not to ask Mr. Robinson if he did know this fact because she didn't want to embarrass him.

When they arrived at their La Compania Café, Gatelink noted another idiosyncrasy of the assistant teacher. When they got to the door of the place, he opened it and held it open for Gatelink. A little confused, Gatelink went in. Mr. Robinson followed and approached the coffee counter to order as if nothing out of the ordinary had occurred. They ordered their drinks as nonchalantly as they could, an Evergreen mocha for Gatelink and a Piazarro latte for Mr. Robinson. The coffee hostess smiled at them mechanically as she rang up their orders and did not betray it if she noticed the shakiness in their voices. They drifted in unspoken agreement to a table farthest from the few other people in the café, who were all in suits and spoke rapidly at each other or cell phones. Gatelink ushered in the conversation with a question that had been prickling her for weeks.

"You're not from around here, are you, Mr. Robinson?"

"Call me George, please," he replied with an affability that seemed rehearsed. "I'm not that much older than you, Gatelink." He paused. "And you're not really trying to start a school paper, are you?" His voice was coy, bordering on flirtatious.

Gatelink smiled, in spite of herself. She should be terrified that she's about to get into a mountain of trouble, she knew, but instead she felt…relaxed. *Disarmed by his charming smile, probably,* she thought, still smiling. She crossed her legs and leaned forward in the large wooden chair whose thick arms held her in like a gentle vise.

"I asked you first," she said lightly, wondering what "George" was. She'd never seen that name in any ads. She had the feeling she'd heard it before, but not as anything for sale.

"Yes, you did," said George, "and no, I'm not. Now you."

"No, I'm not, either," Gatelink said.

"So…what are we doing here? Other than getting high on tasty mochas, that is." He smiled, teasing, and tilted back on the hind legs of his chair.

"Where *are* you from?" Gatelink gestured the question with her hands. "Why are you not listed on any corporation's progeny page? I mean, did you just drop out of the sky? And why do you seem so surprised at everything at school? Why did you open the door and wait for me to walk in first just now—what was that all about? And what is a '*park*'?" Gatelink paused as he laughed, then added, "And, how did you know I was lying about the school paper idea?"

Their drinks were delivered as Gatelink finished her last question, giving George a chance to recover his composure just enough to respond.

"You looked me up on the Internet?" he asked, sounding flattered but with a devilish grin.

"You're answering a question with a question!" Gatelink protested.

"No, I'm answering a *bunch* of questions with a question!" he replied. "But I *will* share my story with you, after I answer your last question first." He blew softly into the large white ceramic mug and took a ginger sip. "Ooh—it's hot! …I strongly suspected you were lying about that because I know that you suggested the idea of having a school play and that it was refused royally."

"You knew about that?"

"Sure. Some of the Board is still all up-in-arms about it and worried you're going to agitate and cause unrest. They warned me about you on the first day."

"Really?" Gatelink wasn't sure if she proud, hurt or angry.

"Oh, don't take it too personally," George said. "I wouldn't."

"Hmmm," Gatelink replied, sipping her mocha and taking it personally.

43

"And, being that you seem like an intelligent person, I figured you'd never go back before that so-called School Board with another good idea that they would undoubtedly shoot down."

"You thought it was a good idea?" Gatelink couldn't believe her ears. She couldn't believe someone agreed with her; even more, that someone else disagreed with the Board.

"Of course. But they'd never approve it."

Gatelink thought for a minute. "Wait—but if you knew, or 'strongly suspected,' there was no school paper idea, why did you agree to talk with me?" she asked.

"Because," George said, smiling. "I'm curious, too." He brought himself forward and rested an elbow on the table and his chin in the associated hand.

"Huh?" Gatelink said. Though she was still confused, she felt remarkably at ease talking with this man. She pulled herself up and fell backward, too relaxed to maintain her posture without the support of the chair back.

"Let me explain. Or at least, let me start to explain, because this could take more time than we've got today."

Gatelink tried not to move a muscle as she sat waiting for him to organize his thoughts and begin his story.

"I'm from Arizona," he began, and Gatelink noticed that immediately his voice had changed. The accent that she thought she'd heard a hint of on his first day was now a full slowish, stilted drawl. "That's where I was born and raised. My parents own a small store where they sell general merchandise. It's the only store in town." He paused to sip his coffee. Gatelink was sure she must have misheard him, because there's no town with only one store, especially not a *small* store, but she had resolved not to interrupt Mr. Robinson until he was done telling his story.

"Actually, they sort of co-own it, with a bunch of other families—whoever has the interest and ability to keep it going. It would be hard for just one family to keep it going on top of managing the farming, too—"

Gatelink's eyebrows shot up like rockets. "I'm sorry," she interrupted him. "Did you say *farming?*"

George looked her in the eye and said calmly, "Yes, I did."

"Well, uh, what do you—mean—um—*farming?*" she stammered.

He sighed softly, sadly. "As I had feared, it seems that before I can relate to you my story and how it is that I came to be in your school, and here talking with you, I'm going to have to tell you a lot of things you don't know, about this country, and the world. To share with you *my* world, I'll have to destroy yours." He paused again, as Gatelink stared at him, her brows raised, her expression suspicious. "Well I don't—I don't mean that *literally*, though—don't get alarmed now! It was just a figure of speech!" He laughed.

"What's a figure of speech?" she asked. The doubt creasing her face had flattened her voice too.

"Oh," George replied, surprised. "I didn't realize you wouldn't.... Well, basically, it means that...I don't mean what I'm saying would happen *physically*, but that the effect of it would feel the same.... Does that make sense?"

"I guess," Gatelink answered, still sounding less than convinced.

"You know, that really wasn't fair of me, actually, being overly dramatic in my statements at a time like this for you. I remember when I found out about how the rest of the nation lives, that it isn't anything like I had believed, it was like a ton of bricks had fallen on my head."

Gatelink frowned and wrinkled her nose.

"There I went again! Sorry."

"That's okay," Gatelink said, straightening up, her shoulders behind her like wings. "But what is it that you're trying to tell me, that you *need* to tell me?" She was very impressed with how mature she sounded saying that.

"Well, first, let me ask you a question, the answer to which I'm fairly certain I already know. But, then, I could be wrong, so: Are you perfectly happy with the way things are—not in your life specifically, but how things are in general, how *society* is, how everyone seems to be, to think?"

Gatelink opened her mouth immediately to respond, then froze. What was she going to say? Should she say "no" and betray her resolve or "yes" and betray herself? She didn't know, so she closed her eyes and heard "no" issue from her lips.

"I can see that that wasn't easy for you, Gatelink," George said softly, his eyes downcast. "Maybe I shouldn't have asked. It's just that…"

She interrupted him again; since it was to stifle an apology, it was mature, she'd decided. "No, no. It's okay, really. I don't mind. It's just that, I've never told that to anyone before, and…I didn't think I ever would, that I ever could. But, you know, I think I feel a lot better, now that I have!" She rolled her shoulders and neck around, for effect, as if she'd just received a massage.

George smiled. "Well, good. It's nice of you to preserve my feelings like that."

"It's nothing," Gatelink replied.

"No, that is not nothing. That is a precious quality to have. It shows compassion and selflessness, and it's a quality far too few people have. It's wonderful that you do have it. And I'm only telling you all this because I'll bet your parents never did, and I know you wouldn't get it out of that school. But where I'm from, things like this, like having this quality, are valued very highly."

Gatelink sat still, stupefied. She knew she'd come across those words—"compassion" and "selflessness" in her old books and must have looked them up in her antique dictionary at the time, but she couldn't remember what they meant. Satisfied to assume they were good things, and vowing to look them up again when she got home, Gatelink let George resume his explanation.

"I had asked whether you were happy with the way things are because the fact is, they aren't this way everywhere, despite what Ms. McUthrie said in class the other day." He waited for her response, having decided to go slowly with this intervention.

"I've been taught that same thing my whole life," Gatelink said slowly, "that the whole world was just like New York and Gatelink."

"It's not entirely untrue," George said carefully. "Much of America is very similar, and a certain percentage of the rest of the world is very similar too."

"But not...*all*," Gatelink said, dumbstruck.

"No," he said, slowly. "I had no idea they started indoctrinating that so early." He shook his head, seeming surprised and possibly a little impressed. "It makes sense, I guess, but..."

"So what is the rest of the world *like*? How do people live?" Gatelink knew her voice sounded suspicious, but she couldn't help it; it sounded so unbelievable to her that what she'd always been told, from so many different sources, was a lie and that she should believe the word of this man who seemed nice but could be crazy.

"Gatelink, I don't have to tell you anymore, if you don't want to hear about it," George said gently. "We can both go back home and pretend this never happened. I'd be a little disappointed, but I wouldn't hold it against you."

Her smile dissolved, Gatelink raised her eyebrows in surprise. She considered George's proposal.

"I want to hear," she said resolutely. "I'm sorry if I sound— sounded—like I don't believe you." She couldn't think of anything else to say. Her words hung lonely in the air.

"That's okay. I understand," he said, sounding like he did. Then he scratched his head. "But where to begin? Hmmm...."

Gatelink waited, sipped her Evergreen mocha.

"Can you tell I've never done this before?" he said with a small, nervous laugh.

"Well, then you're in the right company," Gatelink replied, surprising herself again with her thoughtfulness.

George smiled and wagged a finger at her jokingly, "There you go again!"

There was a pause as he considered how and where to begin what would undoubtedly sound like an incredible story. Finally he said, "Well, I guess as you can see, I'm a little nervous about this too. And I don't know if this is the best place to start but I'm going to start with, uh, what I'm about to say. You can feel free to interrupt me anytime if have questions about anything."

Gatelink nodded. George took a deep breath.

"Corporate *sponsorship*"—he said this word derisively—"of

education, and *people*, only controls 42 of our 50 states of America. And I say 'controls' because it does. But in the other 8 states the people have resisted the monstrous commercial system—not only resisted, but rejected it. In those states—the *free* states—there is still education for the sake of learning, and life for the sake of living. Not like here." He paused again, to regroup his thoughts. "Here, in *corporate* America, everything is done for the sake of commercial interests, for money, for *things*. In the free states, we try not to use money, unless it is absolutely necessary. We still have to meet our needs of survival, but beyond that we choose to put our energies into acquiring and maintaining things we cannot see—greater depth of spirituality, human relations, domestic harmony, love, peace. There, we talk about these aspects of existence; we teach about it in our schools. Material things are necessary for life, but we see that they are not life. Or, I should say, we *believe* that they are not life. People here, in the corporate states, *do* believe that they are life. For the adults here, it is their choice. Children are rarely allowed a choice of how to live in childhood, anywhere—but here, it seems that they are prevented from making that decision in adulthood either, since they never know there's a choice to be made. Many choices." With this, George leaned back and sipped his coffee, his gaze far away, past his companion's left shoulder.

Gatelink was grateful for the lull, which gave her some time to process what she had heard before there was more.

"You mean, *there*, kids are given a choice?" she asked.

"What do you think I'm doing here?" he replied, smiling.

"*Really?*" Gatelink asked. "You've decided to *live* here?"

"Well…no. But I didn't feel I could make a decision without seeing what this life has to offer. It was my choice to come here, for a while. Most people, there as well as here, are content to accept things without questioning, without prodding or exploring. This isn't a bad quality to have—it lends itself to increasing inner peace and outer peace. However, there have always been and will always be those among us who question, and prod, and explore. How this unusual quality, which holds as great a potential for destruction as it does for creation, is treated by a society determines the limits of its greatness."

"So this quality is indulged by your society?" Gatelink asked, incredulous that she could even understand what he was saying; it sounded almost like a foreign language, it was so abstract.

George laughed again. "Indulged…I wouldn't say that. But tolerated, yes. And maybe even encouraged, a little bit. In any case, my parents and community were not ecstatic about my decision to come here to do a Master's, but they would not have dreamed of trying to talk me out of it."

"Why not?" Gatelink asked, in awe.

"That would have been trespassing on my adulthood. What they did do was stuff me with all sorts of advice, much of which turned out to be helpful. They helped me come up with a false bio to convince the university that I was from a branch of Sundaram Blarney in England that limits the information they make available on the internet—an 'experimental' division of the company that serves as a 'control' in one of their corporate marketing studies to 'gauge if the amount of data publicly available is helpful or harmful to their competitiveness.' I had to say that I suck at financial analysis and everything else corporations need and that's why the Sundaram Blarney decided it would be best for me to train to teach in one of their schools. I told you to call me George, which is my name; but as far as the University knows, my first name is SB: Speedy Mergers or something—I don't really remember. It must have been convincing, though, since I got into the Master's program with no trouble. My family also gave me some really good practical advice, like to mail order the corporate states' style of clothing to have on when I took the plane, so as to not draw attention to myself. It did prevent me from drawing looks, I'm sure, and got me prepared for the shock of seeing what clothes look like here!"

"W-What do they look like there?" Gatelink asked, sensing that she somehow already knew the answer.

"Well, in fabrics and styles they're not too much different, actually. But there, our clothes are solid colors, or maybe stripes or flowers or some other design; but there are never advertisements on clothes, never logos or ad-photos. Here, you can't get any clothes without the whole logo-and-photo thing. I know because I've tried, as part of my own personal research project. It's like it's illegal here or something." He paused. "Hey, *is* there some kind of law against it, here?"

Taken aback at being asked a question in the midst of all this revelation, Gatelink hesitated. "Um, I don't—I don't think so. I don't know, really. I've never thought about it."

"Hmm." George nodded. "That's okay. The elders didn't know either. They told me I'd better dress within the social norms anyway, just in case. If I got thrown in jail, they'd said, that could be the end of my exploring days." He chuckled.

"The elders?" Gatelink asked

"The elders...versus here...oh, that's another whole big conversation, and you know what? It's starting to get late. It's past seven, and it's already dark out. Your parents are going to start to worry soon."

"Only that I won't have enough time to do all my homework and could get in trouble and threaten my dad's promotion!" Gatelink spat.

George looked at her with warm eyes. "I'm sorry to hear about that situation. Though I don't get what you mean, I can see that you're upset about it, and I hope you can find a way to make peace with that situation." He smiled at Gatelink, who was gazing at him again with surprise. "In any case...I feel like *I* should be heading home soon. Every day here is a long day for me.... Of course, these last two hours have flown by, but it's the eight that came before it that I still need to recover from. I hope you don't mind." He smiled humbly at her.

"Uh, no, no, of course not," Gatelink replied.

"Great," George said. "Shall we go?" And he got to his feet. As they left the coffeehouse and walked toward the subway platform to catch their separate trains, he said, "If you want to talk again, anytime, just ask. And I'll understand if it's not tomorrow." Then he shook her hand goodbye as they went on their ways home.

Gatelink reviewed their conversation in her head on the subway home. She'd never heard such strange things in her life, but somehow, it all seemed to make sense to her. No—not 'seemed to'—*felt* like it made sense. But it did *seem* strange, and unbelievable. *I wonder if they have no billboards there?* she thought, finding it hard to imagine. *What did he mean by 'if it's not tomorrow, I'll understand?'* she contemplated. *Does he not want to talk to me again? Does he think I don't want to?* Gatelink felt that she couldn't wrap her hands around what he'd said when they parted just as most of what he'd said in the coffee shop still eluded her intellect.

That night, as she tried to fall asleep, she tossed and turned and couldn't stop replaying the conversation in her mind. She felt a thrill of excitement and a sense of doom, all at the same time. As she opened her sticky eyes to see her night stand clock display the time at 3:13 a.m., Gatelink thought that maybe she shouldn't talk again with Mr. Robinson tomorrow—today! She needed to get some sleep; she'd be tired in school today, and cranky afterwards. *Well,* she thought, *now I know why he figured I might not want to talk again tomorrow. That's one thing I don't have to wonder about anymore.* She smiled, and slept.

CHAPTER 6
I HAVE THAT EFFECT ON *HIM*...RIGHT?

Getting up the next morning and getting ready for school felt strange to Gatelink. Everything was different, but everything was the same. As she stood in front of her bathroom mirror and let the Soaper moisten, lather, then rinse her face, it occurred to her that people in eight states of the U.S., and who knows how much of the world, had never used a Soaper, probably never even seen a Soaper. *Come to think of it,* Gatelink thought, *they might not even know what a Soaper is! ...I should start washing my face without a Soaper. After all, washing one's face by hand doesn't seem like it would be that hard, or take much longer. I've been using the Soaper because...well, because it's here, I guess.* Unfortunately, the make-up applicator had already started to go, so Gatelink decided to wait until the evening to try washing without the device.

As she dressed, she couldn't help imagining herself putting on solid-colored clothes—or, trying to imagine, rather, which wasn't easy since she'd never seen such clothes before, even in magazines. She guessed that even if they made magazines in the free states, they wouldn't get them over here. However, she was still wide open to the possibility that Mr. Robinson was playing a joke on her, or worse.

Preoccupied, Gatelink flipped through a company newsmagazine as she ate her breakfast. *What if he's making this all up to try to catch me in admitting my unapproved desires, like the play, to try to help his career?* she thought. Lavish rooms and the exteriors of homes were featured in the center pages of the publication with the names "Alan Black," "Sylvia Petrowski" and "Woshi Suzuki" strewn prominently about the pages. She recognized them effortlessly as the CEO, CFO and Senior VP of the company, and extrapolated that the lavish rooms featured in the magazine must be theirs. Gatelink had heard her parents discussing buying new furniture for the house the night before, planning on how to best emulate their leaders' new summer home furnishings within the Jones' own rather more limited budget.

Looking over at her mother grabbing a "Breakway Cereal Bar," Gatelink speculated, *Does she know about the free states, where there is no corporate sponsorship and people discuss ideas, qualities, lots of things other than things? Does she know and never told me, and never will?* Gatelink mulled over these thoughts in the car, too, all the way to "work," feeling a mixture of bitterness, betrayal and sadness.

At school, there was Mr. Robinson, sitting at his station at the side of the room. He smiled at her, raised his hand partway in a little wave that probably looked suspicious to anyone who'd been looking. She barely smiled back, and turned away. She was feeling angry, or hurt, or whatever, from her thoughts in the car on the way there, and knew that Mr. Robinson was in a way to blame.

Apparently Tablesoft had noticed Mr. Robinson's wave. "Hey Gatelink," she said coyly. "Is something going on with you and the assistant teacher?"

"Going on?" Gatelink replied nonchalantly. "What do you mean?"

"I mean you staying to talk to him after class yesterday, without telling me and Easycalc, and him waving at you just now."

"Oh, yesterday? I wanted to ask him…something about how my Calc test was graded, you know, since he does a lot of the grading." Gatelink contemplated whether she sounded nervous, or guilty.

She figured she must not have, because Tablesoft's face read satisfied, and her tone was teasing when she repeated, "And the *wave*?"

"Oh, *that*, well," Gatelink picked up on Tablesoft's cue, "you know, I just seem to have that effect on guys!" Tablesoft laughed, as expected. Gatelink continued, "It's a curse, but what *can* I do?" Tablesoft laughed some more until the bell rang. Gatelink was glad that Tablesoft seemed to expect her to joke about Mr. Robinson's waving to her, because how else would she have explained it? *Well, Tablesoft, Mr. Robinson and I had a long discussion the other day about how not everyone lives under corporate rule and they actually care about interesting things where he comes from, and I was really interested in knowing more about it, so he kinda likes me because of that.* Though she'd thought this thought to amuse herself, it ended up making her angry, whether at Mr. Robinson, or herself, or something else, she didn't know.

The day was surprisingly humdrum. *Why 'surprisingly'?* Gatelink questioned herself as soon as the thought popped into her head. *Just because I've experienced two major upheavals in my life in the past day, should school suddenly be tumultuous, too?* She avoided looking over toward Mr. Robinson, who didn't wave at her again that day, or the next, or the next. At lunch, Gatelink was more attentive to her friends. She listened, and talked, and tried to enjoy the conversations as much as they were. And sometimes she did feel that she was. At home, things proceeded as usual—she came home, fixed herself a snack, did her homework; dinner was microwaved and eaten by her and her mom, or her alone, if her mom wasn't home by 7:30; and she watched TV a little, and slept. She stopped reading literary books. And life was "fine" for a few days.

Then, questions started to form in Gatelink's mind, unticketed passengers on her train of thought. *What did he mean when he said 'The elders didn't know either'—what's an* elder*?* and *What else is different over there? How much do they know about us? Why are they different; how did it happen that way?* And like unticketed passengers with the gall to board a train, these thoughts were not quiet when she tried to disboard them. They resisted. She admitted to herself finally that she wanted to know more, a lot more.

So the next day at school, Gatelink turned in her Geometry exam to Mr. Robinson with an extra sheet of paper reading only, "Want to talk again—wait after class?" She continued to avoid looking in his direction unless the whole class was, and he continued not to wave at her. After punch-out, on the way out the door, she said to Tablesoft and Easycalc, "Hey, I gotta go to the bathroom before I catch the train. You guys don't have to wait up."

They nodded, "Sure, okay." She left with them and turned down the hall in the opposite direction, toward the restrooms. She waited in the women's room for about a minute, checking her hair and makeup—thought she didn't care too much how she looked right now, she told herself—and then returned to the classroom. As she'd hoped, everyone was gone except Mr. Robinson, still organizing his papers, or pretending to.

"Hi," Gatelink said. "Thanks."

"What?" he said, looking surprised. "I'm just getting my papers together. Thanks for what?"

Gatelink simply raised her eyebrows, with no idea of what to say. She opened her mouth, intending to say something, but nothing came out.

"I'm jus' kiddin' with you, Gatelink," Mr. Robinson finally said, laughing and punching her lightly on the arm. "Relax. I'm glad you want to talk again."

"You are?" Gatelink asked, feeling flattered for some reason.

"Of course I am. I was starting to worry that you'd never want to talk with me again."

"But why are *you* glad? I have more questions I want to ask you, but I can't imagine what you'd have to ask me. My world is what you see around you."

"Ah, but the world around you is always more than what you can see, even here. But," he looked around, "it's wisest not to talk too much before we leave here…. The cleaning crew coming and all." He cleared his throat.

"Same place?" Gatelink asked as they walked out of the room and headed toward the front doors of Headquarters.

"Worked for me," he replied.

"Same way to get there?" Gatelink said, smiling.

George looked a little puzzled. "Uh, yeah, unless you'd rather—"

"No, no!" Gatelink rushed to assure. "It's fine! It's just that people who can afford it usually take the subway everywhere…*here*."

"Even for a few blocks?" he asked, surprised. "On a nice day?" Now that he had taken off his blazer, Gatelink could see that the white button-up shirt George wore that day with the "Crimzon, Incorporated" logo and photos on it fit him quite well. Through the fitted front of it, she could see the outline of strong pec muscles and broad shoulders straining against the synthetic blend. She averted her eyes before he could notice her stare.

"Yeah," Gatelink said, nodding too vigorously. "And before we walked to the place last time, it never would have occurred to me to walk somewhere if you could afford the train fare." She paused, and looked up at the sky as they walked. "Though I think I might like this way better!"

"Hmmm," he said, seeming to be in thought. After a few paces he said, "See, I still have lots of questions I'd like to ask *you*—I just haven't figured out what they are yet!" He smiled. "How fortunate for me that you're able to answer them without my even asking!"

Gatelink laughed. *It is a beautiful day,* she thought. The sun was a fire in the bright blue sky, with not a cloud around to dim its glory. The few other people they saw walking around them seemed not to even glance at it though.

As they entered the coffee shop, the rich smell of the roasted beans massaged Gatelink's nasal senses. She caught herself noticing and appreciating this fact, and remarked silently that this was a new awareness.

"So, have you been having a good week?" Mr. Robinson asked casually as they sat, having placed their orders at the counter.

"It's been okay," Gatelink grinned and nodded. "How about you, Mr. Robinson?"

He grimaced. "Didn't I ask you to call me George, *not* Mr. Robinson? 'George' is also my name, and I'm hardly older than you guys. I don't know why they won't allow me to go by my first name at school." He shook his head and rolled his eyes upward.

"What do you mean 'they won't let you'? *Who* won't let you?" Gatelink asked.

"Well, the Board, of course. Every aspect of teacher-student interaction is regulated, based on psychological modeling, to 'promote development of the type of individuals our firm wants, and needs, for its successful continuance and growth.' …Wow, I've gone over that statement so many times, trying to grasp its meaning, that I've managed to memorize it! … But, you know all this, don't you?" George asked, observing Gatelink's furrowing brow.

"No," she said flatly. "They never told us that." She shook her head slowly, head tilting down. She raised her eyes back to her companion and asked, "You're saying that everything is…'*regulated*'?"

"Ooh, boy," George replied, his forehead wrinkling in discomfort. "You mean you didn't know. Wow. Well, then, this may come as a bit of a shock." He hesitated, whether for himself or for Gatelink wasn't clear, and plunged in.

"How teachers interact with students is regulated—how they address them, how they respond to right or wrong answers, even how much they smile, and whether it's toward individual students or only the class as a whole. How close teachers get to their students or how aloof they remain, is all laid out in painstaking methodical detail."

"But…why?" Gatelink asked the obvious question.

"From what I understand from the classes I've had—and keep in mind I've only done a few months so far in my one-year degree program—it's because people are profoundly influenced by their experiences in the classroom as children. These experiences affect how a person turns out—help mold the clay originally present into its final form. Also, a child's relationship with her or his teacher is similar to a parent-child relationship—it helps determine how a child perceives the outside world to be. The more warmth a teacher emits, the more sociable a child may turn out to be; the more aloof, the more professional. If a teacher smiles often at individual students, and rarely to the whole class, this can foster a sense of competitiveness. If incorrect answers are severely berated, this can create a sense of perfectionism, but will probably erode sociability." He sipped his coffee, which had just arrived, as if they were having a very normal conversation.

"But…why would Gatelink want to regulate that?" Gatelink asked.

George gazed at her for a moment, considering. He said, "Gatelink, it looks like I'm going to have to give you some news about your own world." He paused. "Gatelink Computing and Software, Incorporated, like every other corporation, has a vested interest, a *financial* interest in how its students, its '*progeny*' turn out. …You didn't know about any of this?"

She shook her head, scowling with incipient impatience.

"Well," he spoke slowly, uncertainly, "I'm not even sure *I* should be the one telling you about this but... The characteristics of a person—being competitive or not, sociable, or a perfectionist, or not—affect what kind of job and field of work she or he would be good at, 'contributional' at. Corporations do whatever they can to create people with the qualities valued in their area of production. Financial firms foster competitiveness; medical companies encourage perfectionism; and public relations firms foster try to imbue charm. Computer corporations concentrate on a blend of perfectionism and competitiveness, and don't focus on social connection at all—it's not considered a necessary skill." He snorted softly, almost under his breath, and took another drink of his cappuccino. "There are lots of other attributes, of course, from among which corporations choose for their 'progeny,' and choose the according psychological model."

They both sat for several moments, alternatively sipping their cooling coffees or looking down at the scratched faux-wooden surface of the table, reflecting. Gatelink was definitely surprised at what she was hearing, but it made so much sense she didn't know why she hadn't seen it herself.

"Do other...people know about this, *here*?" she asked George. "I mean, am I the only one who didn't know about this? I knew about the subject matter stuff, once you hit high school, but...I never gave it much thought—it didn't seem like a big deal. But this...I don't know...."

"The Board knows about it, and the teachers, of course," George responded. "I don't know if other people do, or how much they know."

"Why is it that you don't sound shocked at all about this? And especially since you looked so taken aback in class during Corporate History when we talked about the history of the progeny program?"

"Well, I'd learned about these things in my Master's classes. So, I'd already heard about them, in theory. Of course, I was shocked *then*, but that was months ago. And in class the other day, I was more 'taken aback,' as you said, by the propaganda about Fairchild, who, where I come from, is considered to be a very misguided and selfish man who ruined schools and put a nail in the coffin of childhood in most of the country!" The crescendo in George's voice signaled a vehemence that was starting to draw looks. He must have noticed it because he added in a low voice, "But that's a whole different topic," and went back to his drink.

"Hmm," Gatelink murmured, doing the same. When she was almost at the bottom of her mug she said, "What did you mean when you said that the corporations have a 'financial interest' in their progeny?"

There was silence for about a full minute. Gatelink raised her eyebrows and opened her mouth to speak. Before she could, George said, "I know I *shouldn't* be the person to tell you this, but I think that if I don't, you wouldn't find out until you become a parent and the issue comes up…. Gatelink, do you know *why* your parents named you what they did?"

"Sure. The company asked them to. I was chosen to be the highest youth representative of the company. And they probably got raises."

George looked down for a moment, then back up to Gatelink's expectant face.

"Gatelink, your parents got a lot more than a raise. And it was guaranteed. The corporation paid them a few million dollars to name their baby after it—to name *you* after it. Your classmates, named after software applications and other Gatelink products—their parents probably got a little less, due to the lower advertising value of bearing only a product name instead of the company's name."

"The lower advertising value?" she repeated.

"Yeah. The reason corporations began to buy people—I'm sorry, I shouldn't have said it that way—began to put their names on people, was for the advertising. It started with buildings—arts centers, sports stadiums…and at some point those weren't considered 'enough' any more. Companies wanted a new edge. By extending this marketing ploy of naming socially important institutions to slapping names on social beings themselves, the scope for name recognition was increased dramatically. Every time the person's name would be called in class, or in the supermarket, or wherever, it was advertising for the company. This phenomenon started with one baby, and grew over time to encompass millions of babies—*corporate children*, all named after companies and their products. But then, the corporations decided that they wanted control over how their…'progeny'…turned out, since they were symbols of the corporation. And Justin Fairchild had the idea that if the kids were…trained…right in the firms themselves, from day one, that the companies would be able to control what kind of people they became, what qualities they had, even what their interests are, or are not. Hence, their shock and fear at your asking for a school play—not one of the interests you are *supposed* to have."

"Wow," was all Gatelink could say. Any passerby would have thought from the flat look on her face that she'd just lost her job. She felt her muscles go slack.

"I'm sorry to have to tell you that," George said quietly.

"I've never even thought…." she broke off, a choke in her voice, her shoulders slumped. "I mean, I always knew the way I looked was important, but I never really wondered why…."

"Children don't question, not that much," George murmured. "Most people never question anything at all. You are an inquisitive person, Gatelink, but…we all feel we have to accept a certain degree of our reality without probing any deeper, just to keep from going crazy. How much reality we *need* to swallow whole is inversely related to our age. When we're young, we have to accept everything as being exactly what we see and what we're told—otherwise, we'd be too afraid to face the world at all, with that much uncertainty. On the flip side, the beliefs we have early in life persist throughout our lives, even if we are exposed to other possibilities later in life, and even if we consciously try to reject our early beliefs." Gatelink looked up and saw that George was looking very grave. "There are people who have discovered how powerful our early impressions are, and have corrupted the experience of childhood for their own material gain."

"I'll—be right back," Gatelink mumbled, and almost ran away from the table. She looked for the ladies room—it seemed a reasonable place to hide. She didn't want to hear any more of what George had to say just then. *Corrupting childhood?* she thought. It all sounded weird to her. But why was she feeling angry? As she finished up in the restroom,

60

taking her time as she lathered and rinsed her hands several times with big pink foam and icy water, she decided that she was going to go back and change the topic. She'd calmly ask George some of her questions about how things are *there*, as she'd intended. No more talk about *here*; they would talk about *there*. Having concluded this, she felt much better and even smiled at her reflection in the shining full-wall mirror of the restroom. She dried her hands on a disposable cloth towel and returned to the table.

George's expression was soft, sympathetic. "Hey, I'm sor—" he began.

"Don't be," Gatelink interrupted him, with a smile. "I just need time to process, but you have nothing to apologize for." She paused, sipped coffee, and remembered a question she'd kept forgetting to ask. "So, how old are you anyway?"

"I'm nineteen," he replied.

"Nineteen?" Gatelink repeated. "But, you're doing a Master's, right? Which means you've already finished a Bachelor's, right? So, shouldn't you be, like, 22 or so?"

"Over there, we finish school sooner than you do here. Some people, there, believe that the period of schooling is…drawn out, here, to keep people in the position of being a captive audience for commercial indoctrination." He paused. "Of course, I lied about my age on my application for grad school," he added.

"Hmm. So…." Gatelink struggled to recall even one of the questions she'd been planning on asking him. "You know, I *had* a whole bunch of questions that I wanted to—Oh, I remember!" She was glad she could put the tone of embarrassment out of her voice. "What's an 'elder'?" The other questions began to come back to her also, but she decided it was best not to overwhelm George with questions, or herself with his answers. Though she was determined to make the most out of this encounter, Gatelink was aware that her mind was a little woozy already with the strangeness of the information she'd already gotten.

"That's a good question!" George smiled and nodded approvingly. "I'm glad you asked. An elder is a person…well, who's old, who's *elderly*; it's a shorter, and more respectful way of saying it. We prefer to use respectful terms, where I'm from, recognizing that we'll all be old someday, and we all hope to be treated with respect when that day comes for us, too. There is a huge difference between how the elderly are regarded here and there, and what their place in society is. For example, how often do you see your grandparents?"

"My grandparents?" Gatelink asked, surprised. "I was asking you about *there*." She didn't want to talk anymore about where she was.

"I was only asking to make a comparison, which is generally the easiest way to state things clearly," George said briskly. "But if that was too personal, I'm sorry…. From what I've seen and heard here, when people are beyond 'economic productivity,' they just kind of disappear. They vanish. They are considered no longer necessary to society, it seems." He shook his head. "*There,* however, where economic productivity is hardly considered to be the primary determinant of a person's worth, and where wisdom is highly valued, elderly people play a very important role in our lives. We recognize that, although they won't necessarily have all the answers and they will certainly be wrong sometimes, elderly people have a lot more life experience than we do and have had a lot more time to think about things, and maybe figure them out. They are regarded as the keepers of wisdom, which is very different from information. We go to them for wisdom, and we support them in many ways physically and socially in return for this wisdom—in thanks."

"Hmmm," Gatelink murmured, fingers stroking her chin. "*That's* what an elder is…. So what's a 'park'?"

George raised his eyebrows. "Wow, answering questions about there has turned out to be harder than I thought…. A park is a place of nature. Parks where I come from are huge, miles in diameter—places where nature has not been touched except sometimes to make trails for people to walk through. There are trees, bushes, rocks, and all kinds of wild animals, like birds, squirrels and bears. I had heard that there were small parks here, in the corporate part of the country, parks of only several hundred yards, with trees, grass, birds and squirrels, where the flora were manicured but which were still places of nature. But, since I've been here, I haven't seen even one. The land has all been reallocated to 'development.' I slipped the other day when I asked if we should go to one to talk."

Gatelink was plainly puzzled. "What are they for?"

"What are they for?" George repeated, astonished.

"Yes. Why do people have them over there?" she asked earnestly.

"Well, they used to have them here, too, Gatelink," he said in a very teacher-like manner. "What they're for... They're places where people have left Nature unchanged by us, to appreciate the beauty of Nature, and to commune with Nature. To honor it." He had a peaceful expression on his face as he said the last part.

"*Commune*...with *Nature*?" Gatelink said.

"The feeling of connecting with Nature, with the natural world all around us, it's—" as he tried to find the words, George noticed the distinct dubiousness on Gatelink's face. "It's not something I can describe to you...obviously. You'll have to take my word for it. That's why we have them."

They both put their attentions back into their mugs, George, frustrated at his inability to convey, and Gatelink, at her incapacity to receive. They had reached the ends of their drinks when George mumbled, "Unless..."

With raised eyebrows Gatelink repeated, "Unless?"

He lifted his eyes to hers and said hesitantly, "It's really too early to say, but...well, I haven't checked anything out yet.... Gatelink, would you like to visit Arizona, to have a guided tour of *over there*?" He was smiling gleefully at getting these words out, as if he'd just been awarded a medal.

Gatelink's mouth fell open and she was speechless for about ten seconds. Starting to recover, she said, "Woah!"

"You know what, you can think about it. Keep in mind that I'm not even sure it can happen yet. Though...I really think it's gonna be possible. The school has that 2-week vacation coming up in May—it's only 6 weeks away. I'm definitely going home. I don't know if your parents have any plans for your family. I can ask my folks if it'd be okay with them. I think they'd be happy to have a guest from over here. Then I could *show* you about these things that you very wisely want to know more about!" George was looking triumphant again; Gatelink thought he looked especially cute like that. "Are you ready?" he asked, rising.

Gatelink nodded slowly. Actually, she wasn't sure if she nodded slowly, or put on her coat slowly or not; she assumed she must have been moving at a normal pace since neither George nor anyone else indicated there was anything strange in her behavior—but she felt like she was moving in slow motion as they jacketed up and left the coffeehouse. Her thoughts even felt slowed down. The brisk March night air was awakening, however, and when George's words a few moments after leaving the café were whisked off by the wind, she quickly said, "I'm sorry, what?"

He repeated, leaning close to her ear to make his words heard and cupping a hand against the wind, "I said, I'd meant to ask you how things are at home. Last time we talked, it sounded like things were bad. You were upset."

Gatelink smiled slightly and shook her head. "I'll tell you about it next time, if you want to know. It isn't anything terrible. Less so, after what you've told me today, too." She shook her head again.

They had gotten inside the subway terminal and to the point of their separation. George reached out his gloved hands and held one of Gatelink's gloved hands in his, and said, "I'm sorry, Gatelink. You're probably going to feel angry and sad about this for a while. It's part of loss, and you are losing something, with everything I tell you. So, don't beat yourself up about it, okay?"

Woah, Gatelink had the urge to say again, but held herself back. She just smiled and said, "Thanks…George. We'll talk again."

He smiled, and let go of her hand.

On the train home, Gatelink couldn't figure out what she was more excited about—all the stuff George had told her about the school and why she was named Gatelink, which was a bad kind of excitement; the idea of seeing Arizona; or how George had held her hands in the terminal and almost whispered into her ear outside in the wind. The first thing, about the detailed "regulation" of behavior in the schools, and parents getting money to turn their kids into ads…she didn't want to think about that. And the second thing, well, that wasn't even a sure thing, so that wasn't worth thinking about too much yet. Which left only the third thing for her to be excited about. Gatelink knew but refused to acknowledge that she may have ruled out the first two items to be the focus of her current thinking, intentionally.

George is only 19, she thought. *How weird.* But she smiled as she sat in the crowded train, her eyes closed and her mind replaying the sensation of his breath on her ear and his hands on hers.

CHAPTER 7
A TEARFUL TRIP TO THE GALAXY

The next day at school, Gatelink tried to avoid looking at the assistant teacher, though for a very different reason than she had days earlier after the first time they'd talked. On the contrary, Gatelink had successfully managed to avoid thinking about the things he'd said about the corporate country that she knew would make her upset. When she'd got home at about 9:00 last evening and found her mom sitting in the living room watching TV, she didn't confront her about why they'd named her as they had, or whether they knew about the—well, *mind control* the school did on kids. No, Gatelink was more interested in contemplating how cute George looked, and how nice and smart he was, and how he was like no one else she'd never met…and was only a few years older than her! He was only a teenager, just like herself!

She had been occupied with these and similar thoughts since the conclusion of coffee yesterday, and for this reason sought to avoid George's eyes this morning. When she was almost to her chair, however, she slipped and looked in his direction. To her surprise and disappointment, he was shuffling through papers on his desk. She sat down and tried not to let her disappointment show to Tablesoft, who began one of their usual morning conversations about how well someone's Hair Maker was or wasn't doing.

Gatelink observed George throughout the day and concluded that he was avoiding looking at her. *Is he mad at me?* she contemplated. *Did I do something wrong?* She couldn't think of what it was, though. *Maybe it's because I didn't say yes to going to Arizona with him. I didn't say no, but I didn't say yes. What did I say? …Oh, that's right: 'Woah.' Maybe he's mad just because I'm such a dork.* Gatelink made herself miserable with such thoughts for the rest of the day.

Tablesoft and Easycalc noticed that she seemed out of sorts, but then, they had both agreed that Gatelink wasn't acting much like herself lately. At lunch, they proposed the three of them go to the mall that day, or go out to a movie. Gatelink smiled when they asked; she knew that with their workload, none of them could afford to take the whole evening off, and that Tablesoft was actually having trouble with some of the classes lately—Gatelink suspected they were trying to cheer her up, get her back to 'normal' so they could have their friend back again. But she knew it wouldn't.

"How 'bout right after exams, guys? I think I need to keep at it 'til then," Gatelink told them.

Later, Easycalc and Tablesoft concurred that it must be the stress of schoolwork that was getting Gatelink down and making her act strange. They just hoped it didn't last too long. They wanted their routine back, and they were getting impatient.

That evening, Gatelink couldn't stop wondering why George was mad at her. She found her schoolwork to be a nice distraction, and barely even noticed her parents let alone gave a thought to them or what they knew about corporate sponsorship.

The next day at school began again with avoidance, to Gatelink's dismay. But at 10:30, the option of neglect was knocked down as Ms. McUthrie had a personal emergency and put George in charge of the class' Physics Lab. They were working on circuits, and the teacher needed to go around and check that each student's circuit was done according to instruction. The students worked alone at their stations instead of in pairs or groups, George had been told, to encourage self-reliance and competition. They were not learning how to work in teams and to appreciate the varied strengths and weaknesses of others, he had inferred.

He walked around the room as officially as he could manage to, trying to look the part. Only to Gatelink, who knew his age, did the sight strike as a little funny. Gatelink took in a deep breath as George approached her station, and smiled at him as naturally as she could when he moved toward her. She noticed that he looked a little surprised.

He smiled back, examined her project, nodded, and moved on. *He's not mad at me*, Gatelink thought, surprised now herself. She was confused, and had the nagging feeling there was something she was forgetting. *It must be the parallel circuits*, she concluded quickly, refiguring the model.

Through the rest of the day, however, George's avoidance was renewed. *Aaargh!* Gatelink thought. *What is going on?*

Riskily, she dropped a small note on his desk during the bustle of 5:00 punch-out that read, "Wait for me? Thanks!" She told Easycalc and Tablesoft she had to use the bathroom suddenly, after punch-out. Gatelink thought they might suspect something this time, but she didn't care. She didn't know that Tablesoft and Easycalc had gotten so in the habit of making allowances for her lately that they barely noticed another strange action.

Gatelink returned to the classroom, empty except George organizing papers on his desk. He looked up at her uncertainly when he heard her come in.

"Are you mad at me?" she blurted out. *Real smooth*, she mentally kicked herself in the ass.

George looked surprised. "Mad at you? No, but I thought maybe you might be...at me." He was still shuffling papers around, only stopping to look up as he spoke.

Her brow furrowed. "Why would I be mad at you?"

He stopped the paper dance again. "Well, only by transference— mad at what I told you, what I *revealed* to you, about your own life, and transferring that anger onto me, the messenger, the bearer of bad tidings." He sounded a little nervous.

Gatelink looked at him blankly.

"You *are* angry, *aren't* you?" he asked.

"About what?" she asked sincerely.

"Gatelink, have you thought at *all* about what I had told you last time we talked, about the *way* things *are*?" His voice had gotten quiet.

"What's there to think about?" she replied nonchalantly. "The way things *are*, is the way things *are*. There's nothing *I* can do about anything." She moved closer to George and sat on the front of his desk, swiveled slightly toward him.

"Gatelink, give me a second, and we can go outside…" George finished putting the papers together and stacked them in the center of the desk. He grabbed his bag from under the desk and said, "Let's go."

Outside, he said, "Let's walk a little bit, toward the subway station first."

When they had, Gatelink asked, "Why don't you want to talk at the school?"

"Because I think they monitor the classroom—the Board does—with video and audio. And if they find out I'm not who I said I am, I'm not only out, but they may be able to press legal charges for fraud or something, I'm not sure." He waved his hand dismissively before him. "Or maybe not, I don't really know, but hey, better safe than sorry, right?" He smiled. Gatelink smiled back, happy that he was smiling.

"What were you gonna say, before?" she asked, but not really caring as long as she could gaze at his handsome smiling face.

He stopped smiling. "Gatelink, do you remember what I talked about a few days ago, when we had coffee?"

"Sure," she said casually.

"Well, look, Gatelink, if you're not feeling at all upset about it, I think it probably hasn't sunk in yet. Maybe you haven't been giving it much thought. Now, you certainly don't have to. And I imagine that if you do, it's not going to be easy to process, and it's not going to be pleasant. It's going to be hard. But if you don't, or if you *can't*," his voice got softer here, "it wouldn't make any sense for you to come to Arizona with me to visit, if you *could* go. Of course," his tone returned to its previous businesslike tenor, "there are still other factors up in the air, but I wanted to tell you that."

Gatelink frowned, trying to take in all that George had said.

He smiled, and said, "But I'm certainly not mad at you. I gotta go now, though, so hey, have a good evening." He walked off quickly toward his train as Gatelink stood staring after him.

The next day at school, she smiled at him and he smiled at her and everything was normal. *Except that everything isn't,* Gatelink thought, taking her station at this place her parents had been paid for her to attend, to be called by a name her parents were paid to give her. *They even sold the rights to my having my own personality, by making me come to a place like this!* she thought, looking around her through altered eyes. "They basically sold *me*! That's what I meant to them…. And so did everyone else's parents!"

Tablesoft was running late, and Gatelink was grateful for that. She didn't feel like talking. She felt like staring at her desk and burning a hole in it with her eyes. She hadn't been feeling like this ten minutes ago—*What happened?* she asked herself. But she knew; she'd thought all last night about what George had said that afternoon, despite trying to think about *anything* else. This morning, she'd been able to just occupy her mind with the tasks at hand while getting ready, but now, seeing him…she started to think about what he'd told her over coffee, about the school, the names, everything. Her jaws began to hurt, and she realized she was clenching it.

Tablesoft slid into her seat just at 9:00, and Gatelink only had to trade an unconvincing smile with her friend that morning. Matrix Algebra offered Gatelink some relief from her thoughts during Class 1, but Class 2 that day was Corporate History. Looking at her day schedule five minutes before the end of Class 1, she thought, *What am I gonna do?* and looked over at the one person who might understand her angst.

Fortunately, George happened to be gazing in her general direction just then and noticed Gatelink looking up at him with an almost tortured look. He was alarmed for a second, then it occurred to him: Corporate History was next, and the world must have begun to unravel in Gatelink's mind. He shot her back a sympathetic smile, then scowled with an expression that said, "No, I've got to take more responsibility for creating this situation. I've got to do better than that." He stood, not sure yet what he was going to do, and walked over to Ms. McUthrie. Gatelink saw them exchange a few words and then George walk out of the room. Ms. McUthrie didn't look bothered. *What is he doing?* Gatelink wondered, with more urgency than she would have liked.

Only three minutes until Class 2. *What am I going to do?* she thought, with mounting anger. *If I have to sit through this…this…bullshit,*

I'm...gonna— Just then, her instant messenger went off, interrupting her silent tirade. She unclipped it from her belt and read that she was being called to the offices of the Board. She heard another messenger go off and looked up to see Ms. McUthrie reading hers, too. That was standard procedure when a student was pulled out of class to see the Board. Ms. McUthrie nodded at Gatelink without breaking her train of speech. Tablesoft smiled consolingly at Gatelink as she got up and got her things together. Gatelink smiled back a 'thanks' smile, but felt that she could hardly care what the Board thought of her or said *now*, just as long as she didn't have to sit through anymore of that...propaganda.

Gatelink approached the Board's offices not with the trepidation such a visit usually aroused in students, but with an angry indifference— a dismissal of the Board's emotional authority over her. She knew that she shouldn't antagonize this body that did still have power over her life, if no longer her thoughts, but she found it hard to care.

As she reached out to activate the fingerprint-based door system to the offices, she heard a hushed voice at her shoulder, "Gatelink!"

She spun around and said, "George!" but could have said that without turning around—of course it was him, who else would it be?

"Let's go outside," he almost whispered.

They walked slowly and quietly and when they were at last outside George said, "I...uh...felt like playing hookey this class, and...thought I'd enlist you to keep me company." He smiled. So did she.

"I really didn't want to have to hear all that...*crap* right now. Thanks for getting me out of there."

"It was the least I could do."

"Are you gonna get in trouble for this?"

George took in a deep breath and looked around for a second. "I hope not," he replied. "Anyway, it wouldn't necessarily betray me for who I really am, just as a delinquent and irresponsible assistant teacher.... And there are worse things to be."

"Yeah," Gatelink grunted. "Like a liar. Like someone who sells their kid, their kid's *soul*, their *own* souls, and never tells their kid about it." She was close to tears.

"Gatelink," George said, not sure if he should try to comfort her, or how.

71

She started to cry quietly, her eyes clenched closed, arms crossed against her chest with one hand raised up to cover her face. He had no choice now; George put his arms around Gatelink loosely and let her lean her sobbing body into his for support. He was glad they'd walked to a secluded area of the small corporate grounds because there was little chance of their being seen, but there was also nowhere to sit except the soggy artificial grass.

After a few minutes, when her tears were exhausted, George murmured, "Gatelink, are you okay?"

She straightened up and mumbled, "Yeah, sorry about that," wiping her eyes and stepping backward from him.

"It's okay," he said. "It's understandable. And…in a way, it's my fault."

"*Your* fault?" Gatelink asked, reaching into her bag for some tissues. "How?"

"If I hadn't told you what I know, you wouldn't be upset about things, and—"

"And you wouldn't have had to rescue me from 'Corporate History' class," Gatelink concluded, smiling through moist eyes. "I was already kind of upset about things before you came along, anyway. You just confirmed what I already suspected. Or, what I *would* have suspected if I could have *imagined…*"

"I know," George said, sparing her from having to complete the sentence. "You're gonna have to work through this. It's going to take time." He paused. "In the meantime, we've got about an hour until lunch. Do you want to go somewhere to sit and talk, or would you rather be alone right now…?"

"I'd like to talk," Gatelink said quickly. "I—I don't want to be alone right now. I'll be alone all evening and night thinking about this stuff, over and over and over. Besides, where would you go?"

"That's a good question," George replied with a laugh. "I don't know the first thing about where to go to play hookey around here." He turned his head to look around them, seeing only the faux grass and interspersed patches of dirt forming the company's logo.

"Well, I may not know up from down right now, but there is one thing I do know, and that's where to go for a good time around here," Gatelink began to grin. "Come on!" Recovered from crying, she grabbed George by the wrist and led him away from where they'd been standing. She crouched and rounded her shoulders unnecessarily, as if hiding behind the plastic hedges that were only waist-high. George followed suit, probably suspecting the unnecessity. The only person to see the oddly-crouching pair as they made their way to the street was the "garden" maintenance machine supervisor, who oversaw so many different corporate grounds in a single day that he held no strong allegiance to any one enough to care about the strange people on the property.

At the street, Gatelink straightened up. "Are you sure it's safe?" George asked with mock caution.

"You know what, actually, I'm not," Gatelink replied with the same false sobriety. "Maybe you should get down again just in case...." Facing George, she pushed downwards on his shoulders, laughing.

Unbudging but smiling, he responded, "I think I'll take my chances, Gatelink. But thanks for your concern!" He thought to himself, *She's pretty cute when she laughs.*

"Well, okay. You know the risks! C'mon, this way!" Gatelink strode ahead. "We'll have to hurry. It's not far, but there might be lines."

"Lines?" asked George, trying to keep up. "Where are we going exactly?"

"You'll see!" Gatelink called back over her shoulder.

"Of course," he replied.

Eight minutes and three left turns later, Gatelink and George stood in front of The Galaxy. The front window of what appeared to be a store was at least two stories high and frosted black glass with only the name of the place glowing in laser beams printing.

Gatelink was smiling. "I've only been here a couple of times," she said. "You know, they don't give us much time to play," she muttered. "I've always wanted to come back, though," she said, more clearly.

"Is it...some sort of dance club?" George asked.

"Dance club? No. It's better," Gatelink said. "Probably. Let's go." She moved toward the door.

Inside, the place was surprisingly well-lit. There were large concrete tunnels which spanned most of the room, and, indeed, there were lines at three of the six tunnel entrances.

"Do you have money?" Gatelink called out about the loud pop music.

"Uh, how much do I need?"

"Just $100."

"Um, okay, that's no problem."

"I think you'll agree afterwards that it's worth it," Gatelink smiled as she took George's hand and pulled him toward the line-free Tunnel #2.

As they neared the structure, George could read a sign above it entitling it "A Space Odyssey." Only when they got inside the dark interior though, was he able to even guess at what this form of amusement was. The technological splendor of the innards of the place made it no surprise to him when Gatelink poked him lightly in the side of his waist and said in a low voice, "Virtual reality."

George continued to peruse their surroundings as Gatelink opened her wallet and paid for her ticket. She then tapped George on his arm and cued his turn to feed the machine before they could begin their trip.

They spent the next 45 minutes on distant planets and traveling between stars. They felt the dust on the surface of Mars, drifted among the vaporous winds of Saturn. They performed feats of bravery and great technical skill to return to their spacecraft and enable it to break various barriers to return to their own atmosphere. It was exhilarating, and by the end, they were exhausted though they hadn't broken a sweat.

"Wow!" George said as they emerged. "Wow."

"Yeah," Gatelink replied. "Isn't it cool?"

"Wow," he repeated, shaking his head. "I thought hearing about it was strange...I'd never even thought about what it would be like to actually experience virtual reality."

"You know, there's a home version that a lot of people have, but I think the real tunnels are a lot better."

George shook his head and stayed speechless until they had almost returned to Headquarters. Gatelink didn't feel the need to disturb him.

His dazed amazement was enough of a distraction for her.

"So, it's 11:45, and we're almost back to *Hind*quarters," Gatelink announced with a self-satisfied smirk. That was her first vicious pun against Headquarters and not, she hoped, her last. It felt good.

"Oh!" George awoke from his walking slumber. He stopped abruptly. There were just outside the view of the corporation. Gatelink stopped too.

"No one's expecting me for lunch," he began, "not really. And I haven't done too much 'eating out' yet since I got here, so…could I possibly tempt you into sharing lunch with me today?" He grinned sheepishly at her.

"Is that how they ask a girl on a date where you come from?" Gatelink teased.

"Oh, I—um—" George stammered.

"I'm just *teasing* you, *Mr. Robinson.* I'd be delighted to be your companion for this afternoon's meal," she flirted. "But…we are still in the realm of distraction, right?" she pointed and lightly shook her index finger near his face, dramatically. "I'm having fun, and I wouldn't mind having a little more before settling into the misery I'm sure awaits me for some time to come. Maybe *forever*…." She frowned and rolled her eyes downward.

"'*Maybe forever*'—listen to you!" he said, trying to dismiss her concern with the playful tone of his voice. Inside him something wanted to wrap his arms around her and pick her up and make her squeal with laughter, to make her happy. She should be happy, he thought. "But we are definitely still in the…'realm of distraction' as you say. So…now that we know where we *are*…where do we *go*?"

Gatelink laughed, feeling girlish and adult at the same time.

"For lunch," he clarified, laughing too, though not knowing why.

"Um, there's a nice place a few blocks from here, for Italian and French food. So, once again: Follow me!"

"Anywhere!" George replied, infected by Gatelink's giddiness. He suspected that her elation was a defense mechanism against the anger and hurt she was feeling, and he was happy to foster it for as long as she needed it. Besides, it *was* fun.

Lunch was served to an awkward silence, as both Gatelink and George tried to think of a topic of conversation not relating to the cultural differences between them. When they thoughts of things in those terms, everything seemed to be bound in their social structures. Finally, Gatelink said:

"Did I ever tell you that I like to read books? I don't know how common it is to read, over there…but here, it's not very common. Most people think it's a waste of time; it's 'unproductive.'" She paused, not sure if she wanted to ask about how this situation compared to that in the non-corporate states, or whether the answer might sting her with regret and frustration if it was as she guessed. She continued, "There aren't many books written anymore, since TV is more 'efficient' as entertainment, people say. So, mostly, I read older stuff, from the 20th century. I always need to be reading something. I've even thought that I might like to write a book someday." She smiled shyly into her plate of penne and waited.

George quickly slurped his spaghetti. "Really? You want to write? That's fantastic!"

"Thanks." She still smiled into her food, feeling pleased. "And you, do you like to read books?"

"Of course," he said. "I mean, yes." He added, quietly, "But everyone does, there."

And the awkward silence resumed its position as the third wheel. Gatelink and George may as well have not spoken the same language, so unable did they feel to communicate, now that there was this awareness between them. Gatelink ran through what other topics she could bring up: school, parents, childhood experiences—all would have nothing to do with the world in which George grew up, she was sure. He meanwhile, was doing similar calculations and reaching the same conclusions. So they ate, and made trite comments about the restaurant, and the weather.

These few hours helped Gatelink get through the next few days, though—even the stilted conversation in the restaurant. George's presence in the classroom, while a reminder to her of the falsity of everything around her, shone as a beacon of some possible truth. George, meanwhile, seemed to have grown more comfortable in his surroundings. He seemed less nervous, and even seemed to be enjoying himself.

At home, things were unchanged. Gatelink watched her mother and father scuttle about during the rare hours that they were home, working, amassing, spending, doing nothing else. She hated them, and yet she pitied them, too. They looked like they thought they were happy but that deep down they knew as well as she did that they weren't.

The weeks went on, and she adapted to the idea that her life was according to corporate design. But, she told herself, she wasn't. *They may have my life,* she thought, *but that doesn't mean they have me. Not anymore.* She didn't know how to ask about her going on the trip to Arizona, but finally she decided to try.

"Mom, she began one evening in the kitchen as her mother shuffled around the microwave meals in the freezer looking for the one she wanted. "Tablesoft and Easycalc and I want to take a trip during the May break, to a beach in Florida." She had practiced saying it, so that now she sounded confident and natural.

"Oh?" Mrs. Jones replied, not even looking up as she pulled out a red and yellow cardboard box and headed for the microwave. "For how long?"

"For the whole two weeks."

"And…can you afford it?"

Of course, Gatelink thought. *Her only concern is that they won't have to pay. I should have guessed.* "Yeah, I've been saving. We all have. It'll be no problem. It won't cost that much."

"Just make sure you tell me and your dad the dates you'll be gone, and be sure to leave us your cell number in case Headquar—uh, in case we need to reach you. Okay?" Despite her false cheeriness on the last note, Mrs. Jones never took her eyes off the cardboard box inside the bigger metal one and the little digital numbers informing her how much longer until they could enjoy a "heartwarming traditional meal just like Grandma used to make." Whenever Gatelink saw that ad she wondered if they meant that "Grandma" used to serve that same brand of over processed frozen food to her kids, too. *If so,* she thought sardonically, *I guess that is impressive.*

In any case, the 'permission' was there, and with much less effort than she had planned. *I've been reading too many of those old books,* Gatelink concluded. *I'd mistaken my parents for ones like I'd read about, who'd be concerned and suspicious and...protective. My parents are not any of those things. So...I had nothing to worry about, it turns out!* She smiled, but it hurt a little.

It was time to talk to George again. They hadn't exchanged more words than hello since that day her tears made a stain on his shirt. She realized suddenly, weeks later, that she'd never thanked him properly for his kindness, even if her sadness was due to him, in a way. She wondered if that was why he was keeping his distance, but doubted it. She thought she knew him well enough to believe his reason could have nothing to do with his own ego. It could only be for her own welfare, to give her time and space to come to an agreement with this new reality. He was always so thoughtful, so kind.

Thinking these thoughts, Gatelink felt like she'd run into a brick wall the next morning. There before her in the hall right outside their classroom was George chatting and laughing with Ms. Miller, the teaching assistant for one of the younger classes. Ms. Miller was wearing a form-fitting light blue sweater with the LK logo that nicely set off her eyes, Gatelink noticed. She smiled stiffly at the two of them as she hurried by. George called out, "Hi Gatelink," but didn't stop laughing from whatever funny thing had been said between him and Ms. Miller.

Gatelink reached and took her seat with a look of acute indigestion on her face.

"Gatelink, are you okay?" Tablesoft asked her.

Gatelink took a deep breath and exhaled, and said calmly, "I'm fine, why do you ask?"

"Well, because you look like you just swallowed an alligator," she chuckled. "Or at least the teeth."

"Do I?" Gatelink tried to laugh, too. "I don't know *why*—I feel fine. Hey, is this your way of telling me that I'm having a bad makeup day?"

Tablesoft laughed again, leaned over and punched Gatelink lightly in the arm. Artificial as the encounter seemed to Gatelink now, it was comforting, and she felt like she needed comforting right then. Once again, she had emotions without explanations—these seemed to have become non-stop since George Robinson had entered her life. And now, she thought dully, it looked like he had found someone else's life to enter.

Though she felt inclined to avoid him for a long, long time, Gatelink concluded after careful deliberation that she had better tell George as soon as possible that she could come with him to Arizona. *Even if he marries Ms. Miller next week,* she thought, *I still want to see what it's like over there, in the non-corporate states. I'll never believe there is an 'over there,' that there can be, until I see it. This is important.*

So, after school, Gatelink waited fearlessly as the other students shuffled out. She didn't pretend to go to the bathroom; she didn't even consider it. She felt like she was beyond the point of hiding and sneaking around. She was in too deep now—it no longer mattered if she got caught.

George displayed a friendly smile as she approached. *Ah, but did you smile a different way at Ms. Miller this morning?* she wondered.

"I can go to Arizona," she announced. "I found out last night that I can go, easily. And I'd really like to, if it's possible." Gatelink was impressed that she didn't sound hostile at all, though she felt it, a little. *He should be impressed, too,* she thought haughtily.

"That's great!" George replied, sounding pleased. "I was waiting to hear from you first about it, but I've been wanting to tell you that I asked my folks about it, about introducing someone from here, to *there*, and it's all clear. They had to think about it for a few days, toss the idea around town first, but they all decided that they trust my judgment enough, that I wouldn't bring someone, um, inappropriate. So, it's all cool."

Gatelink didn't try to hide her surprise. "Appropriate? Trusted your judgment? What do you mean?"

"Well, it's just that…." he paused, obviously unsure of how to clarify. "A society is sort of an ecosystem. We believe, over there, in trying to minimize damaging influences on this ecosystem. Here, people don't feel a sense of responsibility for allowing destructive factors to penetrate and live in their society, like the harmful hyper sexuality and person-objectification used by the advertising industry, or the ridiculous levels of violence in movies and TV. Kids really shouldn't have to be exposed to that stuff, is how we see it. Here, adults don't take that responsibility seriously. There, we do."

Gatelink's expression turned from surprise to puzzlement to consternation, as George spoke. "So, they think I could be a 'destructive influence'?" she said.

"No, no, Gatelink. I promise you, after you've been there for a few days, at the most, you'll be able to understand what I mean. We'll have this conversation again, okay?" He was putting the last of his papers into his briefcase. "You know, we probably shouldn't have had this conversation in here, actually." He looked around discreetly. "I guess we'll find out by tomorrow if I've been found out." He raised his eyebrows and pursed his lips to express an exaggerated sense of helplessness. "Wish me luck on not getting discovered and thrown in the slammer?" He had now slid his briefcase off the desk and was heading toward the door. He held out his hand for a mock good-luck shake.

"The very best of luck," Gatelink answered, accepting his hand and giving it a few strong thrusts and promptly releasing it.

"Thank you, Ms. Jones," he replied. "Now, can I walk you to your platform?"

"Thanks, but actually, I'm going home with my mom today. For some reason, she's going home before dark today. Maybe the company told her to spend time with me or something," Gatelink said sarcastically.

"Well, I'll see you tomorrow, and we'll talk about the travel arrangements sometime soon." He waved and disappeared down the hall.

Gatelink heaved a sigh of preparation, and headed for her mother's office for the first time in a long time.

CHAPTER 8
MOTHER KNOWS...BUSINESS

The fluorescents were harsh in the offices. Gatelink remembered that, and how her eyes would sting if she looked right at them. *Strange to spend most of your time in a place where you're afraid to look up,* she had thought. *How can you dream if you can't look toward the sky?* But by now, she knew the answer to that question—dreams were the last thing a corporation cared to foster.

"Hi, Mom," she said, entering and putting her backpack down on one of the plush leather chairs facing the large mahogany oak desk piled high with loose papers and thick reports. A desktop and a laptop computer competed with the bound and unbound pages for space on the cluttered desk. Mrs. Jones held her phone receiver in one hand and was pressing a button on the phone's face with the other.

"Just a minute," she said, without looking up. Her tone of voice was businesslike. She made her call, spoke to someone in Tokyo, demanded sales figures to be sent first thing in the morning. She said something in Japanese at the end and hung up.

"I didn't know you speak Japanese," Gatelink said, surprised.

Mrs. Jones looked up. "Yes, they give us enough to get by, with the countries we have to contact. Good for relations, makes people work for us faster, better, when they're happier. I thought you knew all that, Gatelink." Now Mrs. Jones sounded surprised. "Oh Gatelink, you have so much to learn still."

You have no idea, Gatelink thought derisively. The she thought, *Or maybe you do.*

"I guess so," Gatelink said dismissively, looking away and picking up her bag. "You said you were leaving at 5 today, right?" She kept her tone as neutral as she could, though her mother's staring at her was making her nervous and mad. *She barely even looks at me most of the time; now suddenly she's staring? What gives?*

"Gatelink, I wanted you to come to my office for a reason," her mother began, as she rose from her chair and walked around her desk to sit on the front of it. Her navy blue business suit with the Gatelink logo with photos of the computers placed symmetrically in parallel lines, like pinstripes, was slightly wrinkled from the day's wear. Still, she looked very professional, and Gatelink couldn't help feeling a little bit proud of her mom when she saw her looking like that.

"It's time that you start thinking about your future, your future with the company," she said.

"It's time that I start thinking about my future?" Gatelink repeated angrily. "How do you know whether I've *been* thinking about it or *not*? You never asked!" Gatelink knew she was almost yelling. The office was so big, though, that no one else would be able to hear. Still, she crossed her arms briskly in an attempt to calm down.

A cool negotiator, Mrs. Jones seemed nonplussed by her daughter's outburst. "So, Gatelink, maybe I underestimated you. I'm sorry. I shouldn't have." She then paused and waited as Gatelink's eyebrows went up in surprise. Gatelink also was silent, stunned by her mother's response to her tantrum and by the solicitous way she was speaking to her.

"Gatelink, I *know* you're very smart. *Everyone* at the company knows you're very smart. You're at the top of the educational division—the school. And people around here have noticed." She was nodding to emphasize her point. It was Gatelink's turn to stare.

"I'll admit it, Gatelink: I wasn't as good at school as you are. And so, I didn't start out in this office." She gestured around her at the spaciously and poshly furnished room with its own private bathroom. "I had to work hard to get here, for years. I started out in a *cubicle*. I didn't even have any furniture in there except a desk and a chair. God, it was awful!" She emitted a short laugh.

This is the most she's ever said to me at one time, Gatelink thought.

"But they are so impressed with you at the top, Gatelink, that they wanted me to tell you that if you focus your college studies on computer design, which is where they want you, you can start out *here*, in an office like this one, at quite a high salary for starting out!" Mrs. Jones smiled broadly.

Gatelink remained silent, brows still raised.

"Of course, you'll need to play by their rules. You'd need to get approval for your college curriculum and activities, and make whatever modifications they might request. But as long as you just keep doing as well at your studies as you've been doing, then you've got it made!" She finished triumphantly, punctuating her last remark with a salesperson-like gesture of raising her opened hands in front of her to almost shoulder height.

"Vitacomp hasn't talked to you already, have they?" Mrs. Jones suddenly asked suspiciously. "Or Bud Systems?"

"N-No," Gatelink managed to mumble.

Mrs. Jones was silent for a moment, considering this information. The cheerful demeanor quickly resumed. "No, of course not. Of course they haven't. You see, Gatelink, we protect that information carefully— who's at the top of our list, and who we consider...expendable. The company can't *force* anyone to stay, of course, but we don't want our rivals to know who to court the most aggressively, when the time comes." She gave a wide grin. "Those dumb bastards can't hack their way through our firewalls. They probably couldn't hack their way into the government."

Gatelink stared, speechless. Apparently taking this silence for consent, Mrs. Jones became suddenly parental. "Oh, honey, I'm so happy for you!" She stepped forward and hugged Gatelink, awkwardly. Gatelink didn't think that had ever happened before. "And I'm so glad I got to be the one to tell you," she added, pulling away. "I was sure that if they let one of us tell you, me or your father, it was going to be him." She continued to beam, unperturbed by the inscrutable expression on Gatelink's face.

"Well, now that that's taken care of," she said, still sounding happy, "we'd better get going." She returned behind her desk and shoved a short stack of files into her briefcase and quickly packed up her laptop. "I have a manicure at 6."

*****

The weeks dragged on until May break. George continued to assure Gatelink that she would come to understand everything once she saw how they lived over there; she only needed to be patient and wait. He told her that telling her more about there right now might not be wise; she needed to finish absorbing and processing all she had learned about her own world first, or she would only be confused by what she was to see and experience. They confirmed the travel plans: They would get seats together on a flight to Phoenix, and his family would pick them up from the airport. George still had his own car waiting for him back home, a clunky late-20th century model, so getting around while there wouldn't be any problem for them. They don't have subways and taxis everywhere out there, he explained.

Meanwhile, Gatelink pondered her mother's words and actions toward her in her office that day, and her father's proud beaming that same evening. She told George about it, over the one coffee she convinced him to have with her before the trip, and that only because she promised not to ask any questions about there. George was fascinated.

"You mean *she* told you what the company wants you to do with your life," he stated incredulously. "Your own mother?" He made no attempt to hide his dumbfoundedness.

"*She* told me, that if I *played* my *cards* right, I could start out in a big office like *hers*," Gatelink replied, relieved to have someone else to share the shock with, finally. She had thought about sharing it with Easycalc and Tablesoft, but thought better of it. They would just think she was bragging.

"Using parents to recruit their own children into doing whatever the firm thinks it can use the person best at," he stated, shaking his head. "That's amazing."

"She did everything but offer me a sign-on bonus, or ask me to sign a contract," Gatelink said. "Actually, I'm surprised she didn't have a contract for me to sign."

"Probably they didn't want to scare you off," George responded logically. "I think your play idea has them on their guard with you, but your grades are good enough that they don't want to risk losing you to another company."

"So maybe having my mom be their tool was a 'Gatelink-only special'?" she asked ironically.

He drank his coffee thoughtfully. "Hmm, I doubt that actually. They probably wouldn't create a whole new protocol for only one person. It's not efficient. The minor modification of leaving out a contract was probably the only exception they made."

They sipped in silence for a moment. George added, "I wonder...I wonder if they gave her the words to say, if there's a pre-set script all the parents are supposed to give to their kids—the ones the company wants—to entice them, make them feel happy about working at the corporation, make them *want* to work there."

Gatelink looked down. She hadn't thought of that. This was getting worse and worse.

George noticed the effect of his remarks. "This must be hard for you, to see your mother in this light," he said gently. "Acting this way."

Gatelink looked up. "Well, I don't' really like it, I guess you could say." She smiled sadly. "She is the only mother I have."

"I know," said George. "I know." He smiled empathetically. They finished their drinks quietly.

CHAPTER 9
THE HAPPY (?) COUPLE

A week before break, something ridiculous happened. Tablesoft and Easycalc started dating. They made their declaration matter-of-factly to Gatelink that day at lunch. There were no admissions of love; only plans of gain.

Following a grueling 20-minute debate about favorite TV-commercials, in which Gatelink made a sincere attempt to participate for the sake of the friendships, Tablesoft made an abrupt transition.

"Gatelink, we thought you should know that Easycalc and I have started dating, as of yesterday," she said casually.

"We, uh, hope you won't feel awkward about it," Easycalc added, not sounding at all uncomfortable himself.

"What?" was all Gatelink could think of to say. "*Why?*" she said then, before thinking about it. It might have sounded rude to say, but Tablesoft and Easycalc had never expressed any romantic feelings that she knew about, and honestly, they seemed too different to her to ever fall in love.

"We decided it was the logical thing to do," Tablesoft said, biting carelessly into her quiche sandwich. Mustard dripped out onto her plate, unnoticed. Easycalc also decided to return to his eating, leaving the unanswered questions hanging thickly in the air. Gatelink couldn't give attention to food at a time like this.

"Where is this coming from?" she asked, working hard to contain her irritation and remain calm.

"What do you mean?" Easycalc asked, pausing his ingestive efforts but not putting down his sushi roll. "Why does anyone start dating? To find someone with whom they can make a financial team. Both

86

Tablesoft and I are interested in starting such a partnership earlier in life rather than later. We're the same age; we both work for the firm, and…we're already friends." He stopped to smile blithely at Tablesoft, who returned the gesture. "It makes perfect sense."

"A financial *team*?" Gatelink said. "What exactly do you mean by that?"

Her friends looked at her with something between derision and disgust. *Gee, thanks for not hiding yours,* Gatelink thought.

Tablesoft spoke up. "Gatelink, why do you think your parents got married?" she spoke between bites. "Why do you think anyone gets married?" She paused to procure and process another bite. "To share the expenses of living while encouraging each other's ambition and earning power. I mean, parents can only do so much. After a certain point, they're not as useful anymore for these purposes. Easycalc and I have both found that we're reaching that point a lot sooner than we'd each been expecting, sooner than people usually do." She resumed her dining.

"I hope you don't feel offended that I didn't consider you, Gatelink," Easycalc said, "but you don't seem to be at this level yet. No offense, of course—we know you'll get there." He punched her stunned form in the arm. She didn't rebound, but let herself be slanted by the gesture. "And then you'll find someone to consolidate your circumstances and ambitions with." He smiled graciously. "Just like we have."

"Of course," Gatelink stated, pasting a smile onto her face by force of will. She would not let them see her true feelings. There couldn't be any point in that anymore.

As they three munched along on their lunches, quietly and calmly, Gatelink felt a deepening sense of isolation. She felt alone, sitting beside her two best friends in the world, and she wondered if she had never met George Robinson, would she not be feeling this aloneness now, would she never have had to know this awful feeling? If he had never come to Gatelink C&S, never told her about *there* and the truth about *here*, would she still be Tablesoft and Easycalc's Gatelink? Would she have been happy for them? Would she have been the one dating Easycalc, instead of Tablesoft? This she wondered, as she sat eating silently and slipping into her personal abyss.

*****

At last, it was May break. After staying up all night together cramming for finals, Easycalc and Tablesoft were too tired to go out shopping afterward, as had been a tradition for the three every year after finals since the 6th grade. Gatelink could tell they were miffed at her not joining them for the study-fest, but she wasn't going to postpone her trip for a day to catch up on sleep. But Gatelink found that, though she couldn't feel close to Tablesoft and Easycalc anymore, she still hated to hurt them; and so, she did feel a little bad to have disappointed them.

But she couldn't spend too much time or energy on such thoughts, not with so many others vying for her attention.

This was the day she *discovered*. Today her questions would be answered—she would *know*. The phantoms in her mind would have life breathed into them, or they would crumble like dead leaves into the wind. Either way, everything would be made clear.

And she would have two weeks with George Robinson, nonstop! Packing her suitcase the night before, she realized she was going to want to buy all new clothes when she got there, *their* clothes, but still she lingered, pausing to consider each prospective passenger—does this shirt look good on me? Do these pants make me look too skinny? At last she had settled on an ensemble of 30, and was able to lay herself down to sleep. Surprisingly, she slept quickly and well.

In the morning it was difficult to conceal her excitement from her parents. There's no reason she would feel nervous about leaving for a beach trip with Tablesoft and Easycalc. Thankfully, they seemed not to notice as they hustled and bustled around the apartment getting ready to go to work, as every day. They only said, "Bye, Gatelink—have fun, and...uh, be safe," as they left, at approximately 8:05 a.m. Then Gatelink was alone.

Be safe, she reflected on their words. *They're trying to protect their investment.* She snorted. With nearly half an hour before she was supposed to leave, she returned to her bedroom with the intention of dawdling away the next 25 minutes. Finding this impossible, she gave into her instinct and left early. It would be easier to wait for George and what was to come in a noisy airport than in a silent mausoleum.

CHAPTER 10
SMOOTH TRANSIT, ROUGH TRANSITION

The airport indeed was noisy. There were some other May-break travelers Gatelink's age, but the vast majority of people filling the station were men and women clad in dark pinstriped and solid suits with logos and ad-photos, talking in varied volumes into cell phones, punching noisily the keys of laptops, personal messengers and other devices. None of them were talking directly with an actual human being. *So many ways to communicate,* she thought. *Yet no one does.*

A man next to her began to yell into his phone, with increasing use of expletives. No one looked up in surprise or dismay—they just inched away, and carried on with their talking or typing. Gatelink did the same. It bothered her whenever something like this happened, though—not at a conscious level, because she still didn't have any other framework for how society could be, with which she could compare all she'd ever seen around her; but at an untold level in her mind this had always seemed to be not right. Her parents had always approached the situation the way all these other people just had, to ignore someone yelling and even cursing into their phone in the middle of a crowd, or pushing someone else out of the way to get a better place in line.

Once, at a train station when she was eight, a man in a suit and trench coat had pushed her to the ground to get to his line. Her parents had helped her up and warned her not to cry—"we don't know if he's got a gun," they'd said. Gatelink knew that guns could kill people, and couldn't imagine why he'd want to kill her, but terrified anyway she'd kept silent. When she got older and started to watch and read the news, she came to know that there were random mass shootings weekly, sometimes daily, in America. They happened in all different classes of neighborhoods, with all different sorts of people shooting their friends, neighbors, strangers—a middle-aged white male erupts at the office, killing four and wounding three others; a young black woman explodes gunfire at a shopping mall near where she lives; a lonely housewife goes door-to-door with an uzi and a silencer. There were metal detectors and x-ray machines, monitored by computer, at most shopping centers, offices and schools nowadays—really, at all public places—but still it happened, and it happened a lot.

Gatelink felt bad as she thought of these things. She felt angry about them, but she also felt that in a way, they were her fault, that she was somehow responsible. She didn't like this feeling at all, and remembered why it is that she so rarely thought about this issue anymore. *Still,* she thought, *it would be useful to George to hear about this, to help him learn more about here, for his personal project.* She tried to focus on this last thought, as she slumped into a comfortable, plush leather seat in the waiting lounge, looking straight ahead at the quickly passing knees of people heading in all different directions. She would focus on the utility of this last stream of thoughts, and try to forget all the other stuff it seemed to bring up. She glanced at her watch. Still fifteen more minutes until George was scheduled to meet her there. She sighed, and closed her eyes. *I'll just rest them,* she thought. *Maybe it'll help me not to think anymore until George gets here.*

*****

Somewhere in the middle of a dream, Gatelink was alone. She was aware that she might be dreaming, but she couldn't be sure. One thing she could be sure of was that she was scared. She was crouching someplace, she felt like it might be amongst boxes, like in a warehouse, but she couldn't see anything around her, only sense them. And sense that there was someone—something—trying to kill her. She had to hide, and she had to keep running, but above all she couldn't let it see her.

The she saw her parents. They were erect, standing, walking about 20 feet away. There were boxes, or something, separating her from them, but she could tell it was them. Their faces were expressionless. *What are they doing?* Gatelink thought. *I should get them! I should warn them!* But she didn't. She thought it might be because of the look on their faces that she didn't, because they didn't look scared. Still, she thought she *should* warn them. But she didn't. She remained terrified for herself, as they walked calmly past, but not for them. She didn't know why she didn't feel frightened for them, why she didn't feel anything when she looked at them. And then, they were gone, and she was alone again, evading an unknown evil that would surely kill her given the chance.

Then, she was shaking, though she hadn't moved. She was being shaken. She had been found, she must have been found, and she would be—

"Gatelink. Gatelink!" George was speaking loudly into her ear as he shook her with moderate force. "Wake up! You're having a nightmare!"

"Wha-at?" Gatelink responded, opening her eyes fitfully and rubbing them. She looked around, surprised at where she was.

"I'm sorry; I took the wrong train. I'm about a half-hour late. But we'll still make the flight okay, don't worry…. You must have dozed off."

"Yeah, I…" she began, sitting up in her seat. "I just closed my eyes for a minute."

"Well, I don't know how long you kept 'em closed, but it must have been long enough to get you into some kind of dream. Your face was almost contorted with…um, something bad, when I got here. I thought it would be better to wake you up, since you didn't look like you were having much fun. I hope you don't mind."

Gatelink was pleased to note that his drawl was deeper now than the other times she'd heard it. "No, of course not. Thanks. It's funny— I haven't dreamt in a long time, and now I have this really weird dream when I fall asleep in the middle of the airport!"

"Well, these chairs are pretty comfy," George declared, bouncing a little in his, to demonstrate his theory. "I can see how it can happen." He smiled. "You won't be seeing these in the Phoenix airport, though,

I can tell you that." He paused, and bounced a little more. "We have about ten minutes left 'til we have to get going for our gate; you wanna tell me about the dream?"

Gatelink looked at him uncertainly. "I don't know...."

"Was it about *me*?" he replied in a low, mock seductive voice.

"Nooo," she answered, with an amused half-grin. "Though it is interesting that you would assume a scary dream a girl has would be about you...." she teased.

"Hey! Remember that you're going to have to depend on *my* hospitality, now...." he flirted back.

Gatelink smiled and paused for the levity to run its course. "Actually," she said, "I don't remember too much about it—just that I was really scared. I don't even know why I was scared, but think I was hiding from something trying to kill me. And I saw my parents, but they weren't scared, and I didn't try to warn them." She paused. "I don't know why I didn't try to warn them."

"Hmmm," George contemplated. "Well, dreams are usually symbolic; even the people are symbols of something else. Death is symbolic of great change, generally change within a person. And I'm sure your parents *represented* something to you—it wasn't actually your parents that you were seeing. So, I wouldn't feel too bad about not warning them." Observing a lack of positive response to his comforting words, George added, "I'm sorry I can't tell you more about what your dream meant; I don't know that much about dream-reading. But a lot of people back home know a lot more than me. I'm sure they'd be happy to help you understand that dream, if you want to."

"Dream-reading?" Gatelink asked, brightening up.

"Oh, that's right; you wouldn't have heard of it before!" George said in a dramatically cheerful way. "Dream-reading is...well, we *read* dreams because they are our soul's way of talking to us, of telling us things we don't want to hear, but should, or things that we are not yet able to admit to ourselves that we want...or fear. They are one of the ways in which all the parts of our selves come together, and we honor that process. Thus, we never ignore our dreams, but rather, respect them."

"Then…how come when you woke me up, you said you 'thought it would be better'?" Gatelink asked.

"Because nightmares generally say what they have to very quickly, and then just keep going on saying the same thing over and over, to make sure you get whatever point it is you're trying to get yourself to grasp. It's the same way with good dreams, actually, but we try to let others enjoy them as long as they want to last, 'cos, well, they're pleasant." He let out a little laugh. Gatelink wondered if he was thinking about some good dream of his. "But to bring someone out of a nightmare, well, it's only nice."

"Mmm," Gatelink said, processing. She liked this conversation they were having much more than her solitary thoughts before she slept. "So…does everybody read all the dreams they have? Like, even little kids?"

"Oh, Gatelink. *All* of your questions are going to be answered. And very good questions they are, too." He put his hand over hers where it lay on the chair's armrest. "But right now, we've got to ske-daddle. We have to get to our gate." He stood and picked up his bags and hers. "But I promise that we'll talk more as soon as we get settled on the plane."

And so they navigated their way through the morass of maroon and navy blue suits and boarded their flight. George's ticket was for the window seat, and Gatelink's the middle of the 3-seat row; he let her sit first, in the window seat, saying, "I've already seen the sights from up here, you haven't yet. And, uh, I like sitting in the middle better, anyway." Gatelink thought he might have added that last part to make her feel okay about taking the better seat—could anyone prefer the middle seat?

"So," George started, "what were we talking about, back in the waiting lounge?"

"Um, I don't remember," Gatelink said, with a laugh. "What were we talking about? Something about how things are in Arizona…about dream-reading, I think…."

"Oh, you were asking if everyone dream-reads. Well, that's a good question. And you know, I'm not really sure." He let out a lone laugh, almost a nervous chortle. "I've never really noticed too much." His face read troubled.

"Well, you know what they say," Gatelink perked in. "The last thing a fish notices is the water around it. It's like that…. C'mon, don't feel bad about it. Then I'll feel bad." She prodded him with her elbow to make the point. She could tell her advice wasn't working but she couldn't understand why.

"Yeah, you're right," he turned to her and smiled. "Thanks. But still, I wish I could give you a good answer. I know that my parents and brother do, *religiously*. I think my friends do too, but I can't remember any of us talking about it for the last few years. But I guess I've been sort of interested in other things lately," he looked down, as if remembering something sadly.

"Is something wrong?" Gatelink asked. The plane was beginning to leave the ground.

"No," he said, his face suddenly toward her and brightened with artificial speed. "I'm really glad you're going, Gatelink. It's gonna be a lot of fun!"

Gatelink smiled and wondered quietly at his tone as she watched the Earth recede. New York looked beautiful from the sky—a world of miniature intrigues and deceits. *So harmless from up here,* Gatelink thought. She resolved to resist her desire to gather more information about 'there' before it became 'here'—she didn't want to make George more uncomfortable than she apparently already had. So she waited for him to bring it up, at his own pace. His pace, unfortunately, outstripped the flight. They only talked about the plane's interior, the flight service and movies until they landed in the other world.

Gatelink's first impression of Phoenix was that it looked nothing like New York. It didn't even look like a city. It didn't look like…anything. She made a 360-degree turn when they got out of the terminal, unabashed though people drifted by them on all sides and some looked at her curiously. But that was another thing—people drifted; they didn't stomp, as the way of fast-paced walking in corporate America now seemed to her in comparison. Here, you could hardly hear the footfalls.

Gatelink felt an itch at her ankle and tore herself from the stucco structures to gaze downward and saw to her amazement, grass. She scanned the ground and saw grass everywhere but the roads. Her mouth dropped open.

"Um, Gatelink, I hate to cut short your first impression," George said, "but we have to get to the City Center to meet my parents. The time we set was 12:30, and it's 12:25 now." He smiled apologetically.

Gatelink raised her head quickly to her face. It felt strange to see him, here. "Grass," was all she could say.

George nodded and smiled with a look of understanding. "Of course. You're surprised to see the grass. Well, we gotta start walking, but I can tell you about it on the way." With this, he grabbed Gatelink's bags from her unresisting hands and started to walk briskly forward. He seemed to have no trouble navigating the sometimes uneven terrain, but Gatelink stumbled and almost tripped and fell a few times in trying to keep up with her host.

"Sorry I'm walking a little fast, but you know, it is a long drive for my folks, and they're not used to driving much, so, I don't want to ask them to wait, too. Plus, they might take it the wrong way...." his voice drifted off, sounding tense. Gatelink struggled to keep pace on the patchy ground.

"So, the grass," George began. "Well, it wasn't always here, believe it or not. It's actually not native to the land here. Or, at least, we don't know if it is." He paused. "See, years back, before The Separation, folks out here didn't see anything wrong with tearing out the natural setting and filling in concrete to make things more efficient, enable people to walk faster, get where they're going faster." He slowed down a little as he said the last part, and looked around. He said in a low voice, almost a whisper, "Actually, walking as fast as we are now is frowned on by some people." Then he continued at an easily audible volume, "But as I was saying, people thought it was fine to put up sidewalks and filling in the rest of the space with concrete too—the rest of the country was doing it; we wanted to stay modern. But as it became increasingly clear what 'modern' was coming to mean, was coming to entail, all sorts of changes that had been done for no reason but to be 'modern' were reversed. The people voted on it, and the city removed the concrete that had been killing the earth underneath, and growth of new life was fostered. We believe that losing a little time in transport is a very fair price for keeping ourselves in touch with the earth as much as possible. No one needs to get anywhere that fast, anyhow—not in corporate America, either, but people don't realize it there." George smiled proudly as he spoke these last few sentences. After a brief pause, he added, "After all, in life it's the journey, not the destination, that matters most."

Gatelink frowned. She thought she'd heard that somewhere before, but couldn't remember where. Luckily, George was ahead of her, and must not have noticed her frowning.

After a minute, Gatelink realized she should say something, and spoke, "Hey, thanks for explaining that to me, about the grass. It's...amazing." *And really strange,* she thought, but guessed that she should not say, not now that she was here.

George looked at her and said, "You're welcome. It was my pleasure." And he did sound pleased. *Is he, like, really liking this being a tour guide thing or what?* Gatelink wondered.

She didn't have long to wonder, however, because within a minute she was face-to-face with Mrs. and Mr. Robinson and George's younger brother, Tommy.

The Robinsons looked nothing like their older son. Gatelink could pick out individual features that were the same—George's nose was the same as his father's; his chin was his mother's—yet somehow she was surprised he was theirs. His brother was much less of a shock; she would have attached Tommy to George in a heartbeat.

There were hugs for George, which didn't surprise her, but then hugs for Gatelink also. Her outstretched hand had lay still, useless in the air between her and Mrs. Robinson for about 3 full seconds as the older woman delivered a look of sad compassion before smiling gently and pulling Gatelink into a light embrace. It took Gatelink a second to understand what had happened, and by then it was too late to extricate the culpable hand. She reached up with her left and patted Mrs. Robinson's back with her palm, not knowing what else to do. Mrs.

Robinson gave Gatelink a brief squeeze and released her, smiling broadly.

"It's wonderful to have you here, Gatelink," she said.

"Th-thank you," Gatelink replied awkwardly. "It's great to be here."

"Welcome, Gatelink," Mr. Robinson said warmly, embracing her as well. Gatelink was relieved to find his hug of less duration than his wife's. When he pulled back Gatelink was the only one embarrassed.

"We're glad you came to visit, Gatelink," Tommy offered next. Then even he gave Gatelink a quick hug and smiled with genuine gladness.

Wow, Gatelink thought.

"So, whaddya say we get these bags put away in the car and grab us a bite to eat?" Mr. Robinson asked rhetorically, whisking half of the bags off with him toward some point in the distance.

"Sounds good, Dad," George answered, doing the same. Gatelink saw George's father turn back to smile at him as he followed. Gatelink realized she was alone with people she had no idea how to talk to.

"So, uh, George told me about the grass," she said.

"What?" Mrs. Robinson asked, surprised.

"Um…" Gatelink fumbled around for a response.

"The *grass*, Mom," Tommy chimed in. "They don't have grass in the cities over *there*. George said so."

"Oh, of course!" Mrs. Robinson exclaimed. "Of course you'd be surprised at the grass here!" She smiled. "I'm sorry; it's just been such a long time since I've been to the corporate states that I'd forgotten!"

"You've been there?" Gatelink asked.

"Mmm," she said, nodding, but with a look as though she'd remembered something unpleasant. "The national government gives us the 'option' of submitting our census information, but *we* have to go there to deliver it. Each state sends someone. One year, Harry and I volunteered."

"They don't send someone here?"

"No. They say it's 'inefficient,'" Mrs. Robinson replied, in a tone that implied she'd rather leave the topic. "So, this is your first visit to these parts." Gatelink found the way she said this to be somehow comforting; she felt absolved. "Do you have any questions about

98

anything else that you've seen so far? About the city?"

"Yes," Gatelink said. "I was wondering something. The buildings—why are they so…short? They all look only 3 or 4 stories high. Isn't that a waste of space?" Only after she'd said it did Gatelink realize this would undoubtedly sound like a criticism. She bit the inside of her lower lip in self-reproach.

"Don't worry, I'm not offended, Gatelink," Mrs. Robinson said. *Are they telepathic here, too?* Gatelink wondered. "From the perspective of people who live in the corporate states, maybe this is, uh, *inefficient.* It's true that the city has to be wider and you have to travel a bit more to get from place to place, but by keeping the buildings only a few stories high, we can still enjoy the sky, Nature's great canvas." She spread her arms out and looked, smiling at the bright blue picture screen with the hold of yellow sun. "When buildings are too tall, they keep people from seeing and appreciating the sky, from being a part of it. And that's not how humans are supposed to live. No living creatures are meant to live that way. Especially not children." She looked back at Gatelink diplomatically. "At least, that is what *we* believe, *over here.* And that's why, at the time of The Separation, we removed the excess layers at the tops of the buildings of our cities." She smiled with a serene pride. Gatelink noticed that Tommy shared his mother's expression. Gatelink had never seen such an expression as these two people wore as they talked about their history. She didn't understand it, and felt a little threatened by it, but she reminded herself she was here to learn; there was nothing to feel angry about. Their happiness wasn't personal.

"Did George tell you much about The Separation? From what he's told us, I gather they don't teach you about it in schools there," Mrs. Robinson welcomely interrupted Gatelink's reverie.

"He mentioned it, but he didn't really tell me that much about it," Gatelink answered.

"Well, it looks like he and his father are heading back this way," Mrs. Robinson said, turning to look back at them, then back at Gatelink, "so I think it'll have to wait until lunch for us to tell you all about it." She smiled warmly again. *All this smiling!* Gatelink thought. *I've never been smiled at so much before in my life! And it's only been an hour!* She suddenly felt a strange need to be ignored.

When George and his dad reached them, Mrs. Robinson hugged George again. *What is going on?* Gatelink wondered, but no one else seemed to see anything out of the ordinary. *That's because what's out of the ordinary here,* Gatelink thought sardonically, *is me.*

"So, shall we eat?" Mr. Robinson asked, again rhetorically. *It's like he's telling us what to do without giving commands,* Gatelink thought. *Interesting.* "The restaurant's just a short walk from here." He pointed toward a two-story building with a large glass window as the front wall. They started walking in that direction, and soon were seated in a restaurant that looked similar to the ones in New York except that there were dozens, maybe hundreds, of potted plants throughout the dining area. *And who knows about the kitchen!* Gatelink thought.

Ordering was easy, since the dishes were the same, except that there were far fewer meat than non-meat dishes, Gatelink noticed.

"Um, is this a specialized kind of restaurant? Like a vegetarian restaurant?" Gatelink asked as they looked over the selections.

"No. Why?" Mr. Robinson responded casually over the top of his menu.

"Because there's a lot less meat than they eat over there," George explained to his father. "I forgot to mention, Gatelink, that over here we eat a lot less meat, because it's known to be less efficient agriculturally, to be wasteful of the environmental resources to produce, and because there's significantly higher risk of disease transmission through eating meat than non-meat foods."

"Really?" This was all news to Gatelink.

"Um-hmm," George nodded, his eyes still scanning his menu. "It's only sensible."

Only sensible, Gatelink thought. *I seem to recall you chomping down some veal burgers in the Headquarters cafeteria,* But she didn't say anything about it. George ordered vegetarian.

When the food had been ordered and the time for the great wait had come, Mrs. Robinson considerately remembered Gatelink's question.

"Gatelink asked about The Separation," she announced.

"George, you never told her about The Separation?" Mr. Robinson asked his son, mildly chastising.

"Well, it didn't really come up until we got here," George replied with thinly-veiled defensiveness. "It's not like I was trying to hide it."

"Of course not, son. I'm sorry if it sounded that way," Mr. Robinson said sincerely. "I've never had the opportunity that you have, to teach someone from corporate America about us. I don't know where I would start, either."

Gatelink thought Mr. Robinson sounded genuine, but she could see incipient angst in George's face and body language; he looked down at the table with his hands in his lap and his brow furrowed. She wondered why he didn't believe his father.

"George has told me a lot about the Elders, the educational system over here, and how people value different things than we do over there," Gatelink said quickly. "It's just, we haven't had a lot of time to talk, really, before I came with him here. He had to help me understand what things are really about over *there*, first. And believe me, that wasn't easy!" She laughed with this last sentence, trying to dispel the tension she'd seen approaching. It must have worked, because the Robinsons laughed too, and smiled proudly at George. Gatelink looked over at him, seated diagonally across from her on the opposite bench, and saw then he was smiling modestly back at his family.

"Well, we were sure surprised when George told us what he wanted to do, going over *there*," Mrs. Robinson said to Gatelink, but looking at George across from her, "And I still can't say that I'm happy he up and left us for a while, but if he was able to bring the truth to someone over there," she put her hand on Gatelink's, "then I'm glad. We sure are proud of him."

Gatelink wanted to ask why they thought it would be so hard to tell people back there what the truth is, but she wanted first to find out what it was. She needed to know about The Separation. She figured her first question wasn't one she would likely forget.

"So…what was 'The Separation'?" she directed to all of them.

The Robinsons exchanged glances, a silent etiquette of asking who would start, and then, surprisingly, Tommy spoke.

"The Separation was when these eight states broke away from the rest of the U.S., in every way but physically."

"It's when the practice of naming children after corporations began," Mr. Robinson contributed, "that the people of these states, which were less populated and hence less commercialized, rejected all forms of commercialism or corporate control over people's lives. Out of love for their children, more than concern for themselves, people here Separated." Then, noticing the hurt look on Gatelink's face, he added, "I'm sorry."

Gatelink smiled tensely. "Thanks."

After a brief pause, Mrs. Robinson resumed the discussion. "People here saw that such trends were heading in a destructive direction, destructive to the fabric of human society."

"And to humans' relationship with the rest of the world—with Nature, with our own emotions, and with God," George concluded.

They're like a tag team, Gatelink thought. *A relay run. They're passing the baton, finishing each other's sentences. Even George, who looked so uncomfortable two minutes ago, looks like he feels like he belongs.* She realized what she had thought, and why it hurt. *He belongs.* She felt very alone, but tried, for the sake of learning, to keep focused on the conversation.

"So," Mrs. Robinson stated, "we separated. We informed the corporate offices that were located in these states that we would not cooperate with their practices. This is still America, and they couldn't force us to do anything, only try to persuade us."

"Offer us money," Tommy informed. Gatelink was amazed at his level of interest in this conversation. After all, he could only have been 11, maybe 12 at the most—she and all the kids she'd known at that age would have been bored by a conversation about history or politics. At that age, it was all about Virtual Games and Hairmakers, over there. *Ahh,* she said to herself, remembering that those things were not here to occupy a child's mind. *Interesting,* she thought. *What do kids think about, here?* Another question to file away.

"And those people who were, uh, *persuaded,*" Mr. Robinson said, "were free to go and follow their corporate, uh, 'employers.'"

"He means corporate *owners*, Gatelink, but he doesn't want to offend you," George said, not harshly but not gently either. "And I hope it doesn't make you feel bad, my telling you, but if you want to know how we see things here, that's part of it."

"Yes," Mr. Robinson concurred, matter-of-factly.

At this point, their food arrived, and the conversation was postponed until a new equilibrium had been set and a pattern of speaking between bites was established.

"So, the grass? And the buildings? When did that all happen?" Gatelink asked between helpings of her turkey and lettuce sandwich.

"Soon after the corporations were driven out," Mrs. Robinson volunteered. "And those weren't the only things to be reversed, either. Computers were eliminated from homes and schools, once we recognized that video games and the 'internet' were keeping people apart. That was especially harmful for children. We kept one computer in each state's capital, for emergency purposes. So far they haven't needed to be used, to my knowledge."

"With the corporations gone," Mr. Robinson picked up, "there were no more department stores, no more grocery stores. No stores of any kind, actually, since all the small businesses had given up a long time before. Same with restaurants, auto mechanics, dry cleaners— everything was owned and run by big multinational companies, just like things still are, over there. So, as people finished off their food supplies, they had to start thinking about what we were all going to do for food now. See, after we forced them to leave, the corporations wouldn't even sell to us at all, not even at punitively inflated prices— not unless we agreed to the naming program and whatever other 'programs' they wanted to impose on us. They wouldn't even sell food to these eight states—not even food, unless we relented. That's how it was."

"And the fear about shortages got to some people, who hadn't been persuaded by the money, to leave here," Mrs. Robinson said. "Nancy Harrison's aunt, you remember, honey?" she asked Mr. Robinson. "They lost touch with them after that. They felt too ashamed to keep contact, I reckon." She shook her head sadly. "It's a shame. And nobody here would have blamed them for leaving." She said to Gatelink. "That's not how we think here, in terms of 'blame.'" Then, back to her husband, "But I guess Nancy's aunt and her family didn't know that, since they left before The Changes in Thought had even started."

"The 'Changes in Thought'?" Gatelink repeated, puzzlement clear in her voice.

"We should probably tell you about the rest of The Separation before we get into the Changes in Thought," George said, suddenly resuming his role as tour guide. "The people of these eight states decided that they would respond to the food shortage in the only way they could without caving in to the corporations and giving up. They went back to producing it themselves, out of necessity."

"Yes, you told me people 'farm' out here," Gatelink said, recalling. "But I didn't understand, when you told me." She nodded as she took in the insight. "So, it's because the food supply had been under corporate control…."

"Corporate rule, we like to say," Tommy quipped.

"Just like it still is, out there," Mr. Robinson added, sharing a knowing glance with his wife. "If you turn your back on anything they want you to do, over there…your food could be cut off. Everything could." He shook his head, looking disturbed. Gatelink didn't feel so hot with this last thought either.

"On the way home you'll get to see some people's farms," Tommy told Gatelink. "We have all different styles of production here." She looked at the boy yet again. He looked like every eleven- or twelve-year-old she'd ever seen, but he sure didn't sound like any of them. He sounded more like her, or George, or even his parents, than the kids back home his age. She felt disconcerted by this observation, but tried not to let it show. She would talk to George about it as soon as she got a chance.

"Are we ready to make a move?" Mr. Robinson said, seeming sudden to Gatelink. Then she noticed that the food had been consumed, the bill paid, and the table cleared, all during the course of their conversation. She remembered the taste of the turkey and lettuce sandwich, but how was it that she hadn't noticed the rest of what happened, she didn't know. The Robinsons nodded and "Mm-hmm"'d, and said, "that was a great meal" as they got up and pushed their chairs in. Gatelink did the same, and felt a kind of pleasure in the unnecessary action; it punctuated the meal, finished it, wrapped a red ribbon around it. She felt now that it had been special; it must have been, even though she hadn't known it 'til now. She smiled as they all walked out into the sun toward the Robinsons' car, and would have felt foolish if they all hadn't been smiling too.

*****

The drive home was smooth and uneventful. For Gatelink, at least, it was a strange and thrilling experience. It must have been much less so for the other passengers, but the Robinsons still humored Gatelink's wide-eyed questions and open-mouthed stares out the windows with graciousness.

"I've never seen food alive before," Gatelink told them. "It's never even occurred to me that it was alive once. How strange that I've never thought of it before." She immediately began to feel embarrassed, though, realizing she probably sounded foolish to her hosts.

"Not really," George said matter-of-factly. "Folks here even probably never thought about it before The Separation."

Mrs. Robinson smiled at George approvingly. "That's true, Gatelink," she concurred. "You shouldn't feel embarrassed if you don't know as much about this as we do. I'm sure there's a lot you know that we can't even imagine."

Gatelink smiled at Mrs. Robinson to thank her for her effort, diligent though unsuccessful, to make Gatelink feel less ashamed.

Sensing perhaps that her attempt had not worked, the older woman took a tangent. "Though no one knew it then, the corporations did us a huge favor. By depriving us of our customary food source, they made us return to the earth, to agriculture. It enabled us to reconnect with the earth, with Nature. We'd been apart for so long, we'd forgotten what that connection meant, what it gave us, even what it was." She was nodding slowly and somberly at Gatelink as she spoke this. Gatelink smiled slightly and tried not to look confused. She turned toward the window. Ears of corn, sheaves of wheat, bolls of cotton brushed past. Sometimes they would pass long distances of one crop, then a mixture of the plants would abound for miles. The colors were astounding to Gatelink, tossed together like a luscious salad or in uncompromising solid stretches of dull brown. She saw birds, too, and flowers—usually very small purple or white ones on short leafy plants that she wanted to reach out and crumple with her fingers to see if they were really there, such prettiness growing on the side of the road. And everything was swaying, moving, with thoughts and feelings of its own; there were no preordained motions of the neon constituents of billboards, ruled by the binary fancies of corporate workers—no, even through glass Gatelink could see that everything moved with a mind of its own here. It was strange, and she loved it. Past the initial shock of her first hour in this strange land, she was quickly growing enamored of what she saw.

She noticed that the Robinsons were all looking out of the windows too, now that her exploratory inquisition was over, and that they were smiling too. *They're happy!* she realized with a jolt. She wanted desperately to ask them why, or, more exactly: how, but couldn't find the words. She hoped she would learn the answer, or at least how to ask the question, before she had to go back.

CHAPTER 11
OUT OF THE MOUTHS OF BABES

It was three or four o'clock when they arrived at the Robinson house. The sun was still high in its cloudless blue setting. At the doorway, three dogs sat, patient and unchained. As the car pulled up in front of the door, the dogs began to bark and yelp and run forward to greet the occupants of the moving metal box. Gatelink observed as soon as the house came into view that its style was what she'd call 'old-fashioned'—the only ones like it she'd seen there were on housing death row: slated for demolition, but for one reason or another persistently living on. As if reading her mind—*Again with the seeming telepathy!* Gatelink thought—George said, "There hasn't been much construction out here since The Separation. As you can imagine, the machines, the materials, were all under corporate control." He began to unload their bags from the car. "But we don't mind out here. Over there, you all change your style of housing every year, but we say, 'if it isn't broken, don't fix it.'" He smiled. Gatelink cringed a little inside when he said 'you all...your style of housing'—she wasn't sure why. After all, it was true, and really, she was shocked when she saw the house. But still, she didn't like George classifying her with 'them.'

The dogs had a slobbering, licking, sniffing friendliness that Gatelink hadn't expected. She'd never seen a dog in real life, only in old movies. She knew that people used to keep them for "pets," but Headquarters didn't allow people to have pets. It "would distract from the corporate mission" they said. She imagined it must be true for the other firms too, since none of her neighbors had pets that she'd ever seen. When she was younger she'd always wanted a pet, and her parents always answered her five-year-old's please with the company by-line on the issue. When she was old enough to understand, she stopped asking. But she never stopped wanting to ask.

Now she basked in the dogs' unexpected glory. They were one of each size—big, middle and little. The big dog, sleek and black, looked sophisticated and acted anything but. He bobbed up and down, sniffing George and Gatelink from feet to head, trying to discover the truth behind their different scent. He reared up on his hindlegs and offered Tommy his front paws, which the boy reluctantly accepted, as if he were doing a favor for a friend; they did a man-dog dance for a few seconds, which the dog interrupted with an attempt to lick its partner's face. "Oh, Livvie!" Tommy exclaimed in happy exasperation. "You always go too far!" he teased. Livvie drooled in agreement. The middle dog, white and shaggy-haired, was calmer than the other two, but the smallest was a brown-and-white rocket. It shot back and forth among feet and bags being unloaded like a child asking for attention. Gatelink couldn't resist its impulsiveness, and bent down and scooped it up in her arms. Its big floppy ears fell back as it lifted its head to gaze lovingly into the face of its new friend. Gatelink felt a sensation she never had before—she didn't know what it was, but it was very pleasant. Somehow the weight of this little dog in her arms, his helplessness but without fear, his willing surrender that was like a gift, she felt warm, and safe. *And happy,* she realized.

"I see you've met Homer," Mr. Robinson called to Gatelink as he unloaded suitcases and bags from the trunk onto the porch. "He's a very intelligent dog, a Beagle. 'Course, he's never composed any poetry that we could understand, but we figured he deserved a name like Homer anyway. He seems the sensitive, poetic type." He laughed at his own joke.

Gatelink was still mesmerized by the watery brown eyes staring at her. They were so soft, it was like they were liquid. She wanted to touch them to see if they could possibly be solid, as they must. Homer's tongue hung out of his mouth, and leaned to the side, so soft and formless it seemed to take on whatever shape the wind or gravity imposed upon it. Gatelink leaned closer to take a better look at the curious thing, when—"eeuppp!"—it took a taste of her mouth and cheek.

"Hey!" George said, walking up to them and scratching Homer behind his ears. "He likes you!" Homer beamed proudly up at Gatelink.

"He does?" Gatelink asked, still stunned by the sudden saliva. "Then why'd he do that?" Gatelink handed Homer over to George and wiped her face with her sleeve.

"Because he likes you, of course," George replied. "You don't know that about dogs?"

"Well how would I?" Gatelink said in a mix of anger and embarrassment. "Did you ever see a dog over there?"

George stopped walking for a moment, paused in thought. "No," he answered, exchanging glances with his parents and brother. "I'm surprised I never noticed."

"Yup," Gatelink responded, trying to sound neutral.

"But...why would they—" George started to say.

"How 'bout I just explain later, okay?" Gatelink asked, not wanting to discuss the matter. George looked confused. Gatelink picked up a bag and began to walk toward the door, hoping an act of courtesy could camouflage what probably had seemed like one of rudeness. But it hurt her, to talk about dogs while she felt like the Robinsons were judging her, that she was "them, over there."

The door looked like it was made of wood. Gatelink had never seen one like it up close. The doors at her parents' house were made of a synthetic material, silicon or something—it was metallic and almost like steel. They were always cold to the touch. But this door was pretty, with its freckled face and sinewy wrinkles that tried to form ovals but couldn't quite. Subtly, she leaned against it as Mrs. Robinson searched for a key in her handbag. As she'd suspected, it was warm and with its rough texture, it seemed to respond to her pressing against it. It was almost like it was alive.

"Here we go!" Mrs. Robinson declared as she pulled out a small metallic thing Gatelink had never seen before. She inserted it into a handle on the door and turned, then pushed open the door, so Gatelink inferred that it must be something they used to lock and unlock doors out here. Gatelink stepped forward and regained her own weight just in time to avoid a most embarrassing entrance into her hosts' home.

But what Gatelink saved in embarrassment, she got in shock. No sooner did Mrs. Robinson turned on the lights in the front room of the house than dozens of people in plain-colored, striped, flowered and dotted clothes jumped out from behind every visible piece of furniture, yelling, "Welcome home, George and Gatelink!"

The Robinsons, like Gatelink, were rooted to their spots for a moment. Then they broke out in smiles and whole new rounds of hugs began with these people from behind the couches. Gatelink stared on, however, mesmerized not just by the spectacle she had just witnessed but by the plainness of it. She noticed now that Mr. and Mrs. Robinson's and Tommy's clothes were also solid or striped, and conspicuously lacking in logos or photos to accentuate advertisement appeal. She must not have noticed in all her nervousness and excitement. But now, faced with dozens of people dressed in these strange, peaceful garments that didn't demand her attention...she felt lost looking at them. Everyone's faces looked too clear. She stumbled over to a sofa chair and sat down.

From the corner of her eye, Gatelink noticed a girl who looked a little younger than her watch her and then nudge George. With a slight movement of her head, she directed his attention toward Gatelink, sitting dully across the room, and then she turned away discreetly. George said something to the girl, and she nodded her head and opened her mouth in a dramatic, knowing, "O." He smiled to take his leave of her, and made his way swiftly to his apparently ailing guest.

"Gatelink, are you all right?" he asked, kneeling in front of her to be at eye-level.

Relieved at the sight of the logo-plastered Sergio Hamani suit he hadn't had time to change out of, Gatelink felt she could raise her head to say, "The way everyone's dressed...I knew it would be like this, but I didn't know it would be like this.... Everyone looks so vivid, so real, I...it's going to take getting used to, I guess," she said weakly. "Right now, I feel like someone's turned the lights up way too bright." She smiled, embarrassed and apologetic.

"Yeah, I should have guessed," George said, stroking his chin thoughtfully between his thumb and forefinger. "It's just that, I had no

SARINA M. SINGHI

idea that everyone would show up at once, today." He looked around quickly, beaming. "I had thought you might need to be introduced to things gradually.... Do you want to go lie down? Mom already prepared the guest bedroom for you."

Gatelink forced herself to look around at the people smiling and laughing, hugging each other and seeming to have a great time. She knew she wasn't tired, and would feel miserable sitting alone, awake, in a room with all these people out here having so much fun. Though she did have a small urge to run, to hide herself from the clear lucidity of their clothes, she answered resolutely, "No. I'll be fine. I'm already feeling better." And to her surprise, she found that she actually did feel a little better, after saying so. "It was just...oh, I don't know, a kind of stage fright!" She laughed, less nervously than she felt.

George laughed too, and kept the smile after it. "Good for you, Gatelink." He paused then added in a low voice, "You must be stronger than me. I ran and hid for a whole day after I got there." He chuckled along with Gatelink's astonished laugh. "And if you tell that to anyone, I'll deny it. We never had this conversation.... Now come on. I want you to meet some people. Well, I want you to meet everyone, of course, but we're gonna take things slowly. And don't worry: everyone knows you're from a different place, so they won't take anything the wrong way." He uncrouched and offered Gatelink his hand. She hesitated momentarily, reasoning that in light of his confession he could hardly fault her for needing some more time to acclimate before going into active mode, but she took his hand and rose also. *I can do this,* she thought. *I want to do this. It's what I've come here for, not to go and hide. George has a year there—I've got only two weeks. I'm going to see and hear as much as I can, even when I want to run and hide.* She smiled, happy not so much with the situation as with herself, at this moment.

And so Gatelink began to meet her new family, starting with the cousins. There were nine girls and eleven boys there between the ages of fifteen and nineteen. They all looked so mild and content, Gatelink half-expected them to be dumb. But, while two or three didn't strike her as the most conductive wires in the circuit, the others certainly did.

She could tell just from the confident way they said, "Welcome Gatelink, we're so happy you've come to visit us" when they hugged her hello. For her first introduction, with 18-year-old Angela, she made the mistake she'd made with Mrs. Robinson of extending her limb uselessly and had it stared down and crushed. She chose not to make the same mistake for her next 19 encounters, and found them much less painful and even somewhat pleasant, though strange.

The girls were: Rachael, Jameela, Angela, Patricia, Jyoti, Iris, Courtney, Lea and Shanti. The boys were: Jonathon, Mark, Tyrone, Mohammed, Eli, Travis, John, Shashi, Ping, Derek and Noah. If Gatelink weren't already dizzy from their costumes, her head would have been spinning from their names. They were all different, and...unique. This last fact was the part she had trouble grasping. With George, it had been different—he was only one guy, and the uniqueness of his name had matched the uniqueness of him, there. But so many names and no products, no companies to attach them to, no advertisements reminding you of your friend or classmate or teacher and vice-versa in a positive feedback loop—how did people keep everything straight here? How is it that they didn't need to wear name-tags all the time? *They must be going crazy without them!* Gatelink thought.

Her first conversations, with Jameela, Jyoti and Patricia, were general and easy. They asked how her trip had been, had she flown before, where had she gone, what was her favorite subject in school, and seemed genuinely interested in her answers. Then, one by one, her new friends got pulled slowly into a conversation that was rapidly gaining speed among the rest of the group. Wary, Gatelink found herself, too, drawn into the burgeoning discussion among George and all the other kids with their many names.

"You can never fully appreciate their values, George, because you'll never know fully what they are," she heard one of the boys say, a dark-skinned guy in a solid dark yellow sweater with roughly-edged black horizontal stripes in the torso.

"Even if someone handed you a list of their beliefs," a red-haired, green-eyed girl in a solid pink t-shirt concurred, "it could only be partial, because people can never observe themselves completely, let alone others with thoroughness. It's beyond human ability."

"And what does it mean to believe something?" added a boy in a plain white t-shirt and blue jeans, which Gatelink found difficult to focus on. "It's very different than just to know it."

George, who had been standing with an amused smile toward the center of the group, said, "Yes, but…" and he paused with a finger pointed up before him, either for drama or to organize his thoughts. "All I said is that I am coming to appreciate that they have a set of values, just as we do, even though they don't seem to be aware of it, as we, of course, are. At least, more than they are. I contrast this incipient awareness—and I emphasize the word incipient—with my impression when I first arrived there—that because there was no discussion, no recognition, even, of common values, that they didn't have any—couldn't have any, else how could they be so disinterested in them? It doesn't follow logic; the maintenance of the common value structure of a society, especially a large and diverse one, is so critical to its survival, let alone its success. And values can't maintain themselves; it requires dedication, analysis, constant examination and re-examination, and, at last, consensus, to keep a value system going. Or, at least, that's how we think about it."

George likes being the center of attention, Gatelink thought suddenly. *Here, at least.*

"But there, people don't think about it this way for the simple reason that…they don't think about it." He paused as eyebrows went up in incipient exasperation. "And yet, it exists, as plainly as it does here, although unexamined. I have been able to conclude this not only because I did not observe the situation of chaos there which one would expect in a society without a common value structure, but because I figured out how their value system is maintained, revised, and even created." He nodded proudly, now in his element unabashed in self-aggrandizement.

"Really?" exclaimed one of the girls who'd been asking Gatelink about her journey; Gatelink thought her name was Jyoti but couldn't be sure. "How it's created?"

"And...you're not gonna tell us, are ya, Georgie?" a younger looking boy teased.

George appeared to ponder this question deeply for about five seconds, thumb and forefinger encircling chin and head cocked to a side. At last, he generously replied, "Nnnn-now, Travis, you know me better than that! To deprive others of understanding is antithetical to what I'm all about!" He paused again, smiling. Others smiled too, but as their feet began to tap on the floor.

This was a dance they knew well, and enjoyed in its time. George went on, "Their values are perpetuated in things."

The crowd shared a stumped expression, all except Gatelink whose face held a trance-like stare directed at and noticed by no one.

"Things?" repeated one boy, in a light blue button-up Oxford shirt, the style but not content of which was recognizable to Gatelink.

"That makes sense, I guess, based on the huge materialistic focus of the society over there," said another. "But what exactly do you mean, George?"

"Yes, what ex-*act*-ly, George?" a pretty brown-haired girl in a red shirt added playfully. "With all this build up—very nicely done, by the way—we're not going to let you get away with anything less than the exact truth." She crossed her arms over her chest and pouted. Her body language was subtle, but Gatelink caught it; she was sure George did too.

"Well, Miss Patricia," George began, giving the girl the attention she was blatantly requesting, "I have never claimed to possess 'truth,' however 'exact' or imprecise—only my impressions. And, my impression," he turned with flair to face the whole group, "is that, through what they call 'products,' value are created and consumed. Now, nothing is physically embedded in the myriad of unnecessary 'things' manufactured, marketed and bought over there—the 'Break-Maker' machines, the 'Hair-Maker,' the 'Shield.' But with every new gadget that enters the sphere of people's awareness, there is one more player on the side of consumerism, the pull is a little stronger away from a life of thought and love and instead toward one of constant, numbing action. These products, these things, are the new god out there; they are worshiped."

Though completely inactive at this moment, Gatelink was beginning to feel numb. She wasn't even sure if she was blinking. She knew that everyone was so mesmerized by George's storytelling, including George, that she could easily slip away unnoticed…but she didn't. Instead she listened with a morbid fascination.

"They worship things?" a girl asked.

"Not literally, of course. They have no concept of God, or religion, or even worship out there. I think they know that people used to worship God, and pray to Him or Her, and think about Him or Her, but they don't relate that to themselves. They never think long enough about anything that's not about how to make money and what to buy with it. When I say that they worship things, I mean that they give to objects the same regard and importance that religious people do to God and to the words of God. In this sense, everyone out there is very religious." He paused until the widened eyes around him rebounded to their normal shapes and sizes and the eyebrows released the tension of uplifting, when he felt his audience was ready for more.

"The 'products' themselves embody and imbue values, of what is worth doing and what is not. Hundreds of devices to reduce the amount of time of food preparation, and the thousands of available 'ready-made meals,' like 'frozen dinners,' 'canned dinner,' and 'just-add-water meals' inform people over there that cooking food, that loving preparation of your family's and friends' meals is not only unnecessary but obsolete—it's not something that one should do. Why else would so many of such things exist, if it were okay to prepare your own food, or for those you love? And so, by what the corporations produce, they dictate people's behavior. Of course, people don't have to buy these things, that's true, there's no law compelling them to—that's left up to the ferociously competitive nature of people out there. And why are they so competitive against one another, against their neighbors, their family, their friends, even all those they don't know and never will? I had thought at first that people there must be intrinsically different from us in this respect. We certainly don't look at one another this way, with this desperate need to outdo, outrun, outpossess. But as I spent more time there, and talked to more people, more young people, my impression changed.

"The competitiveness is not innate, I believe. Its existence is complex, and the reasons for it are manifold. One reason is quite simply that the corporations create a fear and intimidation in people, which they don't recognize but which holds them tight in its grip like a Venus fly-trap. Through advertising that equates possession with happiness, and lack of it with all sorts of ills, they develop from an early age a certainty that maximum possession is the true path to happiness and the ultimate aim of life, and that they are inadequate without it. The ads over there even say so, outright."

Gatelink frowned, her only movement since George began his soliloquy. *That can't be right*, she thought. *Ads say so, 'outright' that without products we are inadequate?* She tried to think of some of the mottoes that were popular right now. "All you need now is a Perrlo TV to make your life perfect" and "The Mamer Breadmaker makes any home complete," came quickly to mind. *Oh my God,* she thought.

"But, I still don't understand the competitiveness part," one girl offered a welcome interruption to Gatelink's internal monologue.

"Well," George continued in a professorial tone, "in the context of this induced urgency to possess, people there feel very alone, disconnected from each other, and if we look closely we can see the corporations' role in that as well. It has been known to corporate planners for some time that by moving their employees around often—transferring them to different towns, different states, even different countries—they can prevent the formation of community bonds. Also, they enforce long work hours, and offer little enticements like bonuses and promotions to get people to work longer hours voluntarily; this ensures that they have no time to participate in their home communities, or even their own families. This leaves them, and their families, with a hole in their psychology where everyone craves a sense of acceptance and approval—they have nowhere but the Company to look to find it, so they work harder still, for this reason. And they need to buy more, to numb themselves from the pain they feel of being cut off from their neighbors and their own families, not to mention from Nature, and

God. But they never realize that the alienation, they were always and still are in control of."

"It's divide-and-conquer," said one boy in a tone of enlightenment. "Just like it has always happened throughout human history."

"Yes!" George said, proud of his student's astuteness. "And when people feel divided, they tend to feel afraid, and competitive, just as the tribes of ancient times felt competitive against each other and fought, for really no reason other than the conqueror-created sense of 'otherness,' and the fear that inevitably arises from that. Over there, everyone is an 'other' to everyone else, and no one seems to know it."

George's triumphant tone had faded into one of melancholy. Surprised at the sudden silence, Gatelink looked up at his face and saw an expression of sorrow on George's face that was shared by everyone in the group. They were all looking down, mute, pensive—sad. She was more confused than ever.

"I wish I could help them," a girl said finally. Her voice was quiet, assertive, and yet with the knowledge of there being no hope.

"Yeah," said a boy. "The elders never described it that way."

"Well, things may be clearer to see now that the system of control has gotten to be so mature in the corporate states," George responded, obviously refusing to take the comment as a compliment. The funeral air resumed.

Gatelink felt like screaming. No one noticed her, and suddenly it was bothering her. She felt completely outside. Didn't they know they were talking about her, and she was right there?

At last, believing she would not be noticed, Gatelink turned quietly to go. There was still life in other parts of the room, talking, gestures, even laughter, but she was interested in the front door. To be without people for a few minutes, would probably be good. And maybe the silence would have run its course by the time she got back.

"Gatelink!" she heard a voice call out just as she was turning. She turned back and faced George, assuming the voice must have been his. To her surprise, it continued, but from one of the boys in the group, with whom she hadn't talked yet.

"We're so sorry. That was very insensitive of us, to be having this discussion now, so soon after you've just gotten here."

"Yeah, Gatelink. I just got so carried away that I forgot everything else," George said. "Please forgive me."

Gatelink opened her mouth, then closed it quickly. She had no idea what to say. *That's okay?*—but it wasn't. *I understand?*—but she didn't. Suddenly muteness didn't seem such a bad idea.

"Gatelink," said a girl Gatelink joyously identified as Jyoti, "you can say whatever you're thinking." She put her hand on Gatelink's forearm. "It's okay. We want to know what you're thinking and feeling, about our having this conversation, and us having it with you here. We won't get mad—how could we when we're asking you to tell us? It will help you to say it, whatever it is, and we will learn something from hearing it. And not just because you're from corporate America; whenever someone shares what's really in their heart and mind, well, that's the best teacher of life and people that there is!" She smiled, and looked from Gatelink to other faces around them—they all smiled and nodded in affirmation.

Gatelink's face must have shown her uncertainty, because another girl, whom Gatelink recognized as the one flirting with George a moment ago, added, "We all do, all the time—share what we're really thinking and feeling. For example, I think George has grown into the cutest boy in town, in my opinion, and so I have a small crush on him. Which is likely to change, in time, since I'm at the age where crushes come and go. But right now, I wanted to flirt with him, and so I did."

Gatelink's jaw hit the ground, but she saw around her only serene, non-scandalized faces.

"Now do you believe us?" the girl asked, smiling.

After a moment's hesitation, Gatelink said tentatively, "I thought you were flirting with him." She smiled too, stunned that she could say this out loud.

The girl laughed. "It kinda looked to me, from the corner of my eye, that you were noticing." She laughed again, a warm, friendly laugh.

"Wow," Gatelink said. "Okay, now I do believe you." She looked at Jyoti also as she said this.

"I'm Patricia, by the way," the girl said. "Now that we've talked—

and I've shocked you—you'll probably find it a little easier to remember my name. Though, if you don't, don't feel bad asking. Nineteen names is a lot to learn all at once."

"Yeah. Back there, everyone's named after companies or...products, so it's easy to remember names." Gatelink didn't even want to say the word 'products' anymore, after what she'd just heard.

"So," Jyoti said, "if you'd like to tell us what you were thinking and feeling just now, we'd love to hear it, but if you don't feel comfortable, we'd understand that, too."

Oh, what the hell? Gatelink decided. *They are asking. Someone— no, a whole group of people—actually asking me what I think, what my feelings are about something. This is a once in a lifetime opportunity!*

"Where would I begin?" she began. "Well, I will say that I don't fully understand all of what you just said, George, but that it makes me feel bad, because I *feel* that you're right about things, even though I don't *know* that you are. And I feel bad because this is *me* that you're talking about, and I don't like the things you're saying. I mean, 'divide and conquer'—this is my *life* you're talking about! It isn't abstract.... But I don't want these things to be true; I don't want them to be about *me.* I want them to *not* be about me. And I want to know—to *understand*—why you all got silent at the end, and why you 'feel bad for them.' These are some of the things I was thinking and feeling.... Now aren't you glad you asked?" She laughed half-heartedly.

"Of course we are, Gatelink," a girl said softly. "...If you'd said we were all full of shit, we'd be glad, because we'd get to know you better." She smiled. "Of course, we'd feel a little bad, if you'd insulted us, but we'd want to understand why you felt that way."

"That's how we think," a boy explained. "It's how we've been raised to think, to appreciate all perspectives as originating from the same source—from the Great Power, from God—as all being worth understanding. It's how we all choose to think, to accept this way in which we've always lived. We've all decided to keep living this way— we decide this every moment. So does everyone, in every society, whether they know it or not."

"And not to change the topic, Noah," another girl said, "but Gatelink *did* ask a question." She smiled warmly at their visitor. "Why we were quiet after George concluded, and said that we 'feel bad for them'— well, from George's description, it sounds like there is a lot of hurt and confusion underlying the materialism among the people of the corporate states. This isn't a perspective that we had heard before. And thinking about it, we felt no choice but to imagine what the hurt and confusion must really feel like, even though the people who are really experiencing it are probably not aware of it. But we hurt, just to think of their pain, because we have chosen to be empathetic always. We feel bad for them, because…they don't seem to know how to help themselves, and they have these great forces aligned against even their self-realization, let alone contentment and happiness. We don't have such forces in our lives, and we're grateful for that, but feel sympathy for those who do."

"So, you feel bad for everyone who's in pain, even if you don't know them?" Gatelink asked skeptically. "If that's true, how can you even function? I'd think you'd be crying all the time."

"We empathize, we feel pity, but we don't let it devastate us. Because we see how pointless, and how *prideful* of us, that would be. Prideful because it would presuppose that our excessive attention could have any benefit or even consequence. We say a prayer for whomever, and then turn it over to God."

"Uh-huh," was Gatelink's reply. She looked over to George, who seemed to not be able to read her mind right now. She decided not to say what she was thinking and feeling at that moment because, as that one girl had said, they 'would feel bad.' So instead she said, "Why do you keep saying 'we' instead of 'I'?"

"That's an interesting question," said one boy. "A good question. It must be different over there. But here, whenever we're discussing anything relating to our common values, the value system to which we all agree and subscribe, we use the collective pronoun because it's more accurate and, well, nicer."

"But you'll notice," finished another boy, "That when Patricia spoke of her torrid attraction to George"—he said playfully—"she sure didn't use the collective pronoun then. I assure you, there's no *collective* crush on George." He led the group in snickering laughs. "No offense, George, old man," he added, patting George on the back, "but *we* just don't find you irresistible."

"None taken," George assured, grinning.

"But I tell ya man, if it were possible, you'd be the one," the boy said.

"Thanks. I appreciate that, man."

"Maybe," the boy added after a brief pause. There were more snickers as George rolled his eyes. Even Gatelink couldn't help giggling, uncomfortable as she thought she should still be feeling.

"Well, you know, all this fun and games is just fine, but I have a more *serious* game in mind...." George said at last, "a game I have been deprived of for *months* now." He paused. "You know what I'm talkin' about," he added, nodding and grinning.

"I don't know guys, should we give it to him?" one boy teased.

"He has been a pretty good sport today," the boy who'd just been egging him on about the 'collective crush' declared in George's support.

"What, you think that means he'll be any better at *sports*, today, too?" a girl joked.

"I think we should give it to him," Patricia stated.

"Oh, you *would*, Patricia" the girl next to her crooned, promptly receiving a mild elbow to the abdomen for her efforts.

"So it's settled," the 'collective crush' boy concluded. "Football on the field in ten minutes. Do whatever you need to to prepare—change, get sneakers, say a prayer...and whoever's brave enough: *play*!"

CHAPTER 12
SOME KINDA SOCCER

The "field" was not a field, not in the sense that Gatelink had come to expect from the occasional football game she'd seen on TV. There were no markings, no borders; not even a fence to keep the rest of the world out of the game. And though there was grass, just as it *looked* like there was on the fields in those games on TV, there were also trees, shrubs, and weedy-looking plants growing at various places in the "field."

They're gonna play on this? Gatelink wondered. Stumped was confirmed as her emotion of the day.

George sauntered up to Gatelink. "Oh, hey, Gatelink, you should know what we call football is called soccer out there. I've seen the different sports shows they have over there. Have you ever played footba— I mean, soccer, before?"

"No. I've seen it on TV a few times, though," Gatelink said. *I don't work for a sports corporation—why would I ever have played it?* Gatelink wanted to ask, defensively. *If my name were 'Champ,' or 'Sport,' or 'Gearguard,' that would be a sensible question. They're taught sports so they can know how to produce the games that people watch and buy recordings of; I'm a Gatelink.* She wanted to say these things to excuse herself from a blame she knew didn't exist, but couldn't help feeling. But she said nothing.

"Okay, well, uh, the rules are a little different over here, I think," George said, scanning the field as the group took their positions in ramshackle formations on each side.

"Different how?" Gatelink asked.

"Um, since I haven't watched it over there that much, I'm not sure exactly what the rules are there, but it kinda looks different over there, like, what's being played *for*."

"Huh?"

"I wish I could explain it more clearly, but I hadn't really given it any thought until just now. I'll think more about it, and see if I can explain it better, later. But I thought getting us all away from talking for a while might be the best thing right now." He reflected for a few seconds. "You know, I think maybe you'd better just watch us for a while, if you want, until you get the hang of it, and then just jump in whenever you want. Does that sound good?"

"Yeah, I think you're right," Gatelink said. "I already feel clobbered emotionally right now—we don't have to add physically to the list, too," she laughed. George took her hand and led her to a place to sit outside the sphere of play. He sat with her on a short rock next to the tall, large one he'd reserved for her.

"You know, I could sit out the game, with you," he said with a compassionate smile. "Anyone else would offer it too, but we all know that your familiarity with me would make me the only person of possible comfort to you." He paused, but Gatelink was still taking in what he was saying when he continued, "You know, you're very strong to not run away from all the discomfort you must be feeling right now, Gatelink. Everyone here knows that. I just want to make sure that you know it too."

Wow, Gatelink thought.

George laughed.

"Oh my god, did I just say that out loud?" she said.

"Um, yeah, but don't worry about it," he replied. "I know no one says anything like that to you, there. But you'll hear things like this a lot more while you're here, and not just from me, either." Gatelink raised her eyebrows in surprise, but acceptance. "So, shall I sit this one out?" George asked.

Gatelink considered. "No. No, I'll be fine. I'd like to just watch quietly for a while. All the numbing action, you know."

George laughed. "You know when I said that, I wasn't referring to all types of action, right?"

Gatelink made a face. "Of course, I know.

"Well, it's not a bad point you bring up, you know. We need to make sure we get enough action in our days out here, when we're not farming, to balance out all the time we spend thinking, and 'up in the clouds,' so to speak. We need to keep grounded, too. But that's more talk, and that is what we're here *not* to do," he said. "And so, I'll take my leave of you for a while." He rose. "If you want to ask any questions, feel free to stop the game and ask, or just pull somebody aside, if you can get 'em—we won't mind. We don't take this stuff as seriously as we make out to."

With an affectionate chuckle, he was gone. And the first non-televised sports game of Gatelink's life began.

Gatelink was surprised to see the same black-and-white checkered ball she'd seen used in the games on TV. *Must be from before the Separation,* she figured. She watched it arc through the air from foot to foot to head to hip, never still, and never silent. She heard the impact of plastic against the plastic of the goalposts, plastic against the strength of bone and the will of the human pursuit of amusement. People laughed and jeered and teased each other, and shouted encouragements and praises too, when the plays were apparently daring or suavely executed. As Gatelink watched, she could find no pattern in the deliverance of praise or jeers; there was no correlation to the side that the player started on. People jeered and cheered for the other side as quickly as for their own.

But there was a definite pattern of movement for the ball. It made a bumpy journey across the field in one direction, with some signs of indecision as it seemed to change its mind for short distances, and it was delivered between the two branches planted firmly in the ground on one side of the field. Then it made its way to the other side of the field, between the goalposts there, with much the same path of arrival, only reversed. As Gatelink watched for over an hour, the symmetry was unmistakable. She'd definitely never seen this in a televised game. The players' movements did not parallel, however. They were varied, even clumsy sometimes, and definitely not rehearsed. And yet, this pattern persisted. Gatelink kept expecting the score to unbalance, to topple over onto one side or the other and make a victory, and a defeat. But it didn't happen. The players ran and kicked, passed and intercepted, and seemed to not notice this extraordinary coincidence. The score was 20 to 20 when Gatelink decided to take some action.

She stood. Now at eye level with the players, the immediacy of their movements struck her. They were returning to their starting positions in a post-goal fervor, their motions relaxed and happy, yet full of purpose. Gatelink wavered on her feet—she didn't want to interrupt.

She had almost resolved to sit and hold the burning question for however much longer the ball would be airborne when she heard her name.

"Gatelink," a girl was calling to her as she walked toward where Gatelink still stood. The girl started jogging toward Gatelink, her breath a little heavy but somehow, sounding…happy. She was smiling, as they all were except when a look of concentration would supplant that of contentment at the strategic moments of the game.

"Gatelink," she said, "do you want to play?"

"Umm, I just had a question that I wanted to ask, but…I don't want to interrupt the game." Gatelink looked past the girl and saw to her surprise that it was proceeding as if it had full membership.

"Oh, don't worry. As long as there are at least two people on the field, one on each side, that game stops for *nobody*." She sounded affectionate, as she shook her head, smiling. "By the way, my name's Courtney. We haven't really talked yet, and I'm sure you've forgotten. I think after the game, we're gonna make up some name tags to help you with our names." She smiled, and blue eyes sparkled under damp orange hair. "So what is it that you're wondering about, Gatelink?"

"Well…" Gatelink realized she hadn't thought about how to ask her question, only that she wanted to know the answer. "It seems like every time one side scores a goal, the other side does too." She paused, hoping the question was clear from her statement.

"Ri-ight," Courtney said slowly. "That's one of the rules of the game."

"*What?*" Gatelink replied, a little louder than she'd meant to.

"That's one of the rules of football. George told us that you haven't had the chance to play games, over there, but you have seen it on the TV, haven't you?" Courtney asked, now curious herself. "Why, is it different over there? How do they play, where you're from?"

"Well," Gatelink started, "I don't know a lot about it, since people only play sports professionally there, but I'm pretty sure the goals aren't pre-determined. Each side tries to get more goals than the other side, and whoever has the most at the end, wins."

"And the other side?" Courtney asked, fascinated.

"Well, the other side loses, of course," Gatelink replied.

"Whoa," Courtney said. "Weird." She contemplated.

"So, when you guys play, that's a *rule* that after one side scores, the other side has to?"

Courtney nodded. "Is *allowed* to. If one team is weaker than the other, like here, the stronger team helps the weaker one out and has to make it *look* like they aren't going a little bit easier. Often it takes longer for the weaker team to score, and the stronger team has to work harder to try and keep it balanced.

Gatelink hadn't noticed any time lags between the successive goals, but it hadn't occurred to her to look for them. She considered for a moment, and asked the next logical question, "They how do you win, the way you play it?"

Courtney's brow furrowed for an instant, almost too quickly to catch, and released. "We don't worry about anything—we just play for fun and for the skill of it. It's really exciting, when you're playing it, and it takes a lot of finesse sometimes, to keep the balance."

"How do you know when the game is over?" Gatelink asked, puzzled.

"Whenever we all want to stop, I guess," Courtney responded. "They always just kind of…end. Like that. I don't know; I haven't thought about it, really."

"Huh," Gatelink replied. The two shared an awkward silence with a background of yelling, laughing chaos.

"So," said Courtney, the first to recover, "would you like to play, or…"

"No," Gatelink said quickly, then smiled, to not give the wrong impression. "I think I want to just watch for a little while longer, until I feel I've gotten the hang of it. I'll probably join in later. How much longer do you think it'll go for?"

"Who knows?" Courtney said, grinning and shaking her head again. "With how hyped up we are today, could be another hour or two. But, you know…nobody's expecting perfection, from any of us. And, it's really fun. So, if you want to play, you really should. Just pick a side, and run in and start playing. It's as easy as that." She delivered a encouraging smile and turned to jog back into the game, which was now 23 to 24, and nearing another tie from the looks of it.

Gatelink reflected upon what she had just learned. She turned this new information over and over again in her mind and looked at it every possible angle until it ceased to be so foreign anymore—it ceased to be in diabolical opposition to all she knew, and faded into a variant of the familiar. *She* faded it, she *shaded* it, in gray and all its derivations, until she reduced its importance to a size she could fit in her hand. Then she was ready.

She jumped up, almost leapt. It had been about 45 minutes since her talk with …*what was her name? It started with a 'k'…Courtney.* Gatelink half expected the game to stop and everyone to stare at her, she'd been still for so long. But there wasn't even a pause as she scanned the field for George and jogged to take his side, hoping he would fall back into the tutor role he'd grown so accustomed to. *What am I doing?* she thought. *They've been playing for probably their whole lives; I've never played. All I really know is you're not supposed to use your hands. They're gonna clobber me!* And yet, this was the kind of fun that she'd been imagining her whole life, wondering if it existed somewhere in the world other than in her own head. Now that she could see it, and she could hear it, she had to taste it, to see if it was real.

And so, with minor technical assistance from George, obligingly instructional even with one eye on the ball, Gatelink entered the game.

She ran in the direction George ran. She watched the ball, but didn't know what she'd do if it came her way. Bodies ran in every direction around her; limbs flexed and extended in purposeful gestures to enhance speed or access to the ball; heads called out, yelled, ordered, cajoled, teased, laughed. There was a life on the field that was greater than the sum of its parts; was not just a sum of its parts. There was something being evoked here, and she was part of it.

And then it happened. The ball suddenly moved in four successive jabs toward the goalpost 15 feet behind Gatelink. But it was supposed to be heading in the opposite direction. In the flurry of activity it wasn't clear where this progression would end until the last move. It was heading directly past Gatelink's right leg by about one foot, and into the unmanned goal.

"Gatelink!" a girl's voice yelled. Gatelink didn't need to think. Something carried her, pushed her, to the right and in harm's way. Her right foot pulled back, and—*smack!*—reversed the flow of the play and set things right. "Woo-hoo!" members of both teams cheered; "All right, Gatelink! Nice work!" While Gatelink heard them, she could hardly pay attention. She felt a rush of feelings she hadn't felt before she hadn't known—power, achievement, pride…belonging. She was part of something that didn't have a bottom line that had nothing to do with her. It had everything to do with her, with all of them. It felt good— it felt great! She felt like screaming, it felt so good. She did.

"Woo-hooo!" Gatelink yelled, arms upraised and head heavenward, as she'd seen some of the kids do after scoring goals. Someone raised their hand to her in a high-five, and instinctively she slapped it in the air, though she'd never done so before. She felt like she was flying, she was in the clouds, she was high. For a moment, she wasn't Gatelink anymore; she was above herself, above her life, even her life at the moment, in this field with these strange, friendly people. There was a word that she'd seen in one of those 20th century books that she hadn't thought about in years—"transcendentalism." She hadn't understood then what it meant, and she didn't know why she should have thought of it now, but she couldn't shake it.

The game went on for another hour and a half. Gatelink felt great through the whole game, even when she fumbled and was customarily booed, with good nature. The ball went one way, then the other, and

Courtney was right; it was fun. They were on different sides, but they were on the same side, too—they were all playing for each other, and for nobody at all. As the ball moved, as she tensed and relaxed and thought of nothing else but the present moment, right where and when she was, Gatelink felt a calm, a certainty, a security that was new to her. The ball held no demands of her; it didn't ignore her, or lie to her; it was honest, and wanted nothing from her that she didn't want to give. The game was the same way, and these people, too, she thought. She felt free, finally, totally free.

Then people started dropping. *Courtney sure didn't mention this!* Gatelink thought as a boy ten feet from her called out, "Man, I'm beat!" and dropped to the ground, first to his knees, then the flat of his back, with his knees bent and arms outstretched. The game moved around him as it did the cacti and other plants and rocks strewn throughout the field area; people running avoided him and made sure not to kick the ball directly at him unless it was high enough to clear the vulnerable figure. Two shots flew over him within ten minutes after his descent. Soon a girl on the other end did the same thing, yelling out, "Too much for me!" The whole process took half an hour. Gatelink, afraid to lie down like the others had, found herself and Jyoti to be the last two still upright and running. She was wondering if she should say something to end the game, when Jyoti caught the ball between her feet and stopped running. "Whaddya say, champ—should we put these sissies out of their misery?" She was grinning.

"Um…yes?" Gatelink said. As everyone started to push themselves up and brush themselves off, Jyoti told Gatelink, "Oh, don't feel bad that I called them sissies. That's just traditional for the last two up to say about the rest of the gamers. We don't mean it, of course. It's just for fun." She smiled.

"Oh!" Gatelink laughed, relieved of her confusion at the other girl's declaration. Then she thought, *That's kinda strange.* "Um, Jyoti," she said. "Can I ask you something?"

"Of course," she replied.

"Why did everyone fall down on the field like that, to drop out? Why didn't they get off the field, instead?"

"Hmm. We've always done it that way. If the game's still going on, who wants to get off the field and just watch from the side? Just because you're too tired to keep playing doesn't mean you want to be excluded from the rest of the game. And we don't want to anyone to be excluded just because they're tired." The answer was apparently very natural to Jyoti.

"But…doesn't anyone ever get hit, and hurt, being on the ground in the middle of the game?" Gatelink asked.

"No," Jyoti responded, surprised at the question. "We wouldn't let that happen."

*****

After the game, and cleaning up, there was what looked to Gatelink like a feast. When they got back to the Robinsons' house, Gatelink caught a glimpse of at least ten women and men bustling around in the kitchen. The activity level in there almost matched that on the field, minutes before. George ushered her to the guest bedroom and bathroom before she could ask about it, and left to his own necessary cleaning rituals.

Gatelink showered and dressed, in her Oresta Ji t-shirt and jeans, which screamed at her with their pictures and words in a familiar way. She felt embarrassed to wear them, knowing George would definitely be in his "here" clothes by now. She tried not to think about it, and went out to the dining room.

She found the room milling with people, who spilled out into the adjoining rooms. Pots were set up in the middle of the table with plates and utensils and cloth napkins laid to the side. People were holding plates and eating, talking and laughing, standing or sitting, wherever there was space. Gatelink found George leaning against a wall, talking to a boy who, from the piece of paper pinned to his shirt, must have been Derek.

"Gatelink, hey, get some chow and join us," George said.

"Uh, okay," she said, surprised at how comfortable everyone seemed standing so close together. She walked over to the table and observed others lifting plates and loading them up with couscous, vegetables, curry, rice, lentils, breads and a little bit of meat. She did the same. There was no soda to drink, or coffee; only fruit juices. Some had seeds in them. She picked a mauve colored juice that looked to be all liquid, and took a sip. It was delicious, like nothing she'd ever tried before. She returned to her guide. Derek smiled at her and drifted away just as she arrived.

"I didn't mean to scare him away!" Gatelink said apologetically.

"Oh, no, no," George responded, shaking his head and smiling. "Derek assumed that you'd probably have some questions, and would be more comfortable asking me alone. It's okay—I'll catch up with him later. We were just talking about the school, anyway, and that's really an inexhaustible topic." He laughed. "You'll get to know what I mean."

"So, this is a party for you, like a…welcome home party?" she asked.

"Well, yes and no," George replied. "We have big dinners like this a few times a week. But they did make my favorite dishes today, just to do something nice for me."

"Everyone's…pretty close together." Gatelink could have kicked herself as soon as the words came out of her mouth.

George laughed again, with no hint of offense. "Yeah," he said, "compared to how distant people keep themselves over there, I guess that's true. We don't live like this all the time, but we think that to have this kind of closeness, to share a meal together, all of us in this way, is good for us to have sometimes. It supports a sense of connectedness, togetherness; we not only feel but can see that we're not alone, however much we may feel so sometimes, as all humans do. And so, the adults take turns cooking together for these gatherings, and we all enjoy the fruits of their collaboration. Or the vegetables, as the case may be." He picked up a piece of broccoli with a fork, made a quick face at it, and put it back on his plate. Gatelink laughed, as he knew she would.

"It takes effort to do this," he continued. "And sometimes there are other things we'd rather be doing, or we'd rather be alone than be with everyone else, but we always come anyway. No one's forced or required to, but we do, because we believe it's good for our souls, for our spirits, and for everyone else's too. It may seem like a small thing, but it's important." He started to look around, taking in the scene as if smelling a beautiful flower he hadn't in a long while.

"It doesn't seem small," Gatelink said softly.

"Gosh, I've missed these," George said at the same time, now breathing in deeply and exhaling. "I'm sorry, Gatelink, did you say something?"

"No," she said smiling, shaking her head lightly. "So, what do you call this stuff?" she asked, lifting a forkful of couscous.

CHAPTER 13
THE LAY OF THE LAND, AND,
WHAT *IS* IN A NAME

Roosters crowed the next morning at 6:00 a.m. Startled, Gatelink shot up in her bed. Then she remembered that Patricia had told her about the roosters last night after dinner, as the young people sprawled about in the Robinsons' living room and chatted and joked about funny stories from the past, and caught George up on what had been going on in his absence. The roosters had been shipped in at the time of The Separation from one of the other "free states," which supplied all the other free states with farm animals. The roosters were imported for food reasons, for eggs, but they also doubled as alarm clocks, making the concept of electronic alarms obsolete over here. And they "gently persuaded everybody to adhere to the old proverb, 'Early to bed, early to rise, makes people healthy, wealthy, and wise.'" Gatelink laughed in agreement with her new friend, not admitting that she'd never heard this, or any, "proverb" before. Gatelink looked forward to hearing more of them. But she wouldn't ask.

As she lay back down in bed and rolled onto her side, convinced of her safety and that all was well, she reflected on how strange she *didn't* feel here. Though she hadn't thought too much about it, she had expected to be treated like an outsider, a foreigner, even an oddity. Possibly as an enemy. But everyone seemed to treat her just like they did George. Their affection was a little cautious, though, but it was never reserved. They even started to tease her, about how strategic she was in resting at the start of the football game so she'd be one of the last standing; they said she was clever, and they'd have to watch out for her. Everything they said that night was in such a light tone of voice, that she had to laugh when ordinarily she would have felt hurt and scared. It was like they had spiked their voices.

Gatelink showered and dressed in one of the outfits several of the girls had brought to lend to her. "'Cos when we go out to the farms tomorrow, we'll get dirty, and clothes from there probably need to be cleaned in a different way than how we wash our clothes here." Doubting if this were true, or that it was the reason they were offering the clothes, Gatelink smiled and took them happily.

So, on this morning of her second day in this new world, Gatelink wore clothes without advertisements for the first time in her life. In a plain white t-shirt and blue jeans—she chose them first over the striped and dotted shirts, maybe for the shock value—she looked at herself for what she felt was the first time ever. When she looked in the mirror her face was the only one she saw now. There were no beautiful people making a constant comparison to her, shouting silently that she needed to buy more cosmetics or diet pills, a better Hair-maker, or get surgery to try to look better, as good as them; she wore no badge of her imperfections. She wasn't forced to read names and words, to learn about the best mutual fund available or why Stellar Coffee Shops was superior to all the rest whenever she wanted to fix her hair. She was just…Gatelink. Just a girl. Who happened to have a multi-billion-dollar corporation's name. She turned away from the mirror. It must be time for breakfast by now.

Sure enough, breakfast was on the table when Gatelink descended, simple foods with lots of fruits and no meat. It was only the Robinsons and her. Gatelink was surprised to find that they hardly spoke as they served themselves and ate. George looked over at her, and the mind-reading began. "We believe that morning is a time for quiet reflection. That's why we don't talk much over breakfast." Though he spoke at a normal volume, he returned immediately to the silence.

Gatelink kept her eyes lowered to the lavender and yellow tablecloth for the first few minutes, assuming she should. But when she emerged for another roll, she saw that the other diners were looking at each other, and glancing around very normally—they were simply not speaking. But they weren't avoiding each other, either. It was…shared silence. Feeling a little awkward at first, Gatelink tried to adopt their behavior. She thought about the excitement of the whole trip, about how pretty the tablecloth and dishes were, and then, about the taste of the food. She became aware of her own pattern of chewing, something she had never noticed before. By the end of the meal, she was enjoying the communal time alone, and looking forward to breakfast tomorrow.

"So," Mrs. Robinson broke the silence gently, "are you ready for the fields?" She was smiling, but her tone held a note of caution, a hint that the question wasn't rhetorical.

"I think so," Gatelink responded. "No one's expecting anything from me, right?" she asked, accustomed to this assurance by now.

"No, of course not, dear," Mr. Robinson answered. "But the conditions will be different than you're used to, I imagine."

"Yeah, you gotta watch out for the chiggers," Tommy volunteered.

Gatelink looked to the older Robinsons for an explanation.

"You'll come into contact with a lot of insects that you probably haven't before, over there," Mr. Robinson said.

"I barely saw *any* insects in corporate America," George added, returning from the kitchen, where it sounded like he'd been washing the breakfast dishes. "I think I might have seen a really hearty ant once, and maybe a spider, trudging dully in the artificial grass, poor thing, and that's about it." He shrugged his shoulders with a "what-can-you-do" expression that looked half-sincere. She suspected he might be looking forward to her reaction, for its entertainment value.

"But, forewarned is forearmed, right G.L.?" Mrs. Robinson said, wiping the counter with a damp cloth. She said the words like they were in quotes, so Gatelink guessed this was another one of those "proverbs." She vowed to remember it. She only wished she could write them down right away without raising any suspicion. Why was she embarrassed to admit she'd never heard them before? Maybe because the way people here assumed she knew them, and said them like it was a shared wisdom, a shared tradition, made her feel good, and she knew she'd lose that if she became a tourist in that respect.

As they all walked to the car, Gatelink thought, *But what was that, that Mrs. Robinson called me? 'G.L.'?* It was the first time she'd been called anything but "Gatelink" since she was five, and neither she nor her peers had any longer the protection of extreme youth to keep them from getting in trouble for mispronouncing the name of the company or any of its products. And now, the corporate moniker had been abbreviated, beheaded, degraded. And Gatelink liked it.

G.L., she thought. She tossed the nickname around in her head, wanting desperately to speak it aloud to feel the short syllables form and disappear so quickly from her lips, a gift from her host and a blow for Gatelink against the brick walls the corporation had built around her—it was a pick-axe put in her hand. But she wanted even more not to be conspicuous, and have to explain her thoughts, which would have to sound stupid to them, who weren't saddled with names not theirs. *And a saddle is what it is,* the thought occurred to Gatelink suddenly, as if spoken from elsewhere. *Something you use to convert a free animal into one who works for you.* This thought floored her, and for at least a full minute she could only marvel at it. "Huh," she grunted aloud, softly but audibly. She immediately realized what she'd done, and looked around the car, embarrassed. The conversation around her continued, however, jovially and unabated.

*****

The car stopped about ten miles from the Robinsons' home, in a small dug-out lot adjoined to the road. Grass had been cleared away but no gravel or other artificial surface had been imposed, and on a damp day like that one, Gatelink's shoes squished gooily into the earth. Her feet came up reluctantly for each new step, convinced they'd worked hard enough for the day.

The Robinsons seemed to be moving slowly too, but with wide smiles on their faces. Gatelink looked ahead and saw what might be the cause of their mirth—amidst an expanse of tall green stalks, people with white cloths on their heads and what looked like yellow plastic guns in their hands looked up and waved to the new arrivals. As the distance between them eroded, Gatelink saw that the guns were attached to long thin tubes that stretched out of sight. Liquid was spraying out of several of the guns into the ground.

"Marjorie!" Mrs. Robinson called out at a woman with squinted eyes and short black hair.

"Helen! It's nice to see you all here!" The woman replied, stepping forward to hug Mrs. Robinson. Mr. Robinson engaged in conversation with a man next to the woman, and Gatelink took a look around.

It was like nothing she'd ever seen, even in the Virtual Reality Tours. *It would make a good game, though,* she thought. *What would it be called? 'Dirt and Bugs and Long Green Things in the Ground.'*

Most of the ground was moist, and she struggled to find a dry patch to stake out in. "We're de-weeding today," Tommy said to Gatelink as she nearly stepped into him in her quest. "That's why they've been spraying the soil, with natural weed-killing stuff. It won't be so wet tomorrow."

Gatelink smiled a thanks and continued her observations. George also looked around, nostalgically probably, as Tommy walked off in pursuit of some task.

There were, indeed, bugs. Gatelink had seen a few flies in the city, but nothing comparing to this number and variety. Some had really large wings of solid colors, and some of them had intricate colored patterns on their wings that she found incredible. She nudged George on the arm and pointed to one delicately posed on the tip of a leaf. "Are they...real?" she asked quietly, not wanting to alarm it, or reveal herself to the others.

"Yes," he said, doing a fair job of hiding his astonishment. "They're butterflies. Important to maintaining the ecosystem, as every organism is. Unfortunately, we have to try to alter this part of the ecosystem, in the fields, to ensure the crops." He glanced around and sighed. "Sometimes we can, and sometimes we can't. We don't have advanced chemicals, since the corporations took all the chemicals capacity."

"But that was a boon in disguise," Mrs. Robinson pitched in, apparently having caught this last sentiment on her way past George and Gatelink, "because it prompted us to return to natural means. You have to be a little more crafty with 'em, but it's worth it, in the long run. Better for our health, and better for the food."

Gatelink nodded silently, and reached out to touch the leaf the butterfly had just abandoned for greater heights. It was cool and smooth as she rubbed her fingers together lightly on either side of its body. It was flexible, and yet she had to pull it with some force before she could break it. The artificial grass at Corporate didn't break at all. She had tried once when no one was looking, when she was younger.

The stalks themselves were strange creatures. They rose from the earth approximately a foot apart at different heights; the ground was tiered, Gatelink noticed, and gave the impression of steps. Thick green stems in nuances of light and dark green and brown took horizontal directions at their peaks and supported leaves and the beginnings of their fruits. Gatelink reached down from the punctured leaf and put her thumb and forefinger around the width of the stem. They reached around almost half-way. Following a sudden impulse, Gatelink bent down and dug her fingers into the moist soil, up to her knuckles. It was a nice sensation, to be enclosed in this dark spongy stuff from which live things came.

"Getting a feel of the land, huh?" a girl's voice said next to her. Gatelink turned her head, without removing her fingers, to place the voice with a face and, in possible, a name. She recognized Jyoti from yesterday, and noted with pleasure that the girl had a name tag pinned to her shirt, just in case. She was crouching down beside Gatelink.

"Yeah," Gatelink said, wondering why she didn't feel embarrassed and pull her hand out of the dirt. "I've never felt soil before," she said simply.

Jyoti smiled at her, and said nothing. She stayed there with Gatelink for a few minutes, sharing in her moment of discovery.

*****

The next few days passed in the blink of an eye. Gatelink traversed the fields, touched every kind of plant and budding fruit that she saw, and sampled the soils without shame. She took off her shoes, when everyone else did, to relax in grassy areas, and kept them off when she went back to the farms, curious about the sensation—until a snip at her foot convinced her that she'd already gotten the full sensation.

"Chiggers," Tommy replied to her sudden "ouch." "I told you," he smiled and nodded. "But don't worry. Their bark is worse than their bite. They're harmless. It'll just itch for a couple of days."

She helped with picking cotton and tomatoes and learned how to tell when they were ready to be released from growth and when they needed more time. "Everything takes time," people liked to say when advising her to pass over a plant. Gradually, she met more of the community, first the adults and then the younger kids, all of them as interested and eager as Tommy, with a knowing without cynicism she'd never imagined in children. They seemed to have wisdom of the world without the scars that getting such awareness usually left on people. She felt younger to them in understanding, but older in spirit; talking with them left her an odd mix of exhausted and invigorated.

The children seemed curious about the Virtual Reality Tours and the products, like the Hairmaker and the Microsweep, and asked questions when Gatelink brought up these topics, but never asked directly about anything first. When Gatelink asked them why, if they did want to know about life in the corporate states, they never asked her, they told her they wouldn't want to be disrespectful by initiating talk on something she might not want to talk about. Gatelink never heard longing creep into their questions or comments, either; only interest.

They didn't learn about corporate structure in their classes at school, or have to memorize the names of the CEO's and other executives of their parent firm. They learned Math, English, History, Science…and read books. They seemed to have read limitless amounts of books. None of them seemed scared, or confused, or helpless, as Gatelink remembered feeling, and seeing in her classmates as they were told why such-and-such thing that seemed like a good idea to them was denied because of some mysterious "company code" or "corporate doctrine." Things made sense in these kids' world. They knew less of how the world "actually ran," but felt more comfortable in it than Gatelink ever remembered feeling. They knew less of what was possible in it, but more of what it all meant. She envied them for that.

The high school was even more startling. There were rules, and there was structure, but everything seemed to be open to debate. Held in a municipal building, the classes were led by teachers, but run by everyone. After lecture and discussion on one topic was done, there would be debate on what they should do next, what kind of exercises would cement the learning best, and what people felt like doing that day instead of other things. Then they would vote on what topic to cover next, out of a selection of possible issues the teacher was prepared to speak and lead discussion on. Gatelink watched the students agree, disagree, compromise, fold, and even throw up their hands in exasperation at times, all under the advisement of the teachers and in a spirit of working together for a necessary and desired common goal.

The adults were all similar to George's parents. They began to wear name-tags too, to help Gatelink out after she began to meet them on the third day. She was touched by their consideration for her. The adults did not talk with Gatelink much; they seemed to be holding back on what they said to her, she sometimes thought. But she didn't know how she could ask about this to George, so she simply kept it as an observation.

On her fourth day, she decided to take her name into her own hands. More and more she'd been hearing "G.L." instead of "Gatelink," and she'd felt empowered every time she heard it and didn't correct it, didn't protect the company's name. Little by little, she lost ownership of it, she divested herself from the conglomerate of sounds. She wasn't "Gatelink Computing and Software, Incorporated" to these people here, and she wasn't Gatelink, here. She was…a girl, a young woman. She was herself. She was…

"Elizabeth," she stated, stopping George in mid-sentence as they sat on the sofa at the Tinsley's house, the Robinsons' nearest neighbors.

"Huh?" he replied.

"You just called me 'Gatelink.' Well, I don't want to be Gatelink C & S, Inc., anymore. I don't have to be Gatelink C & S, Inc. anymore. If you don't mind, I'd like to be Elizabeth, like Elizabeth Bennett in *Pride and Prejudice*. She's always been my favorite character. She is someone I want to be named after, not a corporation. George, I can be Elizabeth, while I'm here, can't I?"

George sat, dumbstruck for several seconds. "Goo—" he started, then stopped himself. "Wow. Are you sure? Nobody thinks badly of you for it, you know. I hope we haven't been treating you any differently from—"

"No," she interrupted him. "It's not that." She paused, and said quietly. "It's for me." He could see that she was fighting back tears. "I've always hated being called 'Gatelink.' Even when I didn't know I hated it, even before I knew what hate was, I think, I hated it."

As she shut her eyes tightly and flinched, George slid toward her on the sofa and put his arms around her. "It's okay, Elizabeth," he said. "Or, is it Liz?" he asked, running his hand over her hair.

"Liz," she answered, smiling but not releasing from his grip as now unnecessary. "Liz." And smiling, Liz cried.

*****

Liz grew into her new name quickly. One syllable, no implications; she liked it a lot. She spent the next week happily with a name of her own.

She and the other "young adults," as they were referred to and self-referred, took a few days away from the fields to wander loosely around the landscape. There were miles of space with no buildings, no houses, not even roads. They went to places called "parks," where they walked for hours among rocks as big as skyscrapers with surfaces alternately smooth enough to almost reflect and rough and grainy like vertical sand. However big the rocks, though, the sky was always bigger, and never left her sight; Liz found it to be her constant companion in this new world, familiar and yet foreign in its heightened clarity, here. The group stopped occasionally to climb on tall, thick trees which made no attempt to resist the uninvited company. They named the various trees and shrubs to Liz and told her what they knew about how fast each grew and what insect and animal life they accommodated. Liz glimpsed rabbits, squirrels, snakes, lizards and other creatures that held her in awe as they scuttled, ran and slithered through their lives before her and out of her sight, driven by purposes she couldn't begin to imagine. Her new friends dared each other to heights of bravery in climbing certain rocks or sliding down ravines, and sometimes walked quietly, reverently, holding hands or split apart at contemplative distances. At the depths of great canyons they came upon lush oases, rivers and streams of clear water and obvious generosity toward the abundant green life on their banks. Liz rested her feet in these waters and felt Nature's relief, and release. She felt herself as an animal in the world, driven by nothing she could name, sensing a string attaching all things. She felt comfort.

In the evenings, they talked and played games. People chose books and plays to share reading aloud. Patricia painted scenes they had seen that day, and always a few people would be writing in journals or notebooks of more personal stuff. Liz felt herself loosen. There were no expectations of her here, no imposed indebtedness like iron shackles around her wrists.

If anyone had had an interesting dream the night before, they shared it, often reading from a morning journal, and people offered their insights and interpretations. This was done with great solemnity, even when the dreams sounded to Liz's novitiate ears like silly pieces of fluff not worth remembering, let alone vocalizing. To hear them talk even about dreams of not knowing which cat was yours, or losing a button, was fascinating, though. Everything meant something, told something that the soul needed the mind to understand and had used the only means available to it. Meanings were pursued relentlessly. Liz felt tempted to bring up some of the dreams she'd had in those days and the past, but she didn't. Something held her back.

On the ninth day, George and Liz went to see the Elders.

CHAPTER 14
OUT OF THE MOUTHS OF OLD FOGIES

Liz had noticed some older people at the welcome home party on the first night, gray-haired and spritely, but she hadn't seen them since, and now, as she and George walked along a worn trail to the their sub-village, wondered why. She contemplated asking George, but she was enjoying the silence, and George had just taken her hand in his quietly as they walked. It felt warm, and she didn't want to interrupt the sensation.

Gradually they came upon a large house similar in style to the Robinsons' but with ramps leading up to doors in the front and the side. George pointed to them with his free hand as they approached. "Those are for wheelchairs. Several of the Elders have health problems where they can't walk. We don't have the advanced medical technology over here, anymore." He looked down. "When the corporations left, they took that with them."

He released her hand and Liz asked, "How come I haven't seen them since the first night?"

"Oh, I'm surprised I forgot to tell you about that. Usually they do hang out with us, and participate in everything with us, but this week they're on retreat. One week a month, the Elders keep to the Elders' House for rest and meditation, for age-appropriate discussions. They are closer to leaving the world than the rest of us, we recognize, and they work to keep themselves more prepared for it than we need to. And it's good for the younger part of the community to go for some time without their grandparents and grand-aunts and -uncles, to loosen the sense of attachment. It will make it easier for us when they go. Everyone expects that this is how we will live too, when we get to be older."

They had reached the front door. George opened it and Liz entered. She saw to her left a large room, sparsely furnished, occupied by about fifteen to twenty gray-haired people sitting on two couches, the blanketed floor, or wheelchairs. Some were talking quietly to each other, and some were silent, with their eyes closed, displaying serene expressions. George followed Liz into the house, and smiled and waved at the seated crowd.

"George! Liz! Welcome!" a thin woman in a flowered dress called out as she rose and moved toward them. She grasped first George's right hand in both her own, then Liz's.

As she did, Liz blurted out, "How did you know my new name?"

"You're famous around these parts, Liz, don'cha know? As famous as everybody else! And we keep updated on events during our week away." She added with exaggerated slyness, "We have our sources." She smiled and led them into the sitting room.

George sat cross-legged on the floor and Liz silently followed suit. All eyes were open now and on them.

"George," a man who'd just opened his eyes said in a hoarse voice. "It's been too long since we've seen you here." Liz couldn't tell from his tone whether he was happy or angry to see George, or both. Maybe George couldn't tell either, she thought, because he looked down for a second before answering.

"I know, Pop-pop. I'm sorry." Liz's gaze redirected from George to the old man across the room, and she could see a family resemblance in the nose, the chin, the eyes.

"It's good to see you, son," the man said, opening his arms. Without hesitation, George went over and hugged his grandfather, and returned to Liz's side. He was smiling now and seemed at ease.

"Are you learning much, over there, dear?" an old woman a few feet from them asked. "Are you having the experience you were hoping for?"

"I'm learning much, ma'am," George replied. "And all your sage advices and admonishments have served me in good stead."

Huh? Liz thought. *Do you need a different language to speak to the Elders?* She knew George was still speaking English, technically, but fancier than she'd ever heard spoken before.

George chatted with the Elders for several minutes, answering their questions about his general health and how he was taking care of himself there in the same archaic terminology. Liz could just barely understand his sentences and found herself absorbed in the task when suddenly there was a silence and eyes were inquisitively focused upon her.

"I'm sorry—what?" she said instinctively.

A heavyish woman in a lavender blouse and loose khaki pants repeated her question, her voice breaking with age. "I asked if you are enjoying your stay with us, Liz."

"Yes, very much, thank you," Liz responded.

"And what company do…your parents work for there, dear?" another lady asked her. *That's a nice way to put it,* Liz thought.

"Gatelink Computing and Software, Incorporated…uh, ma'am," she answered.

"And that is your full name, I understand?" a man across the room queried.

"Yes…sir," Liz replied, feeling silly using the vernacular but sensing that it was the right thing to do.

A few of the Elders shook their heads gently. "We are sorry, my child," a woman next to Liz said, placing her hand on Liz's arm, as seemed to be a popular gesture around here. "Because you must have been unhappy there, or you would not be here."

Liz hadn't admitted that to anyone but George. She knew that it was a logical conclusion to draw from her presence, but hearing this stranger say it made her feel she had nothing to hide from them, that she couldn't anyway.

"I have questions I want to ask you," she said, looking first to the woman, then to the rest of the group.

"Naturally, you do," a man said. "And we will answer you as best we can."

"Why did The Separation happen? What was the final straw? Why didn't you do what…my grandparents did—must have done? Why did they do what they did?"

"Our actions we can attempt to explain; theirs, we cannot," the man stated. "That is always the truth." His way of speaking was grand, Liz noted. It didn't draw attention; it demanded it. "The growth of the corporate structure, the spread of its hold, was so subtle, so insidious, that it wasn't until they confessed their power and started making demands of us to 'improve their marketing power' that we were forced to confront it."

"Right under our noses we lost control over the supply of any clothing, household goods, even medicine, and then…food," a lady continued. "And we never gave it a thought."

"But when they began to impose their demands," another woman picked up the baton in the relay run of this conversation, "when they thought they needed to sharpen their edge over competing firms by starting to use our children as billboards, we knew we were at a crossroads. We had a decision to make."

"The whole nation knew it," George's father pitched in in a gruff voice. "Of course, they didn't call it a crossroads in their media, like we did. They didn't look it at so much as a decision as an inevitability. Or so their media framed it."

"They didn't have any independent media left out there," a woman added. "But out here, there were still sturdy spirits like my older sister, Julie, God bless her soul, who were informing for free, and stirring up debate."

"We determined, by vote, that we would not let life become only about whatever was dictated to us by a few people who value only one thing—money and what you buy with it," a man said. "That was too limiting for us, and not worth what we would have to lose."

"I know I might regret asking this," Liz said, "but why do you think corporations are so bad? You speak of them like they're evil or something—why? They're just a way of doing business, aren't they?"

"Don't be afraid to ask us anything, my child," said the same lady who'd called her 'my child' before. "And yes, in a way, they are 'just a way of doing business.' That's how they started out, in this country as in others. Certainly, then, no one knew the tremendous implications they would bring."

A man next to her picked up just before the end of the woman's last word, as if starting a chorus. "But people got too good at what they were trying to do. Advertising to make people want your product over someone else's that is too similar; then, advertising just to get people to buy more, to consume what they didn't need or even want. The goal became to convert humans with full, satisfying lives into beings who believed truly and deeply that only buying could complete them."

Another man started, "Corporate structures became more advanced, more attuned to the higher purpose of generating the most profit for the few people at the top. Employee morale boosters like sports teams, parties, things that had fostered some sense of humanity in the workplace, were eliminated. And families were brought into the picture, the corporate picture. Family structure dissolved into corporate structure."

"People began to take lifestyle guidance from corporate guidelines," a woman declared. "They had to, or lose their job, and not be able to buy the things they'd by this point become convinced they couldn't live without."

"There is a saying, Liz, that you probably haven't heard," a man said. "Absolute power corrupts absolutely. If you think about it a little while, later, you will come to understand what it means. Well, the people who ran the corporations recognized the tremendous power they had come to have over people's lives, over society, by virtue of the changes that one by one, everyone had let slip by. You may have read about the kingdoms and empires which dominated throughout the second millennium. They were means of vast control of millions of people by small numbers of individuals. Well, these people at the tops of these corporations, have created empires of illusion and kingdoms of currency. Control through the creation of desires and sole ownership of the means to fulfill those desires. Not so different from every system of empire in history, where control was imposed through force and economic control."

"It's in rebelling against such empires," a woman stated, "that America was founded."

"And now, sadly," a man added, "most of our fellow Americans are content to live in one, right on our own soil. There are no more democratic elections, when corporations choose our leaders—the whole political system of democracy has become a mockery of itself—a shadow."

"Except here," a woman said, and smiled. "We don't have everything here," she gestured at the wheelchair in which she was sitting, "but we do have that!"

"Amen, Anna," the previous speaker commented. "Amen."

"What are the 'Changes in Thought'?" Liz asked, now unabashed to interrupt the Elders' reverie with another question. She thought they might look disturbed at her intrusion into their post-Amen peacefulness, but they didn't. They must have meant what they said about her not being afraid to ask them questions. "Mrs. Robinson mentioned it before, when they were telling me a little about The Separation, but then it didn't come up again." She paused, and added her next query before she forgot to get it out. "And I noticed that, well, it seems like the other kids, and 'young adults,' want to talk to me a lot, but the grown-ups, around Mr. and Mrs. Robinsons' age, are hesitant to talk to me about anything, to teach me anything. Why?" Liz didn't know if she'd gone too far with this last question, since it was just her own observation, and she didn't know if it was really true or just her imagination.

"Well," said an old man in gray pants and a white short-sleeved button-up shirt that matched his all-white hair and trim beard. "You're very observant, Liz. I can see why you must have been very bored over there." He was nodding his head slowly, rhythmically, in approval.

"To answer your last question first," a woman continued, "which does sometimes make the most sense, the Middle Generation, as we call the folks in George's parents' age range, were indeed reluctant to try to educate you about here. You see, children are never hesitant to share what they know, and they should not be, because that is part of the enthusiasm of youth. We never try to curb that. But as people get older, they start to be aware of how incomplete their understanding is, and how many things require age to attain. Like wisdom. In the Middle Generation, one knows much and thinks that one understands much, but one also knows that they *do* not and *cannot* understand everything that they *know*. Children know this, in an objective sense, but subjectively they cannot fathom it—they don't yet have the experience; they just haven't had enough time yet here in our world to truly realize the truth of this. But the Middle Generation—they do not want to give you any misunderstanding. They accede to us, Elders, for that—that is our proper task, as it will be theirs, when they have had enough time on this Earth to think things through, as we have. You see, understanding takes much more than intelligence, or even hard work. People need *time* to absorb even what is most familiar to them, and to be able to distinguish between what is the world, what is the true nature of things, and what is actually them, themselves, that they are seeing and mistaking for the world. With time, people can develop the ability to separate their own thoughts, experiences and desires from how they understand the world, and themselves. But it takes much, much time. The process can only be gradual. We couldn't handle it if it happened too fast."

Another woman added, "This way of thinking, this agreed-upon worldview, arose as part of the Changes in Thought, which is why I suppose Miriam thought it wiser to answer your second question first." The woman glanced over at her predecessor, who nodded back. "The Changes in Thought existed because when we realized how wrong things had become, we had to face that we must have not have been doing things right, to allow the corporate system to go as far as it had. We knew we had forgotten how to think, how to *live*. We were jolted into seeing what was wrong, but we had lost sight by then of what was right."

The first man resumed, "We knew that if we were going to really reject corporatism and protect ourselves from its reemergence and conquest anew, we were going to have to *change*. Though we had gotten to where we *were*, gradually, insidiously, unknowingly we were going to have to willfully remake ourselves, and our broken communities."

Liz was struggling to absorb this all with glazed eyes. She felt like her mind was spinning a little. "So, how did you do it?" she asked slowly, her brows furrowed with the weight of concentration.

"How could a whole people change their way of thinking, of relating, of *being*—their values, their thoughts, even what they choose to joke about, you must be wondering," a different man said. "Well, it wasn't easy, Liz. It wasn't fast, and it wasn't pleasant. We saw that *everything* that we had come to know was *wrong*, needed to be reversed, in our minds, and much needed to be added. We read many books on the topics, from philosophical and spiritual treatises, to so-called 'new age' books and novels. We gathered as much insight and help as we could from our weary parents and grandparents—rest their souls—who had long ago given up on life and found it hard to understand or believe what we were trying to do, what we *were* doing."

"We had community meetings and discussions," a woman said. "Endlessly—for days, weeks, even months on end. We approached this project as if our and our children's lives depended on it, knowing that in a sense—in the most important sense—they did."

"And we changed our values, our beliefs, our priorities, even our desires. We worked hard to learn what we wanted to be. Then we worked even harder to try to become that."

"And we continue to do so," another woman said in a conclusive tone, nodding. Most of them were nodding now, looking deep in their thoughts which were undoubtedly the same one.

"We came to some surprising conclusions, too," picked up the man with the matching shirt and beard. "About ourselves, about what we did and why we did them. Looking back on it now, it only surprises us that it took the corporations to get us to see our own actions and motivations clearly for what must been the first time."

"We realized," a different man said, "that we, and especially our children, had been turning to drugs, and sex, to find something that we had let ourselves lose hold of. We had begun to misuse these material means to try to recapture a sense of connection with the sublime, the unknowable, the transcendent—bliss. We had forgotten that these are available to us, free of charge or addiction, free of unwanted pregnancies, STD's and emotional scarring, whenever we wanted, through approaching what we were really seeking—connection. We relearned how to meditate, how to pray and how to play. We experimented with learning how to 'be,' how to enjoy the very act of being, to recognize it as an act and to respect it, to honor ourselves."

"And addictions fell away," a woman continued. "Like dead leaves that had clung too long to a tree. Addictions to drugs, sex, overworking—gradually, little by little, we learned how not to be afraid of ourselves anymore."

They all nodded. Liz wished she had a tape recorder, so maybe she could listen to the conversation in installments, sound bites, like she was used to. But, she reflected quickly, though the meanings were outside her grasp still, she felt sure the Elders' words would be emblazoned on her mind forever. She doubted she would forget a syllable of what she heard that day.

"Liz," a woman said to her, "I hope you don't mind, but this is the last day of our retreat, and we don't like to do too much talking other than…what brings us here, on the last day. We'll be back in the main village from tomorrow, and I'm sure all of us would be glad to talk to you again. Is that all right, dear?" she smiled too sweetly for argument.

"Of course," Liz replied. "I didn't mean to cause you any trouble."

"You didn't, Liz," the woman next to her assured, with a quick touch to the arm. "We're very happy you came," a man added, smiling also.

As Liz and George left the house, voices raised in a song about questions, answers and the Spirit. It was a quiet walk back to the Robinsons' as Liz tried to sort out what she'd heard, and George wondered why the words had sounded so unfamiliar to him now.

*****

True to their word, the Elders began to reappear the next morning. "Grandpa," as they called him, was a still and somewhat grouchy presence at the breakfast table at the Robinsons'. "His arthritis is worse in the mornings," Mrs. Robinson whispered to Liz in the kitchen over frying eggs. "He's in a lot of pain right now—that's why he's grumpy. He's usually feeling better by the afternoon." Liz nodded and smiled, wondered what 'arthritis' was. She wondered if her grandparents, in a home somewhere or dead, had it—she couldn't remember anything about them from the last time she saw them, over 10 years ago, when they became "economic burdens" and vanished from her life.

In the fields that afternoon, the Elders changed the pace of things. Some of them moved so slowly, Liz wondered if they would just stop moving altogether, like a wind-up clock that has reached the end of its cycle. They participated in the smaller tasks—shelling the peas, picking the tomatoes—and stayed out of the way of the actual soil-work. Liz felt sure, watching them, that their physical output was negligible. Yet the total work by the end of the day appeared greater than it had the day before.

"Do the Elders work in the fields every day?" Liz asked Tyrone as they sat under the shade of a tree, resting.

"Whenever they can, whenever they feel they're able," he replied. "It's good for them to keep busy, to work with us, and it's good for us to be in their presence."

"To be in their presence?" Liz repeated, running her hand over the grass beside her, massaging the uneven blades. "What do you mean?"

Tyrone seemed to consider for a moment. "I understand that it's different over there—how age is regarded. There, it is something people feel ashamed of, as if they should apologize for having lasted so long. People try to look younger than they are. But to us, age is something we respect, and all hope to attain someday. We figure, if you get to be old, you must be doing things right. We respect age, and its implications. When we see the Elders, we're happy we've been able to help them get this far, as they helped us get as far as we have. Everything moves in cycles in this world. Seeing them reminds us of that, that we're all in this cycle, together. And things make sense."

Liz said nothing, and her companion did not seem to expect a reply. They rested a bit more, and returned to the rest of the group, now dropping seeds in zigzagging diagonal holes in the ground. Liz watched the Elders with their skin wrinkled like raisins and their deep-set eyes, and tried to see what Tyrone saw.

*****

"Liz!" the voice chastised. "Not like that! You're peeling away half the potatoes! What are you doing?" The old lady pulled the device out of Liz's hand as they stood in the Robinsons' kitchen, which was almost moving with the vibrations of at least a dozen women, men and children that evening. "I'll show you how to do it, then you try, and don't press so deeply! You're only trying to take the skin off! And did you wash your hands first?"

As she made her way to the sink to lather and rinse, Liz noticed that she was angry. Who was this woman to yell at her, to give her orders? She felt a great temptation to make her thoughts known to the skinny lady with piercing blue eyes that flashed at Liz when she had usurped the task Liz had volunteered to do. But at a counter three feet away, the same scenario played itself out, as the caustic voice directed itself at Patricia and her "lazy way of separating the lettuce." Liz observed Patricia, who sighed softly and stepped out of the way. She caught Liz's eye, smiled and shrugged behind the old woman's back, and moved somewhere else to assist with another task. Still fuming, Liz retreated to the living room. She reflected on the fact that Patricia had not looked angry at all; her response to the old woman's rudeness had been…gentle, indulgent. *This is a strange place indeed,* Liz thought.

After dinner, when it was just the Robinsons and her, the unexpected occurred. A fight.

Liz, George and Tommy were in the living room, reading, when shouts emerged from upstairs. Liz couldn't make out the words, but the voices were unmistakably angry. She saw George and Tommy exchange an inscrutable glance. In a few minutes, they heard a door slam. Mrs. Robinson walked quickly down the stairs and toward the front door. As she passed the entrance to the living room, she called out, her voice quivering a little, "Guys, I'm going out for a walk. I should be back in about an hour or so." She didn't stop on her way out, and she didn't meet any of their eyes. Liz heard the front door slap against a human hand, hard, then close. Mrs. Robinson had probably caught the door just in time to prevent another slam, Liz thought.

"What happened?" she whispered to George.

"Oh, who knows?" he replied at normal volume, shifting casually on the couch where he lay, a copy of *The Brothers Karamazov* nestled in one hand. "They have a big bad fight like this once in a while, then it all blows over." He turned to Tommy. "What, every few months? Least, that was the going rate when I was here full-time. Has it changed any, Tomster?"

"Not a lick, chief," Tommy replied. "Like clockwork. Only not so regular." He grinned at his joke.

"But, something must have happened," Liz insisted.

"No," George looked up at her, surprised. "If anything had happened, anything serious, they would've told us about it. People just fight. Especially married people."

"Yeah," Tommy added, turning a page in his book, *The Count of Monte Cristo*. "They told us once that it was good, to blow off steam. They said when I got married that I'd understand." He looked up from his book. "'Yechhh!' I told 'em. 'No way. I'll take your word for it, thanks.'" He returned to *The Count*. "How do your parents fight, Liz?"

Liz thought of their verbal scuffling in the hall that day when her dad told her about his pending promotion. That was the closest thing to an argument she could remember seeing them in. She never saw them talking to each other enough to fight.

"Doesn't it make you feel bad, when they fight?" she asked, deciding not to answer Tommy's question.

"I think it did, the first few times I noticed, when I was little," George said, looking at her. "But then they explained that when people love each other and care about each other, and disagree on something, the love can express itself as anger, because we're only human. We get confused by our thoughts sometimes when there's a lot of emotions involved. In an ideal world, maybe, we could live without fighting, but the anger, which is really frustration, is only temporary, and it's natural. People don't fight if they don't care, in a family. We're all living too closely together—emotionally, I mean, not physically—for us to not step on each other's toes once in a while." He paused, and added, "Love and hate are not opposites. Love and indifference are opposites."

"I've never thought about it that way," Liz said slowly.

George nodded. "I know. People don't talk about these things over there. Not even in the media, where all they aim to do is shock. I never heard anything about emotions, or families, or love. And it's such an important part of life. I mean, you strip away everything superficial, and what else have we got in this world, but what we think and feel?"

"Yeah," Liz said, not as an answer. She knew the question was rhetorical, and explanatory. "Huh," she added quietly, thinking. George returned to *The Brothers,* and she resumed the copy of the *Tao Te Ching* she'd pulled lazily off a Robinson bookshelf. In an hour, Mrs. Robinson returned with a jar of freshly-made ice cream from the neighbors for them all to share. Liz wanted to ask her something, but she didn't know what. She looked at her searchingly when she thought she wasn't looking, but George's mom only smiled, and her eyes betrayed nothing incompatible.

CHAPTER 15
MY SECRET DESIRE

The day before they were to go back to New York, George took Liz to see her first waterfall.

"It's *my* waterfall," he told her as they stood before the tumbling wall of water and smooth, shiny rocks. "At least, that's what I like to think, when I come here alone. I know no one can own it, but in a way, that's what makes me want to call it mine." He stared into it, as if waiting for it to speak, to confirm what he said, to say, "Yes, when you are here, I am yours." "Everything is so *vast* out here, so…unattainable, that…sometimes I wish there were some part of this beauty that I could just put in my pocket, that I could *have*, that would be there for me always."

"But, this *is* here for you always, isn't it?" Liz asked, looking around in awe at the spongy green carpets on the rocks outside the path of the water, knowing they must be natural but not quite believing it; wanting to touch them, to press into their soft bodies, but afraid. "It doesn't look like it's about to get up and walk away." She smiled.

"I know, but…it's different. I have to come to it. Like everything here. We're all so…powerless." He had a distant look in his eyes, still staring into the mouth of the fall. Liz didn't understand his words but recognized what his eyes spoke—dissatisfaction, and the guilt of it.

"Here, this might help," she said, stooping down to the gurgling waters they stood atop and plucking a small, smooth rock the size of her palm. She lifted his hand, opened it, and delivered her gift.

George laughed, and so did Liz. "You're so pretty when you laugh, Liz, do you know that?" He raised his still-dry right hand and brushed his fingertips along the side of her face. "And so brave. I feel like…you understand me, Liz."

Inside her, something jumped. Her breath lost depth; she could hear it, fast but quiet. Liz hoped he couldn't hear it too. She parted her lips, but she didn't know why; she couldn't say anything.

She felt his hand drift away from her face and land softly on her waist. It moved gently up and down a few inches and his breathing became louder too. Liz didn't move. She heard a "plunk" as the pebble dropped from his other hand into the waiting water and then George's lips were on hers, his hands damp but strong against the back of her shirt and her hips, drawing her to him. The distance between them was erased by his desire and hers—she leaned into him, as she had times before for comfort, but this time with intention. His lips were warm and smooth and then the sense of them overcome by this thick, soft tongue introducing itself to the sanctity of her mouth. It danced around her tongue, in circles, squares, pentagons, shapes she had not yet known. It tickled her and dared her tongue to come out and play; it itched, and then it scratched. Liz's hands had gone instinctively around George's neck, as she'd seen women do on TV and the movies. Her fingers sat awkwardly there, stuck to the fine hairs on the back of his neck by the sweat that had begun to generate in the 45-minute walk to the fall— she raised them to his blond, blond hair and contoured the shape of his head. This somehow made her more excited and she felt almost ready to accept the challenge presented to her tongue by his, when he pulled away.

"Oh, wow!" he panted. "Liz."

Unsure of what she should do or say, Liz ran her fingers through her hair anxiously and waited. After about a half a second, she could stand the silence no longer.

"Um, have you…uh, done this before?" she asked, trying to sound casual.

George hesitated before answering. "Yes, but…never this like. I mean, it's never been like *that* before."

Liz's face look troubled, and he added quickly, "I mean that in a *good* way!" He paused. "And I've never kissed *here* before. This is the first time I've brought anyone here with me, that I've shared this with anyone—this part of myself. My secret desire." He took her hand.

"Thanks for letting me kiss you, Liz. I'll always remember this."

Liz laughed nervously. "So…what do we do now?" she said, looking down and kicking a pebble lightly with her foot. It skipped a few feet and settled into its new home.

"Well, *right* now," George replied, looking around at the trees circling them yards away, "I think we go back home, because they'll be starting dinner soon, and probably organize a *search party* if we're not back within the hour." His voice was more confident than hers, almost normal. George released her hand and turned away from the fall. Liz followed, and he stopped suddenly, and turned around to her. "But Liz, first, I just want to tell you that…I like you a lot, I like everything about you…and I care about you…deeply, I think. And…um, I guess that's about it." He turned back around and traced back the path over the uneven stones that had brought them to their "kissing spot," as Liz would call it in her memories.

"George," she called to him, two or three feet in front of her, after about a minute. "I—I feel the same way about you, I think." But she sounded more sure than she was. Too much was happening all at once— too many new perspectives, new understanding. New information was something she had plenty of experience with, at least, but everything in the last two weeks, and now this.… But she was hoping they would kiss again, soon. She knew *that* for a fact.

*****

Dinner that night threatened to be uneventful. They were having a special bonus round of the big-group dinners. This night, people packed around the living room table, all trying to stay in the same room with the members they were about to lose. There was chatter about what Billy did that day at the school, and how cute it was when little five-year-old Jessie tried to help unloading the soil from the trucks and looked so proud of herself for having put her hand on top of the heavy bags when the grown-ups unloaded them, "to keep them from toppling over." The talk was quieter than usual, though, the words scarcer. Small silences interceded, despite the dozens of willing vocalizers. Liz also was quieter than she had been, lost not only in thoughts that tripped over each other, vying for her attention, but in the sadness that this might be the last night she didn't eat alone. Finally, during the dessert of chocolate pudding, made with chocolate Liz had brought with her as a gift, George's grandfather broke the waning conversations.

"Goddammit, George, you shouldn't go!" he said angrily, pounding his fist on the table. His nearly-empty dessert bowl jumped in front of him. "You've *gone* there, you've *seen*. You've experienced it—you got what you went there for. We didn't oppose your going because we know how curious you are, how you need to see things for yourself, but there's *got* to be a *limit*!" He stopped, and glared at George, who looked back at him, stunned and waiting. "You should be here with us, where you belong. If your grandmother were alive today, you'd make her cry with this selfishness, this thoughtlessness. You have no idea how hard we worked to keep you safe. And you—you go *back* to them!" He spat this last sentence, as if trying physically to get rid of a bad taste in his mouth.

George's expression had dissolved into one of hurt and fear.

"Papa, we talked about this…." Mrs. Robinson remarked quietly, from across the room. "We all did."

"That was *then*," he retorted. "That was a *long* time ago," he went on, turning from his daughter-in-law back to his grandson. His voice became soft, almost beseeching. "Don't you know how much we all miss you, all the time? You're *part* of us. It's like one of our organs is missing. Like our kidney ran away!"

"Pop-pop, I *didn't* run away," George said levelly. "I'm traveling; I'm exploring. I'm here right now, aren't I? I write, and call, when I'm there."

Pop-pop looked at him in disgust, then resignation, and, maybe, regret. He mumbled, "If you'll all excuse me, please," as he pushed back his chair, rose and left the room and then the house. The front door closed softly behind him.

George stared into his pudding bowl for a moment amidst uncomfortable silence. Then he rose too, saying, "I'll be back in a minute," and left through the back door. Liz hesitated less than a second before following him.

The night sky was a dark vault of scattered diamonds. The grass was already moist with dew beneath Liz's bare feet. It tickled and teased her as she walked quickly to catch up with George. He walked ahead with his head down and hands in his pockets. From behind, he looked like his grandfather might, hunched with the weight of worries as people tend to become, *even here,* Liz reflected. He stopped when he heard her approach and about-faced.

"I'm fine, Liz," he said, sounding annoyed.

She was taken aback by the note in his voice. "I know," she said unwaveringly. "I just wanted to see if you wanted to talk."

He sighed loudly, harshly, almost a huff, facing Liz but looking downward. He deliberated for several seconds. At last he broke out in controlled syllables, "Maybe they're right." He turned around again, away from Liz.

"It was only your grandfather who said—" Liz began.

"I know," George interrupted, still facing away from her. "But they were all thinking it. Probably have been for a while. And maybe they're right. What *am* I still doing there?" He paused, and took his hands out of his pockets. "God, I'd like a cigarette," he said.

"I didn't know you smoked," Liz said, surprised.

"Well, I—I just started a few weeks ago, before I came back. I guess maybe I was stressed about coming back here." He shrugged, analyzing the grass again.

"Why?" Liz asked, more because she wanted to know than because she thought it would help him to talk about it.

But like she had brushed Tommy's question about her parents off the surface of the conversation, George similarly manhandled hers.

"I *have* seen; I *have* experienced. I've been there for months already. Theoretically, I *should* have gotten what I went there for, by long ago. But I feel like…I haven't yet." He looked trancelike into the distance. Liz raised her eyebrows and waited unobtrusively, feeling oddly patient. She was compelled by his confession, if that's what it was.

After about a minute or so, George returned his attention to her and answered her unspoken question, "Liz, I really can't explain."

"You don't have to," she said softly, wishing of course that he would.

She put her hand on his arm, gently, consciously, getting a feel for this gesture of theirs that still intrigued and beguiled her. As predicted, it appeared to have a calming effect. "So, what are you gonna do?" she asked quietly, confused even as to how she wanted him to respond, let alone what his most likely answer would be.

"Oh, Liz, can I kiss you again and forget about this whole thing?" Before she could say anything, his hands were pressed against her back and his chest against hers. He approached her mouth with his open, giving her no choice but to match his. She could feel his heart beating quickly against hers; they kissed a hard, passionate kiss. At first reluctant, Liz began to feel a sense of release in this act. She didn't think; she *did*. And it felt wonderful, this warm sensation flooding her body and clearing her mind. She maneuvered her arms under his and explored the tapestry of muscles she could feel through his shirt, long smooth ones and short rectangular ones toward the bottom that cried out to be touched too. He moved his lips to her neck and she had to moan, so sweet was this pleasure that had lain hidden from her but somehow could be released from her own, simple neck that she'd always taken for granted. She was sure she never would again.

"Oh, Liz," he whispered into her ear and moaned softly himself as he slid his hands down over her hips and then her buttocks on his way back up to her back. He returned to her waiting, parted lips and ran one hand through her hair.

After minutes this way that seemed like blissful hours, George pulled away brusquely.

"Liz, we shouldn't be doing this," he said.

"What?" she wanted to scream. "This wasn't *my* idea!" But she still felt too happy to even think this fully.

"Not like this," he said, heaving a sigh. "What am I doing?" He was clearly asking the question of himself.

The lust starting to fade quickly with the removal of his body from direct contact with hers, Liz's mind began to demist. "What are you *doing*?" she said harshly. "What *are* you doing, exactly?"

"Oh, man!" he ejected, hitting his forehead with the base of his palm. "What is wrong with me!" he said roughly.

"What is *wrong* with you? What, for kissing *me*? Is that what you mean?" Liz almost spat out. Somewhere, she suspected strongly that what he meant had nothing to do with her, but her pride and insecurity wouldn't allow her to entertain this scenario just then.

"Yes!" George replied, sounding almost relieved at what she'd said.

"My *God*!" Liz retorted, hurt. She turned on her heel to go. Though, what she'd say to everyone waiting inside she had no idea.

"No, wait, Liz!" George cried out. "That's not what I meant!" He laughed quickly. "Ah, Liz. I've been wanting to kiss you for weeks, maybe months. Definitely since the minute you asked if you could 'interview' me for your 'paper.'" He smiled, and she had to too, at the memory. "But right now, after what Pop-pop said to me…my emotions are running high. Yours probably are too, from all the newness of being here, and knowing you're going back tomorrow." Liz noted the use of "you're" instead of "we're." "This just wasn't a good time for me to kiss you. My head's not clear. My *heart's* not clear. I'm sorry, Liz."

"Well, I am too. I guess," she said. She started to laugh, too. "But hey, it was fun, wasn't it?"

"Yeah," George said. "It was."

Liz knew she should have felt happy with his answer, but somehow it cut into her.

"Well, to answer your question," he said smiling, "I *am* going back with you. I don't know for how long, but I'm not ready to come back here for good yet." He paused. "And, if some people don't like it, well…I'm not hurting anyone by being there."

Though Liz had just heard to the contrary inside, she decided not to say anything. They walked back to the house in silence, not holding hands.

*****

Inside, the dishes and people had been cleared away from the living room. They found Mrs. Robinson alone in the kitchen, washing dessert cups. "Oh, there you kids are!" she said cheerfully when she saw them enter. "It seems like you've been out there forever!" She smiled. She stopped rinsing and turned to George. "George, you know that Pop-pop is getting advanced in years, and he doesn't—"

"I know, Mom," George cut her off, but gently.

"And, well, we want you to be happy, son. We all do. Your grandpa too. We do miss you, you know that, but we don't want to keep you here by force." She frowned slightly, maybe dissatisfied with what she'd said, or just distaste at the thought of keeping her son against his will. "We love you honey, whatever you do, and wherever you are."

"Thanks, Mom." He went to her and hugged her. "You know I love you all, too." As they pulled apart, Liz wondered if George noticed the expression that had suddenly engulfed his mother's features, dampening and distorting them. If he did, he didn't show it.

CHAPTER 16
A RETURN TO PRODUCT LIFE

The rest of that evening passed without fanfare. Various friends and family drifted in and out through the Robinson living room in approximately half-hour shifts, smoothly and seamlessly like gentle river ripples. They teased George about various things, and joked about the benefits of his absence from town on its economy and society. He smiled through it, and seemed to genuinely enjoy the company and conversations. Everyone told Liz they were happy to have met her, and wished her all the luck in the world in her life, and that they hoped they might see her again or be able to keep in touch. She had expected them to be tentative in their approach to farewelling her, but they weren't. They were sincere, and must have been making an effort not to put pressure on her or to say anything they didn't fully mean. Their restricted language was conveyed with such warmth, however, that the effect was that of a full and genuine goodbye that meant both 'Goodbye Forever' without reproach and 'See You Later' with hope, at the same time. *It was artistic*, Liz thought later of that evening of taking leave. *They're artists and scientists of human communication.* She knew she'd never forget that night, any of it, or the impression it left on her, everything it taught her, which took her months to fully unravel.

*****

In the air, there were no more distractions. Without people to engage her curiosity and with George beside her surveying the clouds with apparent intention, Gatelink returned to the words she had heard in Flagstaff, still only moist with the dew of comprehension. The words of the Elders loomed large in her mind. "Absolute power corrupts absolutely," they had told her. "Think about this later, and you will understand." *Absolute power,* she thought, *would mean control over everything, I suppose. But the corporations, do they really have control over everything?* she wondered. *I mean, we work for them, sure, and they control everyone's incomes, in that way, but that's the extent of it. ...Isn't it?* She remembered George's long discussion with the other kids about the companies "creating values." She wasn't so sure about that. She was stunned then, even by the implication, but as the sands settled in her mind she began to re-evaluate her doubts.

Creating values, Liz mused, and snorted in her mind. *I bet that was just George showing off to impress the others. I wonder if he even believes that or if he just thought it sounded cool.*

She knew she would miss her days in Flagstaff, though—of that she had no doubt. She had had fun, been allowed to enjoy herself, even encouraged to. Liz suspected that had she, or any of them there, not been willing to enjoy life, they might well have been forced to, even— worn down by teasing and cajoling until they submitted to some degree of leisure. Workaholism was not an accepted value there, and yet, they were never wanting.

But Liz was at the moment. She buzzed for a flight attendant to bring some packaged peanuts or pretzels, and noted the other passengers on the flight for the first time. The cabin was scarcely occupied; the seats were maybe 25% filled. She wondered at the flight even running at so low occupancy. The other passengers were all suited, however, in pinstripes with "Barney & Tarek" logos and "Citrix" mottoes wrapped around their tense figures—they could probably pay enough to keep the flight going. Liz recalled an announcement at the start of the journey about continuing on from Tokyo or Singapore; this flight was obviously a connector. Planes equipped to travel so far without rest stops were more expensive than these, their only reason for still existing, and the only reason for there being any flights from New York to Phoenix, Liz suspected.

Liz and George had brought a change of clothes with them, to camouflage them when they got out of the plane. Liz was in no hurry to put hers on, and George didn't seem to be either. He continued to stare out the window while Liz perused the typing or sleeping strangers. *These are my people, they are where I come from,* she thought, trying to feel some emotion in regards to this statement, some solidarity. She felt nothing, though—not relief, or anger at seeing them, knowing exactly what was in their minds, what was making them tick. She felt a quizzical distance from her compatriots as she watched them, working to gather more products, or asleep but dreaming about them.

As she meditated on this observation, George broke out of his reverie and pulled Liz in to a different train of thought.

"We'll be landing soon," he said, facing Liz and stroking her knuckles sideways with one fingertip absentmindedly. It tickled—Liz liked the way it felt. "Weird, huh?"

Liz reflected that she'd never heard him say 'Weird, huh?' in Flagstaff, and couldn't imagine him speaking so casually, so *lazily* over there. "Mmm," she replied. "Yeah." She pulled her hand away. Now, she wanted to think.

"How long are you going to stay there, in New York?" she asked George. He looked at her for a long moment, expressionless, then said, "I don't know yet." He continued to gaze at Liz with a blankness. "Why do you ask?" he said levelly. Liz thought of replying that she was "just making conversation," but she knew that George wouldn't buy it.

She shrugged. "I wondered, suddenly," she said. "I don't know why."

"Hmm," he said and turned back to the window. Liz had forgotten about the other passengers for the moment and wondered for the first time about George.

✶✶✶✶✶

George came home with her up to the door of her parents' house, dressed strangely in his "Vision Quest" casual shirt and slacks. They had been mostly quiet on the way home, holding hands now and then. At the door, he held one of her hands in both of his and said softly, "Thank you for coming with me, Liz. I hope that…" and he trailed off, unsure of what he hoped, apparently. He kissed her lightly on her closed lips, quickly but without hesitation, and smiled. With that, he left her to her house of lies.

Liz entered the house to near silence, with muffled sounds of voices and typing from within the depths of the place. It was 10 p.m., and her parents were in their home offices, she knew. If they heard her enter, they gave no sign; they stayed mired in their work, where they were needed, or, rather, where they thought they needed to be. They assumed she'd understand, Liz felt sure. She didn't go in to see them. *What would be the point?* she thought. *Even if I knew what to say to them now?* Instead, she'd walked slowly through the rooms packed with stuff, most of it logoed, to the relative sanctuary of her bedroom. There, she did some cleaning—clearing, really—until it was a place she wanted to sleep. Her "Soaper," her "Hairmakers," her portable waistband DVD player with supersonic speakers, and many other products she had believed she couldn't do without were retired to a large wastebasket that she put at the curbside for the morning pick-up by the mobile sanitation machines. When the room looked more like the one she'd slept in for the last couple of weeks, she washed her face and brushed her teeth with her own hands, and changed for bed. She wore the plain pale pink pajamas she brought back with her from free America, a gift from Mrs. Robinson. She was sure she wouldn't be seen in them; her parents hadn't come over to her part of the house for many years. As she lay down on her bed, she thought of a boy she had seen on the plane being ignored by his mother, his curiousity about sights from the window no doubt deemed unnecessary to the woman's personal goals.

I could have talked to that boy, she reflected. *I could have sat down and answered his questions, told him he wasn't wrong for wanting to know more than what's going to help you get ahead in the company, and it wasn't wrong for him to expect his mother to care about him beyond how he could advance her career. He was probably only with her for some job-related thing; maybe they were at a VinDyne joint educational conference for kids and parents. His mother probably wouldn't even have noticed if I'd gone and talked to him, and if she did I'm sure she wouldn't have cared. So why didn't I do it?* She remembered that George had distracted her, and she'd begun to toss around the various impressions she'd compiled about him, instead; as if by doing so, she could solve the puzzle he had become to her—even to himself, she ventured. But that little boy had gone on wondering and hurting, thinking that he was wrong, that he was alone, and that he should stop what he was doing and thinking and feeling, but couldn't. He didn't know what she knew. And she knew he would want to, if he could.

What would she do about it? Could she do anything about it, she wondered. And, more immediately, what would she do about her? She was back here, in the land of things—but did she have to be? *Could I have stayed there?* Liz wondered for the first time. *Even with George coming back here, could I have stayed there? They might have let me. I was able to help out, probably as much as anybody else, once they showed me what to do.* But the work was hard, she admitted to herself; sometimes it was even grueling. *For a few days, it wasn't too bad, but to do it all the time…. And what about all the programming I've learned how to do, all the computer languages I've mastered? I've worked so hard at that stuff, and I gotta admit, I'm damn good at it. And…I like it,* she realized. *I love it.* Liz dwelt on this last fact for several seconds, a factor she had not taken into consideration previously, had had no need to. *For all the treachery and disgusting lies, I really do love going to school, in a way; I love the work. Would I really want to give that up completely? It was only two weeks that I was there, in Flagstaff, and already I'm thinking of giving up everything that I have, that I am? …You'd better go to sleep, Liz.* She picked up her headphones, put them on and said, "Bach" aloud to her audio-activated CD player, which obeyed dutifully. Strands of 18th-century Austria drifted into her ears as clearly as the day they were born. She was glad she hadn't thrown the CD-player out.

*****

Mrs. Jones must have remembered that Liz had come back, because she heard her mother's voice call out through the large rooms that morning, "Gatelink, are you ready yet?" Liz was sitting on her bed, fully dressed in her ridiculous ad-plastered clothes. She'd been ready for a full hour already, so trained by the roosters' crows in those two weeks that she had outgrown her alarm clock. She sat and thought, about everything and nothing; she let thoughts and feelings enter and exit her consciousness, not pinning any of them down, trying to let her mind be clear. The kids did that back in Flagstaff. They called it "pre-meditation." It wasn't up to the level of meditation like the grown-ups did and the Elders were really expert at, but it was an exercise. They had told her about it, but never asked her to try it—they'd never imposed anything on her. She hadn't tried it then, still thinking it sounded a bit wacky, but now, with this stretch of time before her and nothing else to steal her attention, she'd decided to do it. It was pleasant, strange. When her mother announced its end, Liz rose feeling calm, relaxed and curious about what the day would hold.

Mrs. Jones was brisk and efficient as ever that morning. She had laid out a cursory breakfast for Liz, maybe more for efficiency than charity. Liz chomped at the sausage links gratefully as she watched the older woman toss her dishes in to the sink for cleaning by their Avantgard Dishcleaning Device and check her makeup in the hall mirror, as if the Facer didn't do it perfectly every time. Liz watched her rapid actions and tried to imagine her another way, moving at a comprehensible speed, smiling at her daughter, talking with her as if she mattered. When Mrs. Jones did finally look at Liz, it was to see her smiling strangely at her, serenely. Liz could read the surprise on her mother's face, and was not surprised herself at her mother's decision to ignore even her own unauthorized emotions.

"Gatelink, let's go, huh," she said, her face businesslike again. She wasn't going to give in to curiosity. Yes, it was strange that Gatelink was *smiling* at her, for no reason, but to spend time thinking about something like that wouldn't be very valuable.

So Mrs. Jones drove herself and Liz to work, thinking only of deals she had in the making and the new car she was going to buy if the current deals worked out. For her, it was just another drive; for Liz, it was another life.

Liz shook her head slightly as they made their way past billboards and digital boards that covered the field of vision. She sensed her spine straighten, her muscles tighten at this spectacle of her everyday life that she'd shed so readily from her mind, in Flagstaff. Her face turned fully toward the window, Liz closed her eyes. Her ride to school from now on would be dark, and commercial-free.

*****

A little groggy from keeping her eyes closed, Liz left the car for Headquarters that day curious. Though logically she knew that she knew exactly what to expect, she also felt that she didn't. She was changed. She had touched the earth, thrown seeds, worked with her hands and her body; she had talked and laughed with people who cared about ideals, values, society, and who never talked about *things*. She'd been where none of her peers had ever gone, where no "progeny" had dared to go before. And now she was back where no progeny had ever dared not to go.

The building was concrete, steel, chrome, glass—imposing as she remembered. Ads for Gatelink Computing and Software, Inc. generally and for their subdivisions and applications and other products were tastefully inserted in the precise center of each hexagonal brick of the various materials, occupying about 60% of the space. The pavement was dark but colored, with the same mottoes and images. Liz noticed for the first time that some of the color combinations in the images were quite nice, if you ignored everything else in what you saw. She smiled at this realization, walking into Headquarters feeling serene, feeling "Zen" as she'd heard some kids say in Flagstaff. She was feeling okay about things. She'd had an *interesting* experience in Arizona, and maybe now that her curiosity was satisfied she could return to her life here in New Jersey and New York and everything would be fine. Things weren't so bad.

Until…. She had forgotten about Tablesoft and Easycalc, her friends, her nemeses. The aliens who had taken their places. When she entered the classroom, Liz saw that her station was already occupied. Easycalc was thumbing through a stack of papers on the desk. Tablesoft was doing likewise at the adjacent station, her own. They both looked up as Liz approached.

"Oh, hey, Gatelink. What's going on?" Easycalc said casually. "We didn't hear from you during break at all." That "we" took on a whole new meaning since their declaration before break, Liz thought.

"Hey guys," she replied uncertainly, standing between the two stations. "What's up with you?"

"How come you didn't call us at all over break?" Tablesoft asked, and Liz thought she might have seen a fleeting look of hurt on her friend's face. "Did you go somewhere?"

"Oh...no," Liz said. "I was just feeling really beat." She had no idea why she was lying, but it seemed like the right thing to do. "Sorry," she added for emphasis.

"Yeah," said Easycalc, skeptically. "You were probably hard at work nailing the extra credit program they gave us, *weee* know," he said in an exaggerated, knowing voice. "Not like you *need* it. As *everyone* knows." He and Tablesoft laughed, and Liz noted something she hadn't seen in them before: envy. She tried to laugh too, but heard only a strangled chortle emerge from her throat.

"Um, are we trading seats?" she directed to Easycalc, hoping her tone was lighter than she now felt.

"Oh, yeah," Tablesoft answered smoothly. "We were hoping you, um...wouldn't mind. We already cleared it with Ms. McUthrie. We told her we were officially dating now and wanted to be closer together so we could work together—she said sure right away."

"And...my stuff?" Liz asked, sensing that her consent was irrelevant.

" Here," Easycalc replied, smiling and cupping a short stack of books and notebooks with two boxes full of computer disks atop them. He stood and picked up the pile to deposit in Liz's anticipated arms. Liz followed expectation, and carried the small but heavy burden to her new station three rows away.

It's now official, she thought, disconcerted. *I've been shunned.*

Liz watched the "couple" surreptitiously through the morning from her alienated position in row five. Word seemed to be out about her being at the top of the class, or maybe about the "offer" the firm made through her mother, because Liz felt a chill toward her from all directions. Except from Ms. McUthrie, who called on Liz more than ever to answer questions, and smiled only at her that day. Liz considered answering some of the questions incorrectly, but never seemed to have enough time to dodge the correct answer, which would come barreling at her from within the depths of her intellect. To say "I don't know" would be too much of a lie; Liz worried that she wouldn't be able to pull that off. If people knew that she was faking a lower performance, they might resent her even more, she suspected.

So the morning went on with Liz answering questions, correctly and regretfully, and trying to decide if she should join Tablesoft and Easycalc for lunch as she had every day of her life in this building. They never turned to look at her once as they huddled together occasionally to discuss problems, pointing at each other's screens and typing in notes. The other unresponsive place Liz looked that morning was at George's empty station. *Where is he?* she wondered. *I just assumed I'd see him this morning; I didn't even ask him last night. I hope he's okay.* After about a minute, she thought, *I wonder if he went back.* She felt a jumble of emotions at this possibility, and decided not to entertain it without more information.

With still no sign of George by lunch, Liz concluded that it would be necessary to try to eat with her old friends. As they stood to go, she walked quickly over to them. They exchanged a glance that Liz couldn't read. The three of them walked to the cafeteria in near silence, with only intermittent, non-committal remarks on how a certain lesson was presented that day. Liz noted that neither Easycalc nor Tablesoft made any comments on the difficulty of any of the lessons or assignments, which they usually did on the walk to lunch. But they weren't unfriendly. Through lunch also, they chatted in single-sentence paragraphs about the same topics they always had—hair, shoes, appliances. But they were cautious in what they said now; they thought before they talked, maybe even censored themselves. They spoke as if they had a spy in their midst.

*****

When by the end of the workday, George still hadn't materialized, Liz began to feel anxious. He was her lifeboat here. She doodled furiously and excused herself for the bathroom several times during "Corporate History." As the class animatedly discussed the different systems of accounting the firm had used since its inception and the basis for each "evolution," Liz scribbled pictures of the trees, squirrels and other sights she had lost in the last few days. She felt able to get through the day, but at the end of it rushed out without the formality of a goodbye to Tablesoft and Easycalc. She realized as she caught her train that she had forgotten to punch out. *Huh,* she thought. *Isn't that something? Well there's no way I'm going back now to do it. I'll just have to see what happens.* She was sure Tablesoft and Easycalc would be scandalized if they found out. She snorted softly to herself on the train, and watched the concrete whiz by.

Inside the empty house, Liz felt safe and comfortable in calling George. She rummaged through her bag to find the piece of paper on which he'd written his phone number for her weeks ago; it was on her Palm Assistant, but that was long gone now. At last, she found it, and spoke the digits to her cell phone. George answered on the third ring.

"Hello?" His voice was hoarse.

"George?" Liz asked, starting to doubt the veracity of the number.

"Liz?" His tone perked up noticeably. "How are you?"

"Well, I'm okay, but how are *you*?" she asked. "You weren't at school today." Liz knew she was stating the obvious, but didn't know how else to ask the question.

"Yeah," he said. "I'm sorry I wasn't there to help you, um, readjust. How'd the day go? Was everything okay?"

Liz sighed. "Not exactly," she replied. "But first, tell me why you weren't there." She decided she had to cross over into accusatory to get her point across.

"I'm just...not feeling well today. I couldn't sleep last night—at all. Every time I started to fall asleep, I had a nightmare that woke me up. And I've been throwing up all day." He paused. "I'm gonna take some medicine for it tonight, though, so I should be fine. I'll definitely be there tomorrow."

Liz considered this information for a moment. "What were the nightmares about?" she asked quietly.

"I—I don't remember," George stammered. "But I'll be fine after tonight. I'm sure it was just...readjustment.... But how was work today? Everything okay? You've never called me at home before."

"I hope it's okay," Liz said quickly, taken aback that he would even comment about that.

"No, of course," George replied, also quickly. "So, what happened?"

"Well, first I come in to find that Easycalc had taken my station, already approved by Ms. McUthrie, to be nearer his 'girlfriend,' his 'partner.'"

"Partner?"

"I'll explain later. But yes, Tablesoft and Easycalc told me a few days before break that they had decided to 'date'—to 'make a financial partnership.'" Liz snorted again for the second time that day, surprising herself with the gesture.

"Huh," George said thoughtfully.

"Yeah. The way they told me about it was all *mired* in *propaganda*, too. But anyway: they made comments to me about how I 'didn't need to do the extra credit assignment over break.' They were icy to me, and the rest of the class was even worse. And Ms. McUthrie couldn't seem to call on me or smile at me *enough*! I thought it might feel strange to come back, but not *this* strange," Liz concluded glumly.

"Oh God!" George emitted suddenly.

"What?" Liz said. "Did something happen?"

"Yes," said George. "Something did happen—at Headquarters, while we were away." He paused. Liz couldn't see him, but from his tone of voice could imagine he was shaking his head. As she opened her mouth to question him again, she heard him say, "Liz, everyone knows you're at the top of the class."

"Huh?" she said. "I am?"

"Yes. You must have known you were near the top before midterms. Well, midterms were graded over break and must have put you in the lead. And the Board decided to let your peers know, and in a way they won't soon forget. They probably sent memos to their parents, in terms very denigrating to their own kids."

"But...why?"

"Something I learned in my Labor Theory classes: companies that thrive on internal competitiveness of their employees, they like to foster that competitiveness by holding up the #1 in a vaunted, and hated, position. They tell everybody else that they're no good, basically, compared to the primo one, and it makes everyone more determined to become #1 themselves. Supposedly, it makes people work harder. That result is backed up by statistics—they've done controlled trials. It's pretty interesting, actually."

"*Very* interesting," Liz said brittly.

"Um, it wasn't used in schools before, though—this strategy. This is new, what they're doing," he said.

"And they're doing it to *me*," Liz moaned.

"And to the rest of your class," George stated. "They probably don't realize it, but they're really not enjoying this either."

"So what do I do, George?"

He paused for a moment to ponder. "There really isn't anything you can do," he said finally. "This thing is bigger than us. It's like a force of Nature."

What? Liz thought, but she was too thrown off by George's last statement to speak.

"But I'll be there from now on, Liz, to help you through this. I promise."

"Thanks, George," she responded. "Now, you get some sleep, and I'm gonna hold you to that promise tomorrow, huh?"

*****

That evening, Liz wouldn't let herself do her homework. Even though she'd missed the thrill of solving the mathematical and programming puzzles that the work always amounted to, looking at the Gatelink Computing and Software, Inc. disks that held her assignments made her want to throw them out the window. So she did something she'd never done before. She sat at her desk and pulled out an old-fashioned paper notebook.

Pen poised about paper, she wondered what she was about to do. She'd seen almost everybody writing in journals over there, from ages five to ninety-five. Patricia wrote plays. And somewhere, in the landscape of Liz's mind, she was still dreaming about the play she tried to make happen, four months and a lifetime ago.

"Four people sitting in a room, at a posh conference table," she wrote. "Fairchild: 'This is brilliant, Toshiwa, sheer genius. They won't know what hit 'em. We can make them into anything we want, if we start out that young—we'll get them to buy whatever we tell them to, *do* whatever we *tell* them to, *want* whatever we *tell* them to! It's brilliant!' The four men clap and cheer."

Liz put down the pen and looked up from her pad. *Wow,* she thought. *I'm writing something.... I'm writing a play!* She smiled. She felt a thrill that was almost physical, an exhilaration. What she was doing felt dangerous. And it was all hers.

*****

Liz spent three hours at her desk that night, barely moving except to write and to turn the pages. Whenever the words stopped, she would stop, close her eyes, lean back in her chair, and breathe. Deep, even breaths, in and out, for relaxation, like she'd learned to do as part of pre-meditation. And eventually the words would start to flow again, people would come to her and demand their place in her story. She would have to listen closely for their words sometimes; other times, she would hear them as clearly as her own. Over the course of the hours, a story began to unfold. It was about The Separation, what bits and pieces she had been able to glean from over there, and over here. She watched as families came apart; parents lost their grip over their children, over themselves. The quest for "Things, things, *things!*"—as one of her characters, a young man and progressively disinterested father of two, said several times—was outright. It was not camouflaged in terms like "progress," "wealth," or "well-being." Her characters were shockingly honest; their decisions and motivations were laid bare. They were unafraid to say who they were, who they really were. Liz drank in their honesty—got drunk on it. Even as she hated them for ignoring what they really *knew* their children needed, for letting themselves be convinced that being parents were not their privilege or even responsibility, she loved them. There were no propaganda in their world that wasn't exposed for what it truly was; their world was pure. *Children need things in black-and-white,* Liz thought. *Children can't see through manipulation, not when it's all around them, when there's nothing else for them.... And they know it—Fairchild and his bunch, and all the people who let him win, and still do....And now,* it occurred to her, *so do I.*

Liz was surprised at how easily she slept that night. Through a growing sense of excitement, she felt a strange calm, and a new mantra. *Everything's gonna be okay,* emerged in her consciousness with a suddenness that drifted oddly into consistence. *Everything's going to be fine. I'm gonna find my place.*

CHAPTER 17
DAUGHTER-ENFORCED
MOTHER-DAUGHTER CHAT

Over the next weeks, the play took form. Liz kept her head down at Headquarters and steadfastly refused to do her homework more than half the time, though she wanted to. She learned how to think quick enough to start giving wrong answers in class. So far the authorities hadn't come down on her for her aberrant behavior; "they're probably too shocked to know what to do," George hypothesized when Liz told him about it. "I'm sure they never expected *this*!" And he laughed.

Liz continued to chat civilly but coolly with Tablesoft and Easycalc, following their lead. She noticed that her wrong answers in class didn't seem to allay the hostility toward her, but feed it. Nevertheless, she pursued it, believing it was the best course of action at this time, and the only thing she *could* do. She felt better doing *something* about the situation than doing nothing.

Liz felt a growing desire to talk with her parents, or at least, to try to get them to talk with her. When she felt like the play was on solid enough ground that she could risk a major upset to her psyche—which she expected—she cornered her mother in her home office one evening.

"Mom?" she called out softly over the large oak desk with intricate engravings and embossing.

"Yes, Gatelink?" Mrs. Jones replied after looking up for only an instant. She didn't stop watching the computer screen.

"Why did you name me 'Gatelink'?" Liz asked innocently.

"What?" her mother replied, taken aback. Her eyes were on Liz now, her fingers above the computer keyboard, arrested in the air.

"Why did you name me 'Gatelink'?" Liz repeated the question in the same guileless tone. She had prepared herself for this meeting.

"Why would you ask that?" Mrs. Jones replied, not hiding a puzzled expression, which faded as she returned her gaze to the screen. "Look, Gatelink, I have a lot of work to do here, so…"

She assumes she doesn't even have to finish her sentence, Liz thought. *I should just feel ashamed for bothering her and walk away. Well, sorry, Moms….* Liz did the unthinkable. She pulled a chair from against a wall to a place before her mother, with no desk, no kitchen table, nothing between them—physically. Mrs. Jones looked away from her screen to her daughter, her brow raised high, her jaw slack. "What are you doing?" she said.

"I'm trying to talk with you, Mom. Didn't your mom ever talk with you?" Liz was trying to stay serene. *So far, so good,* she thought.

"Not if she was in the middle of a multi-billion dollar deal, she *didn't,* no," Mrs. Jones said harshly. But Liz was not to be deterred.

"*Was* she ever 'in the middle of a multi-billion dollar deal'?" Liz questioned.

"Yes," Mrs. Jones replied. "Often." She was still facing Liz, who thought she saw a flicker of pain shoot across her mother's face. Mrs. Jones seemed to relax suddenly—she slumped a little in her chair. "Gatelink is a good name, you know. I would be proud to have it."

"But…did you consider other names when I was born?" Liz asked, deciding to try a different tactic.

Mrs. Jones looked at her for almost a minute, as if considering her answer. "No, Gatelink, we didn't. We wanted to give you the best, so that's what we did." She began to shift in her seat, back toward her monitor, away from her daughter. Liz knew she had to act quickly. Her approach so far hadn't been as fruitful as she'd been hoping, so she would have to re-strategize.

"I heard somewhere that people were all paid to name their kids after companies and their products," she said quickly.

Mrs. Jones stopped in mid-swirl, and refocused on Liz, with an intrigued smile on her face. "Where did you hear that?" she asked.

"Is it true?" Liz countered.

"Yes," Mrs. Jones replied frankly. "It is."

"So…really, you named me 'Gatelink' because you were paid to," Liz stated.

"Really…yes," Mrs. Jones answered dispassionately, her arms crossed in front of her chest. She was looking at her daughter in a new way now.

"How much?" Liz asked, sounding nothing more than curious.

Mrs. Jones looked to the ceiling for a moment, recollecting. "3.2 million dollars," she said finally.

"Mm-hmm," Liz responded, contemplating her next move. "And did you have any…reservations about not naming me yourselves?"

Mrs. Jones looked confused for a moment, then suspicious. "Do you think we should have?" she demanded. "Do you realize how much 3.2 million *was* back then? And what an *honor* it was for us—and *you*—to be selected to be the *first* at Gatelink? Everybody at the firm wanted their kid to be chosen to be 'Gatelink,' you know. Everybody."

Surprised her mom was still talking with her and wanting to prolong this rare experience, Liz decided to try to tread a little more lightly. "Yes, but—had you ever thought about giving me a name that you chose, just because you liked the sound of it, or it reminded you of someone you admire, or any of those reasons? I mean, I know that people weren't always given only business names. You weren't."

At this Mrs. Jones stiffened visibly. "No, and my parents couldn't afford to give me even *half* of what we've been able to provide you. Yes, before I was pregnant, before Headquarters made the offer, I probably did dream silly dreams of what we would call our daughter or son…." her voice had gotten soft, maybe wistful. It returned to its previous crispness, "But things aren't like that anymore. Things are better. The company has been very good to us."

Liz nodded to appease her mother, who seemed to be getting upset by the conversation, to Liz's astonishment. Also to her surprise, Liz began to feel a little bad for her mom, for the frown and the troubled expression that had come across her face. In spite of herself, she found herself feeling sorry for this woman who gave up her daughter for things. *Somewhere inside her,* Liz thought, *she must wish she hadn't, or she wouldn't be getting…defensive…right now.* So Liz rose to take leave of her mother, with one unthinkable parting gesture that she'd learned from her friends in Flagstaff. She leaned toward her mom and hugged her around her tensed shoulders, than delivered a short kiss to the side of her face before pulling back. Mrs. Jones' bottom lip fell about a half an inch as Liz smiled intentionally and said, "Goodnight, Mom."

*****

One late evening in her room alone and probably presumed to be doing schoolwork if her parents even wondered, Liz realized that the words she had just written were the last in the play. Everything that she had expected to come to pass in the world of her drama had, with a few surprises. She was happy with it; she'd been happy writing it. But it was done now, and she knew that it needed an audience—and a cast.

She went to the first person she thought of. She and George had gone out several times in the last few weeks, but each had been pre-occupied, neither fully listening to the other. Liz hadn't told George about the play yet, but with it finished now, she needed him to celebrate, and to help.

Liz leaned forward in her chair at the Bangalorean diner and whispered excitedly to George the details of her unlawful act. He smiled, much more present than she'd seen him since they got back to New York, and told her in hushed tones how terrific he thought that was. "Liz, that is wonderful news! I can't wait to read it. Have you written the folks back home about it yet? I'm sure they'll be tickled to find out!" Apparently unaware that he'd inappropriately referred to Flagstaff as "back home" for Liz as well, George held her hand where it lay resting on the noisy red, green and white tablecloth. "You really are something, Liz. You're the most amazing young woman I've ever met."

"Thank you," Liz said, liking the feeling of his hand on hers. Since the night of their return, they had both avoided touching each other.

"I want to put the play on," she said, suddenly assertive though her hand still lay with his cupped above it. "I don't know how yet, but I…I have to." She paused. "Will you help me?"

George laughed brusquely, and withdrew his hand. He used both hands to pull his chair in as he straightened up, a pretense to needing to reclaim the appendage. "You're kidding, right?"

Liz looked back, dismayed. "No. Why would you think that? I thought you always thought my idea of putting on a play was a good one."

"Gatelink, in Flagstaff it would be a good idea. I can understand that you went to the Board with the idea, once. But now that they've told you, in no uncertain terms, to drop it, and…for what this play is *about*…" He looked at his empty waiting plate and shook his head. "Gatelink, I'm not sure what the consequences could be." He looked up and added quietly, "and if I helped you, I could be putting myself under scrutiny. If my background were found out…. I'm not ready to leave here yet."

"So you've said," Liz responded coolly, consternation clear on her visage. "And it's Liz."

"Maybe you should think about this some more," George said, brushing the correction aside. "I think you need to find out what you'd be risking—you heard what the corporations did to us during The Separation. No food, no medicines; they took everything away. The same thing happens to people here—it's just not publicized."

"It does?" Liz hadn't thought about this.

"I've heard about it, like, third- or fourth-hand. People try to move out west, but not everyone's as exceptional as you, Liz. Plus, it's supposed to be harder for people when they get older, to adjust. Some of them find they can't do without all their products, and…well, I'm not sure what happens to them."

"Hmm," Liz answered him.

"Just think about it some more, Liz. And…be careful."

CHAPTER 18
THE "DOCTOR" IS *IN*

That night Liz had a mission. She'd heard her parents listening to a call-in talk show on the radio once, while they were driving to some corporate awards ceremony with her in tow. It was a psychological-type show; the host was a Human Resources Specialist, or Organizational Management Director, or something like that. She'd mentioned this to the kids in Flagstaff—they'd been fascinated by it. *Funny that I'd never thought anything of it,* Liz thought to herself that night. *People calling in about disputes with their colleagues or feeling anger toward their boss, and it's considered a show about human psychology. Yeah, from the free-state perspective, it is pretty weird. But it might help me tonight.*

She found the radio station's site on the Internet and looked up information on the show. It was heard twice a day; it would be on again in about half an hour. They had an interactive web-page for it where people could post questions, but that would be too easy to trace back to her. Liz knew how to scramble the phone digits really well, and felt pretty confident it wouldn't be traceable, especially if she didn't stay on too long. But on-line tracing technology was much more sophisticated, since people used the Net more than they used phones anymore—she was sure she could be discovered if she went that route. *I'm lucky they still do a phone show for this program. I guess because it's a 'psychological' show and all*, Liz thought. *They want the 'human touch.'* She tried to pre-meditate for the twenty-eight minutes she had until the segment started. Realizing that that wasn't going to work, she closed her eyes and listened to a CD she liked for the remaining twenty-five.

At last, it was 10:00. She said, "Radio AM 1-0-7-4." She kept her headphones on, just in case her parents happened to be walking near her bedroom for some reason. She listened through the introduction of the show and the ten minutes of ads, rolling her eyes and groaning in frustration the whole time. Finally, they were taking calls. She took a deep breath, and dialed, first the scrambler code, then the station's number.

"W.A.M.U., What's-Your-Problem. Do you have a question for the doctor?" a shrill male voice squealed from the other side cheerily.

"The...doctor?" Liz asked, hoping she hadn't misdialed. With all the commercials, the one-hour program came to about ten to fifteen minutes total, a small window of time.

"Well, okay, you got me, he's not *really* a doctor, but he's just as good! And he cares *just* as much!" The saccharine voice replied. "He wants to help *you* with *your* psychological problem today. Now, do you have a question?"

"Um, yes," Liz replied hesitantly. "I do."

"Aw, *nuts*!" the voice muttered angrily. "Gary *homo* over there just got one in, which means *he* gets the first-caller *bonus*! Shit. Well, anyway, hold on. We'll get you in next. I'll still get somethin' outta this." Liz heard a click and was regaled with more ads. She turned down the volume on her phone and held a headphone over one of her ears. A woman with a low, sad voice was explaining that her co-workers wouldn't listen to her anymore, and she was excluded from the projects and any recognition by the Board of her company because of it. She made some muffled noises toward the end of her soliloquy that might have been crying. The "doctor" told her something about asserting her needs, sabotaging her peers' work if that's what it took to get herself heard, that no one could fault her for it under the circumstances. Liz tried not to listen too hard; she had to formulate her own question.

"Okay, honey, you're on!" the screechy voice returned, a little quicker than Liz expected, and too briefly. Suddenly she wished she'd written notes.

"You're on with the doctor," the host said to her, his voice more deep and comforting on the phone than it sounded on the radio. "What's your problem?" In his smooth syllables, even this phrase didn't sound offensive. *I guess that's why they can call it that and people will still call in,* Liz thought wryly.

"Well, it's not really my problem. At least, I hope it isn't," she began. "My sister works at the same firm as I do. Her daughter, who's fifteen, is well, a rebel, I guess you'd say." Liz paused as she imagined a woman actually calling in with this problem would pause in distaste. "She's written this...play, or TV show, or something, I don't really know, but it's something the Board of my firm expressly forbade her from doing. She was dumb enough to ask them if she could. It's a very *anti-social* kind of play, saying it's bad to focus so much on all our products, that corporations are devious and controlling." Liz thought she was doing an excellent job of sounding disgusted. Perhaps she'd play a role in the drama after all. "And now she has told my sister that she means to put it *on,* to lure other children into her anti-social scheme, and put it on publicly, in open defiance of the Board. I hope that my sister will be able to talk some sense into her, or bribe her enough to keep her quiet, but my question to you is: could it affect my career and my progression in the company if the girl does what she says she will?"

There was silence from the other end for about 5 full seconds. *I wonder if they're starting a trace,* Liz thought.

"That is an unusual question," the "doctor" responded.

"I *know*, doctor," Liz replied, convincingly, she thought. "Can you help me? Tell me if I should be worried, if I should bother to get involved in this mess and try to shut the girl up."

"Ma'am, if your niece does what she's said she will, you'll have a lot to worry about. If she's saying anything against your firm, the company will have no choice but to protect itself. And if she's denigrating businesses as a whole, and if she really does do so publicly, well, you can expect her and *all* her relatives to be cut off from the corporate structure. Removed, if you will, as an undesirable element."

"What do you mean, 'cut off?'" Liz asked.

"I mean fired, blackballed from working in any other corporation, and quite possibly banned from purchasing any corporate products." His voice was hushed. "Caller, this a very serious problem, this kind of illegal, anti-social behavior. I've seen it before, and it never ends well."

"You have?" Liz said, surprised into forgetting to keep disgust in her voice.

"Yes," the host said very somberly and with finality. Liz could see that he wasn't about to offer any more information on this morbid topic. "Now, I hope I was of some assistance, and good luck to you, caller," he recovered cheerily. "And now we'll hear some important words from our benefactors, which you *don't* want to miss." Persuasive as the "doc" sounded, Liz did shut off the radio, choosing to remain forever ignorant of the "important words." Nothing could be more important right now than the ones she'd just heard.

So what if I got 'removed'? she thought. *I don't need to stay here. I'm sure I can move west—I'm sure they'd help me settle out there.* She laid on her bed, arms crossed sternly across her chest, and faced a hard fact. *But this isn't only me that we're talking about. This would be my parents and... whoever else I don't know about. They would be 'cut off,' 'removed.' They wouldn't know what the hell to do with themselves, even if I told them. I wish that weren't true, but I know it is. How much do I care about that? ...God, I really don't know.*

Gratefully feeling tired, Liz let her eyelids drop slowly and allowed herself to get lost in tangled dreams she'd forget.

*****

The next round of exams arrived at school and Liz threw them. She scored exactly 76% overall, as had been her plan. But to her chagrin, there was no announcement the next day of the new number one.

It couldn't still be me! she thought woefully. Liz complained to George of the foiled plot to escape the *persona non-grata* status she'd fallen into, and how much she was not enjoying it. He was surprisingly less sympathetic then she'd expected.

"You know, Liz, they might be on to you. Forget *persona non-grata*, you're probably still a *persona suspecta* with the Board. I don't think you realize how important that is. If you don't watch your moves, you could jeopardize your whole future." He paused to sop up sauce with a piece of bread in the Russian restaurant where they were having early dinner. "You probably shouldn't have thrown your score by that much," he added matter-of-factly.

Liz stared at him.

"George, this is really bothering me," she said, her voice somewhere between hurt and annoyed.

He looked up from his food. "I'm sorry, Liz. I guess I… just have a lot on my mind these days. I'm sorry that things are tough at school. I wish I knew how to help you, but I don't."

They ate for several minutes in silence, almost through their small meals. George broke the quiet. "Have you been thinking more about…what we discussed the other day?"

"Yeah," Liz said. *He won't even name it,* she thought. *Huh.* "I called in to an H.R. talk show."

"What?" he said in mid-chew. A small piece of steamed spinach spilled out of his mouth, garnishing the remaining food on his plate.

"I scrambled my number, don't *worry,*" Liz said exaggeratedly.

George seemed to relax again. "And…what'd you find out?" He was chewing normally again.

"You were right," she said, nodding her head slowly, with a loud exhalation. "It would be the end of life as I, my parents and any aunts, uncles or cousins they never bothered to tell me about, know it." She said this sentence in one long breath.

"So, what are you gonna do, hon?" George asked, forking more quail lasagna into his mouth. He sounded semi-interested.

"I don't know," Liz responded. She thought of adding, 'What do you think I should do?' but decided against it. George had already shared that opinion with her, and from his attitude and even his body language, she felt she could assume that it hadn't changed.

"I'll let you know," she said, smiling to convince herself it was okay that she didn't feel she could talk to him anymore.

CHAPTER 19
THE GATHERING CAST

In the following days, Liz thought of little else than the notebook burning a hole in her desk. Scenes from the play enacted themselves in her mind spontaneously, as if on their own accord, whenever she started to relax or otherwise daydream. The appearances of the actors changed—one day, the father character would be short, thin and balding and the mother stern-looking; the next, he would be large and hairy and she would be docile. Even the child character—she, herself—would change: sometimes she was skinny and brown-haired, and sometimes she would be played by a plump redhead. She imagined Tablesoft and Easycalc having roles in the drama. This thought made her feel good for some reason, though she knew it could only happen via miracle.

Maintaining appearances with Tablesoft and Easycalc was becoming harder and harder. She didn't know if it was because they were distancing themselves, but their lunchtime conversations were growing more strained. But George insisted that it would be too dangerous for the two of them to lunch together. It defied protocol for a teacher, even a teacher's assistant, to eat with students, especially with just one student in particular. *Especially a 'persona suspecta'?* she'd wondered when he delivered the explanation. But she hadn't asked. She couldn't risk alienating the only friend she had left over here, and George's reactions weren't exactly predictable anymore.

George was dining with increasing frequency with Ms. Miller, the pretty teaching assistant Liz had seen him chatting with several times. *I guess it's okay for him to dine with just one teaching assistant in particular, though,* she thought bitterly sometimes. To be fair, she admitted to herself that they never actually sat alone together; but even at a table crowded with the other teaching assistants for all the other classes, it still looked like as far as they could see there was no one else around.

Letters to and from her friends in Flagstaff were a lifeboat for Liz. She and Patricia, who'd struck Liz dumb with her candor in confessing her crush on George, had become surprisingly close in the weeks since Liz's return to corporate America. Though only two letters had been passed in each direction, the maximum allowable by the sparse postal service to the non-corporate states, Liz was surprised that she and Patricia had much in common, other than their perhaps past interest in George.

But Liz felt limited in these letters. They were George's people much more than hers—that was only fair, whether or not it was right. And while she felt that she didn't know quite where he was these days, she presumed they must feel the same way about her. Growingly, she had the impression that George was up in the air somewhere, adrift, and she had no idea where he was going to land.

Liz was engaged in such thoughts one day on the train ride back to her parents' house when something caught her eye. A young man who looked to be about her age pulled a paperback copy of *Catcher in the Rye* out of his computer case, glanced around surreptitiously, and proceeded to begin reading. Liz had noticed this event several times before on her train—not many times, but a few. She had never given it too much thought before. But now she mused, *If he likes* Catcher in the Rye, *if he finds reading old books to be worth doing at all and prefers it to watching the wrist DVD player he must have from the expensive looks of his clothes, I wonder if he'd like my play....* She stared at the boy's downturned forehead, trying hard not to waver despite her social training to do so. After some minutes, he looked up, and turned directly toward her.

Don't turn away, Liz told herself, not sure what she'd do next. The boy looked back at her, at first suspiciously, then merely curiously. She could see now that he was younger than her, maybe 14. Liz rose, crossed the aisle, and sat down next to him. "Hi," she began simply.

"Hi," he answered cautiously, a question in his voice.

"That's an interesting book," she said, raising her eyebrows and nodding once in the direction of the paperback.

"Have you read it?" he asked, surprised.

"About a year ago," Liz replied. "It kinda stays with you, though. Good books always do."

"Yeah," he said, smiling and nodding a little. "My name's New York Gazette."

"My name's Gatelink Computing and Software, Inc.," she answered shaking his hand. "Guess I don't have to ask who your parent company is." She laughed.

He looked scandalized for a second, then seemed to relax. "Yeah, I guess not," he responded with a chuckle. "Me neither, huh?"

Liz had decided not to share with him her *real* name yet, until she could trust him. She had to scope him out first. "Do you read a lot?" she asked him.

"Um…yeah," he answered hesitantly. "I guess you do, too, right?"

She smiled and nodded. "My friends don't though," she said. "I don't know anybody else at my school who does, either."

"Me too," New York Gazette said in a tone of incipient understanding. "I don't know why. I mean, TV's okay, but doesn't it get *boring* after a while?"

"I *know!*" Liz replied conspiratorially.

"Are you reading anything right now?" he asked.

"I've been reading this late 20th-century British book called *Harry Potter* which is fantastic!" Liz told him.

"Really?" New York Gazette said. "I've heard about that book. Or…I must have *read* about somewhere. Where would I *hear* about it?" he scoffed.

"Well, my stop is coming up next, but I'd like to give you my e-mail address," Liz said as she began to rummage around in her bag for a piece of paper and pen. New York Gazette quickly pulled out his Palm Assistant and handed it to her. She smiled as she accepted it and began to punch in the appropriate keys. "You'll have to let me know how you feel about *Catcher* when you finish it," she added. New York Gazette asked to give her his e-address, and she had to explain that she didn't have her Palm Assistant with her to enter it into there. "It's a long story," she said by way of explanation, starting to wonder if she'd been too hasty in throwing out all of her toys in that ecstasy of contrition. She landed on a small slip of paper finally and passed it, with a pen, to New York Gazette. He had just enough time to write and return it before Liz's exit appeared.

*****

The next day, Liz could only think of going home and checking her e-mail. She didn't want to open it at school, for fear of someone looking over her shoulder or, worse, the Board catching it on a random review of student e-mail accounts. She didn't know if it was forbidden to make friends with students at other corporations, but she'd certainly never heard of it happening or the firm ever encouraging it. *It would probably be seen as an 'anti-competitive act,'* she thought wryly.

Liz held her breath as she opened her e-mail account that evening. There was a message from New York Gazette. It read simply, "Gatelink, it was nice to meet you. I met another like-minded individual this morning, inspired by your example. Maybe we can all three have lunch, this Saturday?—NYG"

He abbreviated his name, Liz thought. She knew it was expressly forbidden at Gatelink C&S to abbreviate one's name, and suspected that it must be true at all corporations. "This is a good sign," she murmured. She typed back, "NYG, How about 1:00 at The Russian Palace, on NC Bank Boulevard at C & R Supermarket Lane?—GC." As she clicked "Send" she felt the excitement of new possibilities.

*****

Liz barely noticed the next few days. She awoke, showered and dressed, pre-meditated, went to work, doodled as she tried not to pay too much attention, came home, read books, imagined, and slept. She smiled more at Easycalc and Tablesoft, and they seemed to respond, maybe in spite of themselves. She began to smile and say "hi" to her other classmates, which wasn't standard operating procedure. She'd begun to feel more free and more clear about everything, though she couldn't imagine why, and she found that she wanted to be friendly. Her peers responded unevenly, which didn't bother her. She had a feeling she wasn't being nice only for them. Ms. McUthrie had given Liz a few disapproving looks at her unsolicited salutations to her colleagues, but she hadn't said anything yet. *No doubt she doesn't have clearance from the Board,* Liz thought. *I guess I'll have to wait until after their next meeting to see if she will say anything.*

Patricia, in her last letter, had expressed enthusiasm about the play, begged for a draft of it, and asked Liz to let her know if she had any success in trying to put it on. "I'm sure it must be difficult and dangerous to do so in Corporate America," she written. "So I plead with you, my friend, to not take yourself to task if you are not able. When you next visit us, I'm sure we will have a wonderful time bringing your script to life." Liz had smiled at these nice words, but knew that Flagstaff was not the place for her play. It would not resonate there. They could say the lines, but it could never be a story from their hearts. They would have less trouble putting on an ancient Greek tragedy authentically; those were, at least, stories about people as they've always been, not as what they had now become in Corporate America.

On Saturday morning, Liz hummed to herself as she brushed her hair by hand, without the aid of the "Brusher" she'd used for as long as she could remember until the last few months. It felt good to feel the bristles against her scalp then caressing the length of her strands, to sense the connection of her hands, of her own will and intention, with the sensation. It was a simple pleasure, one she'd almost never known.

She was going to meet her new friends today; maybe, her new allies. Liz grimaced, again, at having to wear the ad-strewn clothes of her world, more so today because it clashed so much with her intentions. *But, this is a covert act of rebellion,* she reminded herself. *Not overt.* She certainly didn't feel ready for that, yet.

Mrs. and Mr. Jones were surprisingly still at home as Liz prepared to leave at 11:30 a.m. She sauntered up to her mom as naturally as she could and planted a kiss on her right cheek as she'd seen George and

Tommy do each morning in Flagstaff. Before Mrs. Jones could reply, she did the same to her father on the other side of the living room, buried in his section of the *Wall Street Post*, and left.

The weather that day was beautiful. The sky was a clear blue like the turquoise stones Liz had seen out West. *Wherever I go, it's with me,* she thought. She smiled as she gazed upward while walking on her way from the train to the café. Without looking around, she could tell she was the only one on the street doing so.

NYG and his friend weren't there yet when she arrived at The Russian Palace and so she took a table in the most secluded corner available. She picked up a menu and scanned it with her eyes but not her mind. She let the letters drift into and out of her brain without taking root or meaning. She already knew what she wanted anyway. The menu was just to keep her from having to look at all the ad-smeared people around her who looked like they thought they were happy, for the moment, until they were informed of something else they needed to buy to be *really* happy, or once they achieved whatever purchase they were already planning. She knew exactly what each and every one of the conversations going on around her were, and she wished she didn't.

By the time her guests arrived, Liz had drifted off into a reverie about the squirrels she had seen in Flagstaff and, she felt, gotten to know in a way. Of course, she couldn't have been sure they'd been the same squirrels she'd seen time and again out there, but she liked to imagine that some of them were repeat appearances and that she knew something of their lives and affairs by watching how they interacted with whichever bushy-tailed companions she saw them with that day. Pleasant as these memories were, however, Liz was glad to postpone them at the still unfamiliar voice of New York Gazette and his friend.

"Gatelink, I'm sorry we're late," NYG began, seating himself. He gestured to the other boy, who was likewise taking a chair. "This is MapMaker. He didn't know how to get here, so I went to pick him up first. No point in one of us getting lost, right?"

Liz smiled. She wasn't the only one who already felt a sense of solidarity.

MapMaker grinned too, a bit sheepishly. "Don't be fooled by my name," he advised. "My parents may work for Maps-R-Us, and I may work there too, for the time being, but I'd be more comfortable reading Chekhov in the original than making my way around a map; and I don't know Russian!" Liz burst out laughing. New York Gazette did too. MapMaker's joke wasn't so funny but his flamboyant delivery made it irresistible. *I'm having fun already,* Liz thought. *Real fun.*

"It's quite all right," she said. "I haven't been waiting long." A little trick of white-lying to smooth the situation over, something Liz had learned to perfection in Flagstaff. She pointed to M.M., as she'd already nicknamed him, in smiling mock accusation. "I like that Russian joke, you know," she said. "I might want to use that some time," she added, knowing full well she had no one else in Corporate America she'd feel safe using it with these days.

"Well, normally I do charge a nominal fee for such service, but I guess I could make an exception, just this once," MapMaker bantered back. The conversation flowed and ebbed seamlessly around deciding, ordering and eating the stated purpose of the gathering. Above the food, however, books were discussed, authors compared, themes uncovered and tilted in different directions. Ideas emerged. Social observations were tentatively tossed about. Liz led.

"It's kinda something how different things are now, huh? From Hemingway's time, I mean. You'd never hear those conversations today, right?" she ventured.

"Nope," MapMaker picked up. "You sure wouldn't. It's all about who's got what, how great some *product* is. It's like we're all…"

"Automatons," New York Gazette concluded.

"Nice one!" MapMaker nodded appreciatively. "Orwell?" he asked, raising a piece of bread slathered with squash sauce up to his lips.

"I think so. I'm not sure," New York Gazette answered. "Might be T. S. Eliot."

"So you guys have noticed it too?" Liz asked cautiously.

"If by 'it' you mean the degradation of the human mind to a mere calculating machine, and the fact that the closest people get to appreciating or even noticing beauty in the world is to notice the colors in catalogs, then yeah, I've noticed it," MapMaker replied with a forthrightness that startled Liz.

"Me too," New York Gazette concurred. He reflected for a moment. "I've never heard it said before. It sounds even truer coming from the lips of another. Though I know, I know, 'sanity is not statistical.' I'm not sure I ever bought into that though, or that the whole novel wasn't disproving of it, but it does feel good to hear someone else say my thoughts, finally." MapMaker and New York Gazette seemed to be in their own little world.

"Well, I think so too," Liz said, a little louder than she'd intended, before they forgot her. "And I'm happy to hear that you two share this view. Happy, and…a little relieved." She had the full attention of her companions now. "Because now I can share something very important with you—important to me, at least, and, something that could be important to others too, I hope." Liz was starting to feel excited. She took a sip of water to calm her down, or to build the suspense—she wasn't sure which.

"Things aren't like this all over," she began. Her new friends, sensible enough to see that she would explain, watched her expectantly. Liz told them briefly about George without betraying his identity or how she knew him, and everything she'd learned from him, then about what she'd seen and learned in Flagstaff, in a "free state." They sat riveted until the end of the tale, 45 minutes later. Liz cautioned, "I know this must be a lot to take in all at once, and I only tell you it all now because I'm so eager to tell you what I want to do about it, what I want to do with this knowledge I have, and how I want to ask for your help."

"Whoa!" said New York Gazette.

"I second that!" said MapMaker. They hadn't dared speak while Liz was divulging. "Maybe you should just give us a minute to digest this all before you ask us for anything," MapMaker said. He sounded irritated. This angered Liz at first, until she remembered how she'd felt when she'd lost the floor out from under her.

"You're right," she said, and chewed silently for several minutes.

"I always thought the whole world was a little *off*," New York Gazette mumbled, "but I never imagined that I was right." MapMaker shook his head slowly a few times, looking down at the table.

Maybe this was too much, Liz thought. *I didn't hear this all at once. But now that I've started, I can't stop here. I might lose them.*

"I've written a play," she said slowly. "About The Separation." She paused and then, not being silenced, went on. "It's about the effects of the decisions the adults made on family and especially on children, represented through three different families whose lives interact before and after The Separation, in greatly different ways, between the families and within. I want to document the effects of the decision to go corporate had on children, how it changed everything, to the best of what I know. I think it could help other kids to see it, especially younger kids, who haven't been brainwashed into refusing all their options yet. We have options, and I want to let other kids know."

Liz waited. Her guests said nothing. *They're still in shock,* Liz thought.

"Look, you don't have to say anything now. I just wanted to tell you. I can't do this by myself, of course, and I don't want to. I'd be happy to meet again to talk, like we did today—I'd be more than happy to. This has been great. It's been a breath of fresh air after weeks in a stuffy closet. But I hope you want to help me do this, too, and that I— we—can find other kids to do it too, and a way to put it on. I really believe in it. I believe we can do something good." She paused, then added, "I'm open to revisions on the play, too. I started it, but it doesn't need to be mine. It just has to get done."

"Liz, this is a lot—" New York Gazette started to say in a low voice.

"I know," she interrupted. "It's out there now, that's all. And…it is dangerous. Getting caught would mean involved parties and all their relatives would be denied from the whole commercial-corporate system. Excommunicated, if you will." She grinned at her use of the obscure word. MapMaker returned the smile weakly. "It's not for everybody," she said. "It's not for the faint of heart."

*****

196

Days passed. Liz kept her eyes open on the trains but caught no more readers in the days that she waited to hear back from New York Gazette and MapMaker. Whatever the outcome, though, she had decided, she felt better having approached them with the idea than not. Perhaps they would choose not to participate in her liberation; but in a way, they already had.

Liz did not expect anything at school to surprise her for a while, until it did. Kindness came to her from the last place that she would have expected anymore. At lunch on the Thursday after the Saturday meeting with her potential partners in crime, Liz received the most unexpected words from Tablesoft and Easycalc.

"Gatelink," Tablesoft said somberly over a turkey croissant, "we're worried about you."

"What do you mean?" she returned, taking in their solicitous stares with more amusement than alarm.

"You know, we shouldn't have…been mad at you, when we found out you were valedictorian," Easycalc said. Liz thought it might be the first time she'd heard either of her friends describe an emotion of theirs since they were stealing crayons from each other in first grade. The thought made her suddenly sad.

"We know it must be a lot of pressure to be in that position," Easycalc continued.

Where is this possibly going? Liz wondered.

"We all have our ups and downs. And you seem to be hitting a 'down' lately, Gatelink," Tablesoft continued. "A big one. We've noticed. Everyone's noticed, I'm sure."

"We know you're not always the most, well, business acumen is not your forté, Gatelink," Easycalc said. "And people who are a little more…oriented in that direction, like me and Tablesoft, are easily aware that falls in academic performance are invariable followed by declines in salary."

'Huh?' Liz felt like saying. She understood Easycalc's words, of course, but was startled by the formality—the professionalism—of his language. "We just wanted to bring that fact to your attention, and to ask if you could use any help with your work."

"You've always been there for us when we were struggling, learning C++ or mastering GAMS," Tablesoft added, "and, though we're not used to the idea of your needing help, we want you to know that we want to help, if you need it."

There was a pause as Liz took in this turn of events. As much as they could, as much as they knew how, her old friends Tablesoft and Easycalc wanted to help her. They wanted to be there for her, though they couldn't comprehend what she truly needed.

"Thanks, you guys," she said. "Yeah, I guess I've gotten into kind of a...slump. I think I just haven't been feeling well lately, you know. Or maybe these new problems we're working on are just...too much for me, I don't know." Again, Liz commended herself on a fine performance. Maybe she would give herself the lead in the play. She tried hard not to smile and giggle at the thought, which would surely blow her cover. "And thanks for reminding me about the salary thing. You're right, I hadn't really thought about it. Maybe I'll start skipping TV and just start putting more time into studying. Maybe that's what I need to do."

"Well, just remember that we're here, if you need us," Tablesoft stated maternally.

"I will," Liz replied, and she thought she saw a look pass between them that said, "It worked." She pushed the thought from her head.

*****

That evening Liz got an e-mail sent the night before, soon after she logged out for the last time and went to bed. It was from New York Gazette. It read, "Have thought about our conversation. Would like to learn more. Meet again? Have found another person who might be interested, but think it would be better for you to explain, describe. I'm excited about the prospects. Regards, NYG, aka, Nathan (à la Nathaniel Hawthorne)."

Liz was immediately aware that this could be a trap—that the 'other person' could be a corporate official of some sort, or even the police. She had no doubt that if they chose to, the companies could enlist the cops and even the laws themselves in their favor. But she couldn't ignore the simple pregnant words at the bottom of the message, "aka, Nate." Her new friend had dared to name himself, and to put it in writing, to put it in cyberspace. It could have been done to throw her off guard, by corporate decree, but it wasn't necessary. It was hard to imagine any Board sanctioning the creation of a pseudonym, even as part of a sting. It was a risk worth taking, she concluded.

The acceptance from MapMaker came a few days later, after Liz had identified another reader on the trains and made her approach. The girl, engrossed in *The Muse Asylum*, a book from the turn of the 21st century, had seemed wary of Liz but consented to exchange e-mails. From her name, Sills: Expert Litigators, Liz deduced that she was a law firm 'progeny,' and had perhaps been bred for suspicion and interrogation. Sills: Expert Litigators had waited until their lunch the next week to pull out her investigative prowess on Liz and stun her with it. Accustomed to analyzing numbers and programs, not human motivations and the validity of facts, Liz had to admit that she admired this skill that Sills: Expert Litigators wielded so effortlessly. If Liz weren't so sure of the truth of her story and her plans, she might have faltered under the pressure of the debate. Sills brushed away the compliment Liz offered her about this; "I'm not even in the top 10% of my class," she said.

Surprising Liz, she added sarcastically, "Boo-hoo."

At the end of two months, there were six people including Liz in the group. *It's time*, Liz decided, *to assemble.*

"I would like for us all to meet together, this Sunday. Any suggestions as to where?" she e-mailed them. The members of this illicit group were in varying stages of information due to the lack of uniformity in Liz's disclosures to them, but they all knew the dangers of what she had proposed. She had made sure tell them all, sensing that uniformity in this one statement was paramount. Like Nate and MapMaker, who'd declined to rename himself just yet, the other three initiates had all hesitated as well, but propelled by curiosity or a sense of rebellion or a sincere desire to help themselves and possibly others, they'd all written to Liz and asked their share of the risks and rewards. Not one person she'd encountered with her story, and her play, had turned away yet. Except, of course, the one person whose support she had thought she could assume—George.

Liz and George had been seeing less and less of each other, and somehow it seemed natural to both of them. Liz knew that George had begun to dine with Ms. Miller outside of Headquarters now, too, and she was surprised at how she barely minded. He might have guessed that she was seeking him out less often now too because she was putting time into an endeavor he similarly didn't like—the play—but Liz doubted that he even wondered about it. They still smiled to each other and talked sometimes after school, but it was always about Flagstaff, about how people there were doing and what they were up to. It was like they didn't want to acknowledge each other in the present moment; they didn't want to face each other *here*, where they were in corporate America, so at odds now.

Jeremy, who'd changed his name dramatically from the original, "Pests Out Manufacturers and Distributors, Inc.," for which "Pests Out M & D" was the company-approved abbreviation—"they must have had mercy on my poor, rich parents," he'd explained sardonically— was the first to reply with a solution. "I have a Discreet Location," his message to all of them read. "Yes, Liz: Discreet, not Continuous. A little math humor, not bad for a natural-born-bug-killer, huh?" After several blank lines, he continued. "Okay, you've had time to recover from your gales of laughter. So: Yes, I know of a place where we can meet. Actually, I kind of own it, which is perfect for our purposes. It's an old warehouse in Connecticut, that hasn't been used for about twenty years. It was given as a prize one year for the best work on identifying shortcomings in the current anti-ant formula, for seventh grade chem. At the time, I was happy and proud as anyone else would have been, though seeing the reward—and the assignment—now, for what it was…. But that's topic for discussion…at said location! If it meets with everyone's approval. I'd be honored if you all would accept this contribution, and make this empty trophy full of life and meaning. Directions by train and car are attached. Yours truly, Jeremy."

Liz suspected that some of the other members, Sills: Expert

Litigators and Coffeelover's Café Latte, would be scandalized by his use of a non-corporate name; they weren't at that level yet. But they would all, she hoped, feel glad for Jeremy's—or, Pests Out Manufacturers and Distributors'—offer. She hoped they were all looking forward to their first group meeting at least half as much as she was.

The days until the meeting prolonged themselves like a computer virus, and were just as reluctant to die. Liz by now was sleeping with her eyes open in classes, blocking everything out in an attempt to use the time for a better purpose—to dream. Ms. McUthrie had stopped calling on her, and moved on to a more cooperative candidate, the new "number one." The stealthy dirty looks had likewise been redirected, but there was no corresponding contrition or even courtesy toward Liz for what she'd done to try to restore harmony in her school life. The hostility had just found a new home, *one that probably laid out welcome mats for it,* Liz thought grimly. Easycalc and Tablesoft were nicer to her now, and even looked at her with pity now sometimes. She was the prodigal son who'd come home and been chastised, and they were comfortable with her again. Though she felt the falseness and contingency of their friendship, still it was a relief to Liz, a burden lifted. She found herself able to laugh again with her old friends, even at their materialistic jokes and making fun of people. Now that she wasn't stifled, now that she'd found compatriots in this strange new country they were building together, Liz could appreciate that her old pals were giving her everything they had to give, everything they had left of themselves. It was enough.

Mr. and Mrs. Jones had been looking more at their daughter lately. The glances were furtive, sometimes strained and worried, sometimes derisive, sometimes scared. Liz imagined some of the thoughts that were running around in their heads in regards to her, the dictates of these glares. They thought she was going nuts; they thought she had become an "anti-social" rebel of some kind and would expose them to the righteous wrath of society's keepers; they thought she was on drugs. As the looks escalated, grew more overt, Liz continued to hug and kiss them at least once a day and say "I love you, Mom/Dad," as they typed or signed or read. She liked to think that their shoulders had gotten to be a bit less tense to her touch, that smiles played cautiously on the corner of their mouths when she kissed their cheeks and professed her affection.

The group decided on Saturday afternoon for the first meeting. That way, they'd still have Sunday to mull and recover before going back to face the lions on Monday. Saturday, when it came, was an ambiguous day; the sun hid itself coyly behind clouds for minutes or hours, then would saunter back into sight and seem to promise to remain. Liz marveled at the sky on days like these since she'd learned a way to look at them, in Flagstaff. "God wants us to see her as fickle today," she'd been told there by more than one person. "She's teaching us patience, and that it isn't all about what *we* want. And that the one constant in life is change."

Liz thought about this last statement that helped to redefine what she had previously thought of as merely "partially-clouded skies" as she walked the three blocks from the train station to Jeremy's warehouse. She didn't know if she'd noticed much changing for most of her life, especially the things around her. They were in constant flux. And her body changed, of course, as it grew, but people seemed to stay the same. Or, like Tablesoft, they seemed to get stripped away; as they got older, they lost layers of themselves like the folds of an onion until they were a stark, functional core. But that wasn't change, not like change happened in Flagstaff, where people grew wiser, became more calm, less "attached." In corporate America, the process was forcibly reversed.

The warehouse was larger than Liz had expected. It was three or four stories high and nearly the length of a city block. Small dark windows punctuated strips of graying wall. Inside, she noticed that the windows still looked dark, and the walls just as dingy.

Liz arrived fifteen minutes early. She thought she should be there before the others, since it was at her behest that they were coming together. Jeremy must have felt some of this responsibility also, having volunteered the place, because he was already there when Liz walked in. He was examining some of the old, dusty equipment apparently abandoned there, and jumped when he heard Liz's footsteps.

"Hey Jeremy," she called out, still about a hundred yards from him. *The echo must have carried my footsteps,* she realized. "I didn't mean to scare you—sorry 'bout that!" The high ceilings and far-flung walls amplified her voice so that it sounded like she was shouting. She made a mental note to adjust to the environment.

"I know you didn't, Liz," Jeremy smiled and called back, his voice adjusted so that it reached Liz's ears at just the right decibel. "It's just kind of…freaky being in here alone."

"How long ago did you get here?" Liz asked.

"Oh, about ten minutes ago. I'd never actually been here before, and thought I should get here early in case there were cobwebs to brush off or anything." Gesturing around him, he added, "but I should have known that a pesticide maker's warehouse is the last place you'd find any insect life, even if it's been empty for twenty years!"

"That is pretty impressive," Liz said, now at the center of the floor, next to him.

"Yup. So are the rates of cancer and nervous system disease that have been conclusively linked to their products," he said. "But don't worry—the warehouse was never used for making the newer pesticides that I'm talking about. No, these were much less dangerous, and less *profitable*. Hence the emptiness of the place." He sighed. As he shook his head lightly a lock of brown hair fell over his hazel eyes. Liz had an urge to reach out and ruffle it back into place.

"Is that true?" Liz asked. "How do you know that?"

Jeremy laughed with a tinge of bitterness. "We all know it, at Pests Out. They use the cost-benefits ratios to teach fractions. We're taught that the benefits outweigh the costs. But that's because we're looking at it from the firm's perspective."

"And the kids are taught that the firm's perspective is *their* perspective," Liz finished Jeremy's statement for him. He smiled at her sadly but in friendship. "Yeah," he said.

"And if they or their family gets cancer or some other disease caused by the pesticides?" she asked.

"The company doctors never tell them. We've got one girl in my class with a lump in her breast you can *see* when she wears a tight shirt—they give her treatment and tell her it's a skin condition, like a big *wart* or something. I noticed that they gave her a raise at about the time the lump appeared, too—for 'perfect attendance' or some bullshit like that. She's got all the virtual reality games and whatever else she wants, and she's happy."

"Do you think she really is?" Liz asked seriously.

Jeremy paused. "I—"

The arrival of Nate and Coffeelover's Café Latte, as yet unrenamed, postponed his response. They looked pretty chummy, standing a little too close to each other as they halted at the threshold, squinting to adjust to the low light level. *The sun must be making an appearance outside,* Liz noted.

"Hi Liz!" Nate said, the two striding across the dusty floor. "And you must be…Jeremy," he continued, reaching out for Jeremy's hand.

"Hey Liz," Coffeelover's Café Latte said, only when she was directly in front of Liz. She spoke softly, something Liz had noticed about her immediately. "Hi Jeremy," she said, shaking his hand with much less force that Nate had put into the task. "My name's Coffeelov- um, sorry. I meant that my name is *Charlotte*." She smiled, shyly.

"Charlotte?" Liz said. "What a nice name!"

"As in Brontë?" Jeremy asked, still holding onto her hand, gazing at her high cheekbones and long curly blonde hair.

"Have you read her?" Charlotte asked excitedly.

"She's one of my favorites!" he replied, at last letting go of her hand.

How convenient, Liz thought as she inwardly groaned.

"So, just MapMaker and Sel aren't here yet," Liz stated, breaking whatever "moment" Jeremy and Charlotte may have been having.

"Sel?" Nate asked.

"Sills: Expert Litigators," Liz responded. "I took the liberty of abbreviating for her, for myself," she said.

"Though, we should probably call her by her full name when she gets here, unless she asks us to call her something different, right?" Charlotte said tentatively. The boys beamed at her, and Liz did another inward groan.

"Oh, yeah," she said, and forced a smile. *I guess it's not her fault these guys are fawning all over her,* she told herself. "So, is there any place to sit down around here, do you think?" Liz asked generally, glancing around.

"Funny you should ask that," Jeremy replied, "because just before you all got here I found…this." He walked around a bulky machine that towered above them to reveal a folding table with four metal chairs around it. "I had the foresight to wipe them down of their decades-old dust, too." He looked very pleased with himself. *He's so cute,* Liz thought. "And as for the two latecomers soon to be among us, I think I saw a solution in that office over there…." He jogged to an office about thirty feet away and returned wheeling two decrepit office chairs that screeched as if protesting their release from retirement. One had its faux leather skin torn in several long gashes where its cotton flesh poked out, the other bore a seat that uncannily resembled a deflated tire.

"Won't they be happy," Nate said with a grin. They sat.

"This is great," Liz lied, shifting in her seat, trying to get the most comfortable angle possible against the uncooperative metal.

"Yeah," said Charlotte, equally unconvincingly. "It's cozy." Liz appreciated the solidarity.

"So, has everyone read the play?" Nate asked, directing the question primarily at Liz and secondarily at the other two. All affirmed with nods or a "yes." They all looked toward the door at the sound of footsteps. Sills: Expert Litigators was making a beeline for the table.

"Hi. I'm Sills: Expert Litigators," she announced, waving to the table and eyeing the two empty seats, sizing them up, along with her new peers. "It's nice to meet you all."

There was an awkward pause in which the original four, self-renamed, could read each other's thoughts. "It's nice to meet you, Sills: Expert Litigators. I'm New York Gazette, out there, but in here, I call myself Nate, for Nate Hawthorne, whom I've always loved."

Sills: Expert Litigators smiled a little uncomfortably, and shook the hand Nate had stood to extend to her over the table.

"My parents and classmates call me Pests Out Manufacturer and

Distributors, but I like to go by Jeremy, when I can," Jeremy smiled and similarly rose to shake Sills: Expert Litigators' hand. "You can call me whichever you feel more comfortable with," he added.

How nice of him, Liz thought.

"And I'm Charlotte, also called Coffeelover's Café Latte." Charlotte reached her hand without rising, since she was close enough to do so.

"And of course, I know Gatelink," Sills: Expert Litigators said, nodding at Liz. "Uh, Liz."

"Whichever," Liz said, smiling graciously, following Jeremy's lead.

By the end of the introductions and Sills' taking a seat, MapMaker arrived and a new round of greetings commenced. MapMaker presented himself as "Adam, formerly known as MapMaker."

As dramatic as I remembered him, Liz mused. They all immediately wondered if the name issue would become a point of contention with Sills.

"So, has everybody read the play already?" Nate asked again, presumably for the benefit of the newcomers.

"Yes," they all said. Liz held her breath. They were going to discuss the script, *her* script. She knew she shouldn't take personally whether they like it or not, and that whether people liked it wasn't even the point, but she wanted them to like it. So she asked, "And…what'd you all think?"

Sills spoke up first. "Well, it's a little dramatic."

"But that's the point," Nate replied. "It doesn't have to be subtle. It doesn't have to be George Bernard Shaw. It *should* have the intensity of Ibsen. God knows, the real story does." After a pause he added, with less passion, "The *real* story always does. *I* should know. I work for a news-making machine."

"What do you mean?" Sills asked.

She's starting out easy, Liz thought recalling the interrogatory force of this law firm progeny.

"Do you guys read the papers much?" he started. "I'll generalize 'cos I know they all work the same way. The *actual* news, the *real* events, are sent to all the corporate sponsors for review before even being considered for publication. Whatever can't be spun to market one of their products, is tossed. It's deemed 'extraneous.' Anything that could be derogatory to a sponsor is of course eliminated, and covered up so other papers with rival sponsors can't get it. If there isn't enough to fill the pages, they make stuff up. 'Eighty-four-year-old woman on 9th and Broadway protected herself from a potential robbery yesterday with the help of Armand's Alert, and a lot of gusto. Elaine Grisho has been living alone in the housing development for the Old and Infirm for the last 22 years, and says she's never had this experience before. She caught only a glimpse of the potential assailant, but described him as....'" his voice trailed off, implying that the rest of the sentence was expendable.

"Is that a true story?" Charlotte asked naively.

Nate shook his head. "I wrote that one. It was the first one of mine they published. I was in sixth grade. Our assignment was to write a believable news story 'to highlight the usefulness of Armand's Alert.' Mine and a few others were chosen for the next day's paper. I felt proud, of course, when they told me, and my parents finally seemed to notice me and have something nice to say to me. But when I saw it there, the next day, on page 32 next to an article about an insurgence of killer ants right outside the city, which I would have believed before…it was the beginning of the end."

"And then you discovered Ibsen," Sills remarked insightfully.

"And then I discovered Ibsen," Nate confirmed. "And Dostoyevsky, and Orwell—I began to discover morality. And that what I was being trained to do, stank. In that place," he looked tortured, "the kids are taught that there's no difference between lies and truth, and it's all in service to a 'greater good'—serving the sponsors' interests, and thereby maintaining the solvency, and 'honor' of the firm. Can you believe they even use the word 'honor'? No one there even knows what it means. I think it was written into the by-laws way back when that this would be the line they fed to everybody. It must work, 'cos they keep doing it. And meanwhile we take courses on Effective Lying starting from third grade. You know, Liz, what you told me about what you learned about how teachers interact with students as per company guidelines,"—Nate looked at Liz as he said this. Liz noticed eyebrows go up on Sills and Jeremy. She must have forgotten to tell them. She'd have to remember to. "—made me start to analyze what was going on in my classroom even more. And I realized that the teachers were pitting us against each other, to come up with the best stories, the most believable stories, the most product-selling stories. It wasn't just the bonuses and the raises, but being 'cool' was defined for us as being able to spin, to manipulate, to lie." He paused again. "My friends, if you can call them that—friendship isn't encouraged as much as collaboration for optimal results—don't read books. They don't think for themselves, I sometimes think. They just do, make money, spend it. They could tell you the prices and upgraded characteristics of every teen-oriented commodity out there but couldn't give you an honest answer as to how they're feeling that day. I don't know if it's because they aren't aware enough, or because they can't remember how to talk without intention anymore." He looked at Sills. "*That's* the real story, in all its Ibsenesque glory. Or should I say, grotesqueness." Nate crossed his arms and slumped slightly in his seat, frowning.

"Wow," said Sills. "That *is* dramatic." Silence overtook the place.

"I...I know what you mean," Charlotte said to Nate softly. "Kind of. At least about the 'being cool' part." She paused. "I haven't really described this before to anyone, so I might ramble a bit—sorry," she said, looking around at all their faces. "But, at Coffeelovers' School, image is everything. What a person looks like, how she talks, even how she walks. The teachers tell us that presentation is the most important thing to the company, that it's the most important thing, period. We get grades on our appearance. We have classes on image and presentation. They start in second grade." She paused again. "They tell us that image is the only thing that counts in this world. It makes people willing and even happy to pay $15 for a $2 cup of coffee. It's the 'ultimate kind of power,' and it's this kind of control that we Coffeelovers kids are so fortunate to have the chance to have someday." Charlotte looked down at her hands, her fingers swarming over each other like snakes. "Everyone else seems to want it, at my school. They don't want anything else than exactly what Coffeelovers can give them, what it tell us we should want. I've been feeling like a retard for a long time, because I don't want what everyone else does. I've tried to convince myself to…but I can't."

"What *do* you want?" Sills asked, not gently.

Oh, turn it off, Liz thought, annoyed. She immediately caught herself and felt bad; Sills probably couldn't "turn it off," she knew.

"I don't know," Charlotte responded, looking lost, first at Sills, then at Liz. Liz nodded at her slowly, sympathetically. She considered reaching out and laying a hand on top of Charlotte's to comfort her. In Flagstaff she would have, since anyone else would have done it in such a moment. But here, she didn't feel confident enough.

"These things take time," Liz said simply.

"I thought the play," Adam broke in, smiling at Liz, "was terrific. As a work of art. You have a great eye for detail, Liz. I thought you gave the characters…flesh. Not just minds, but hearts, too—emotions. I could feel the struggles of the Ramirez parents; I could see my own parents or grandparents—if I knew them—rationalizing to themselves but feeling dull and wrong on the inside. I really enjoyed it, uncomfortable though it made me feel."

Liz smiled in return. "Thank you, Adam. That means a lot to me."

Jeremy smiled too. "I second all that," he said. "When I was reading it, I felt like I could see it in my head, like with all good writing. It made me…angry, and…sad, but I felt really good afterwards. Like…I wasn't nuts. At least, not as much as I'd been feeling." He laughed.

"It was…cathartic for me, when I wrote it," Liz said. "I hoped it might provide that for some other people too—if there was anyone else like me out there, here." She smiled to each of the pairs of eyes around her. "I'm so glad that…there are."

"I'm glad you found us, Liz," Nate said. "I'm glad you found me."

Sills: Expert Litigators had been looking troubled for the last several minutes. Finally, she spoke up, "Um, this is hard for me. I know that you've all 'renamed yourselves.' And I think that's great, I really do. But…all my life I've been drilled in the legal repercussions of breaking the rules. I know coming here would get me in trouble with the Board at my firm, but…I feel like I could plead ignorance, say I thought it was something else—I'd have an out. If I change my name—I'd lose that out. I—I can't do that yet. I think I will, someday, but…it's hard. It was hard for me to come here. I do have respect for rules; I do think we need rules. But…I was suffocating." She stopped, her head hung low. She looked ashamed.

"Sills: Expert Litigators," Liz said softly. "You don't have to explain. They've given us all different…hang-ups." Liz was surprised at how it felt to say that. "We're glad you're here, and we don't mind calling you by a really long name." She laughed, and so did Sills, who looked at her again. "Right, guys?" Liz directed to the other four.

"Of course," Nate said.

"You know, before we get to the play itself," Liz said, "I want to tell you guys a little more of what people told me in free America, and the lessons I learned just from being there, about what peace is like, and how they work to have and keep it, over there. I might have told some of this stuff to you already, so sorry if I repeat, but I think you'd all be interested."

"You know Liz, you should probably write a play about free America, about what it's like there. I'd love to act that out," Jeremy said quickly.

"I think you're right," Liz said. "All things in their time. That's one of the things that I learned over there, that you'll never learn from your parents or your schools, or anything, over here." She paused. "I want to tell you what it's like to sit in the middle of Nature, how it makes you feel awed and humbled like nothing else can.…"

They read the first two scenes of the play that day. It was exhilarating for Liz to hear the words she'd written spoken and brought to life by her new friends. She felt so happy listening to them, being part of something she so believed in, that she didn't want the afternoon to end. But by 8:00, she had to agree with her new friends that she was exhausted too. "All good things must come to an end, just like all bad things do," she said as they all left the warehouse together.

"One for your next piece," Nate said.

CHAPTER 20
NEW BEGINNINGS
(WHAT ELSE, IN THE LAST CHAPTER?)

The group had decided to meet again next Saturday, same time, same place, and to feel free to keep in touch over e-mail until then, if they felt inclined. On Sunday, Liz read, and started her first journal. She felt free enough to do it now. She felt "genuine." She stared at the word in her paper notebook after she wrote it, surprised. She wasn't sure what she meant by it, but it seemed right. It felt right. She wrote down her feelings in her paper notebook, and in a letter to Patricia and some other friends in Flagstaff she was trying to keep. "I feel different now," she wrote to Patricia. "When I left Flagstaff to return here, I didn't know what I was going to do. But now I know. Nothing has changed, yet everything is different. I feel like I'm getting control back, over my mind, over my life. Over myself."

As she went into the week, Liz found that she minded things less. The vacant looks in her classmates, the hard ambition that occasionally took its place, meant less to her. She forgave. She even forgot, or at least, it felt like it sometimes. Alone, in her bedroom at night, Liz would close her eyes not to lose her consciousness but to heighten it, and she would forget everything that had ever bothered her about the world. She would see herself playing as a child, having fun; she could *feel* like it had never changed. With the ability to forget, she could remember now things she thought she had lost forever. She had heard about this practice called "forgetting" out West, but never thought she would be willing it herself someday.

Small miracles began to happen. Her mother smiled at her. It was just once, and just for a fleeting moment, but she had looked Liz right in the eyes when she did it, unexpectedly, during dinner. Mrs. Jones had been sitting down to eat with her daughter at least once a week lately. Still the three of them had not sat all together for a long time, if they ever had, but it filled Liz with hope to share a frozen lamb dinner with her mother.

For the next Saturday meeting, Liz brought her Flagstaff clothes with her. The other members—several of whom had professed an interest in seeing the strange "un-ad clothes"—were mesmerized. As Liz had been, they were taken in by the meditative plainness, the stillness, of the garments.

"Go ahead," Liz said to Sills, holding up a solid red shirt to her shoulders to see how it looked. "Put it on. You can change in one of the old offices or in the bathroom. Here, let me get you a pair of jeans to go with it."

Sills hesitated, but didn't need to be asked twice. She returned wearing a serene expression to match her new attire. "God, it's like...Valium!" she remarked. Luckily, Liz had some shirts big enough for the boys to wear too. That day they rehearsed scenes two through five in the clothes of a different culture.

Rehearsals continued for many more weeks with no talk of the future of the play. Liz had seen a few more readers on the trains, and lost only one, who seemed to be very shy. She grew bolder, too, and ventured to the few bookstores there were in the city, looking for potential recruits. She always had bought her books on-line, and was surprised at how much traffic there was in stores for the written word. Of course, the hours of operation at such shops were very limited; profits couldn't justify keeping them running more than a few hours a day, she figured. *Even in the Underground, business is business,* Liz thought ironically.

Liz was able to spread the word about what she knew and what she'd learned by singling out readers as likely to be open, curious, dissatisfied minds. She knew there might be many people who'd be receptive that she wouldn't find, but she didn't see how she could help that. Whenever someone in the burgeoning group told her how glad they were they'd found her and the group, Liz resolved to be content with what she *could* do.

One Saturday, at their seventh meeting, Liz chose to break the tranquility of their times together. The group had grown to fifteen, thanks to the outreaching by Liz and the other members, and they had gotten through the entirety of the play several times. Lines were almost completely memorized, props and costumes had begun to be injected, and the acting was getting more and more fun to watch. Some improvements had been made to the script, also—shrinking or stretching of dialogue, smoothing or roughening of lines, all of which Liz took in stride as best she could and, after initial internal resistance, admitted were very good changes. The play was becoming professional—or, at least what Liz imagined professional must be for a play. It would soon be aching for an audience.

As Greg—a new member whose legal name was Fisette and Forst Ice Creams of America—pulled the makeshift curtain he had gleefully rigged to a highly situated pipe, Liz took advantage of the moment. The curtain's fall signaled the end of a scene, and in this case, the dramatic finale. Jones, a little boy in the story who had been newly named Homatrix Reconstruction Services, Inc., had just come to fully understand his parents' new relationship to him, and looked tragically to stage right, at a framed picture of himself and his parents playing lovingly on their lawn with the dog they were no longer "advised" to keep. As they always did, the group clapped for themselves and each other as soon as the curtain began to sway from the beam. Some members had taken to yelling, "Bravo! Encore!" which they'd read used to be common after a performance.

Liz clapped too, but as soon as the sound subsided called out, her hands cupped around her mouth to carry her voice from where she stood at a distance to view the whole stage. "Hey guys? I want to ask you about something. All of you." Liz walked to meet them, and a huddle formed in the center of the room. Shafts of sunlight shot overhead, the intersections in brilliant contrast to the rest of the warehouse; Carrie, student at Alpha Omega Cleaning Supplies, Inc., had brought a power-washer to dispel some of the darkness over all of their heads. The industrial strength halogen lamps Nate brought in worked better, though.

"Um," Liz began uncertainly, "something I mentioned to you all when we began this…adventure." Fourteen pairs of eyes looked curiously into hers, trying to gauge the nature of what she was about to say. "I mentioned that…part of why I wrote the play, why I was compelled to write it, was to try to reach other kids, especially kids younger than us, who are only starting to get lost." She paused, hoping against reason that someone else would read her mind and pick up there, so she could avoid being the bearer of hard news. "Well," Liz went on when the miracle didn't happen, "it's not totally ready yet, but it's in pretty good shape right now. It's in great shape, in fact! And, I think it's time we started thinking about…an audience."

Charlotte's eyes widened. "An *audience?*"

"It was always my idea to put it on—" Liz said.

Sills: Expert Litigators broke in. "*Your* idea, yes. And in the beginning, when none of us were thinking too seriously about it, it sounded fine. But…do you realize what kind of a risk that would put us all in? Put our parents in?"

"Uh, yeah," Greg interjected. "I gotta agree. They are kinda dickwads, but they could get in like, serious shit, for something they didn't even do. It wouldn't be fair.

"But *we* wouldn't be the ones *punishing* them," Akiro said, on of the newest members. "That's not our intention, so how could it be our fault, if it happened?"

Sills, exasperated, snapped back, "Because we *know* it would happen. We know it would happen if we got caught at this stuff, even this stuff we're doing here. But this—this is safe. We're not putting ourselves out there, in here; we're not sticking our necks out, saying, 'Catch us!'"

Silence followed this outburst. A few people drifted away to nearby chairs donated for the Warehouse activities. They mostly rubbed fingers against their foreheads or chins, lost in unpleasant internal debates. At last, Jeremy said, "I agree that it would be a good thing to do—it would be something *right*. I think the possibility of getting caught is the only thing that's holding us back."

Sills snorted. "Brain surgeon," she muttered.

"Is that really necessary?" Keisha said coolly. Keisha was the newest member but had quickly become one of Liz's favorites. She was the most mature one of them all, in Liz's opinion—herself included.

Sills looked momentarily embarrassed. "Sorry," she said to no one in particular. *It's the training,* Liz imagined she must have wanted to add.

"I agree with Jeremy," Keisha proclaimed loudly. "Just to be sure, maybe we should take a vote on whether that one issue is the only objection, or whether there are any others."

"We should do it by secret ballot," Sills said quickly. In response to the rest of the group's stares, she said simply, "I always thought that would be a cool way to take a vote."

"It couldn't hurt," Keisha said generously, scoring yet another point in Liz's book. "Do you have paper, Sills: Expert Litigators?"

The "secret vote" was a resounding yes. The only fear was that of getting caught and costing their parents everything they had that they valued. Anna, another new member, suggested a vote to assess how many people felt ready to take that risk right now, and to start forming a plan. These results were not as conclusive. The outcome was 10-5 in favor of not being ready now if ever. Liz stifled a sigh.

"There's no need to rush things, I guess," she lied. "I just wanted to see how we were all feeling about this. Maybe we could all give it some thought. I know it could be risky, but if we play it well enough it doesn't have to be. And just think what a relief it could have been to you when you were younger, and even now for that matter, to know that you weren't the only one seeing things differently, to know the truth."

Some members nodded. Several looked uncomfortable.

"But I want to say again how glad I am that I found you, all of you. It's been so wonderful getting to know you all, hearing your stories, sharing our anger and our dreams, and working artistically together. Even if we never go public, I feel like this is the best thing that I've ever done."

She smiled, and her smile was returned. "And I'd say we're all pretty tired...of hearing me talk, huh?" Liz laughed. As the group began to mill around, sharing private jokes in groups of two or three, laughing at goof-ups during the performance, Keisha walked to Liz, who was struggling to keep her smile, and touched her on the arm. Liz looked up at her, startled. Liz had told the members about the gestures of communication people used out West, but none had been used among them until now. Keisha smiled, and said softly, "They'll come around. I know they will. It'll happen, Liz. Your dream is a good one."

*****

George sounded surprised. "Is anything wrong, Gatelink Computing and Software, Incorporated?" he said.

"I just…wanted to talk to you. We haven't talked in a while. Wait— did you just call me Gatelink?"

"Yes," he replied evenly.

"Is someone else there?" Liz asked instinctively.

"Yes. I have a friend over. Now isn't really a good time…."

Liz heard some metallic object clatter to the floor in the background; then a laugh and a female voice call out, "Oops! Sorry!" and laugh again. The laugh was high and sloppy. *Ms. Miller,* Liz thought.

"Oh, well…okay," she stammered into the receiver. "I'm…sorry about that."

"You said it's not urgent, right?" George said. "Can we discuss this later?" Liz noticed that his words were slurred slightly.

"Oh, yeah, sure. Of course. Well, I'll just…see you later."

"I'll see you in class Monday, Gatelink Computing and Software. We can talk about your *test score* then." The receiver clicked, and Liz put down the phone. She tried to picture what George must be saying right now to the busty Ms. Miller. Would she have asked why a student was calling George at home, or would she not have even noticed, or care enough to ask? George would be telling her that "due to Gatelink Computing and Software, Inc.'s recent fall from valediction," she was seeking assistance in the class work in a big way, trying to get her edge back. She was going kind of nuts about it, actually, but he just felt so sorry for her that he didn't report her for harassing him at home for help. "She's really a smart girl," she could hear him saying. "It's really a shame. I hope she can get herself out of this slump before it really damages her career with the firm." And then he would kiss Ms. Miller like he'd kissed Liz that day at the waterfall and comforted her. Part of Liz wanted that George back—wanted that part of him back again. She knew that part of him was still in him, but he was exploring a different part now. And she couldn't predict which he would decide he liked better. She had to forget about him, for now, and any possibility that he would help her with her plans.

Because she was making plans. In the three days since the last meeting and the disappointing referendum, Liz had received messages from all four of the other dissenters who'd voted to go forward now. She'd heard from one person already whose mind she'd changed with her little speech afterwards, too. "They will come around," they'd all echoed Keisha's sentiment. "Let's start planning now. I want to help other kids to know the truth about life, too, to know their options, before it's too late for them like it is for my parents."

To reach other kids on a mass level, in a way that wasn't too risky to the group, would be tough. Liz had hoped she could count on George's help, that when he saw how there were other people here too who believed in what she did, what part of him still must, that he would finally join her. He knew much more about how the corporate schools worked than she did, and how they could discreetly disseminate information about what they were doing, how things really are run here, and the play. "We have a right to know the true history of how we got here, of how things got to be the way they are, and what's been given up to get here—what we've been denied, and are denying ourselves," Anna had written to Liz in her e-mail of support. *George was never denied these things, though,* Liz thought. *Maybe that's why he can't understand what I'm doing. What we're doing.* Liz e-mailed her five co-conspirators and suggested they meet on Thursday to brainstorm.

On Wednesday, a batch of letters arrived from Flagstaff. Liz had told them all about the play, the group, and the warehouse; they wrote and told her how proud of her they all were. *It's nice to hear it from someone,* Liz thought as she read the letters. They also asked how George was doing; he hadn't written back in some time. The letters said that everyone there still remembered Liz, and missed her; they hoped she would come back to visit soon, and would remember that she always had a home in Flagstaff. "By the end, you were planting and picking just like one of us," Tyrone wrote in his letter. "Even aside from how much we liked your good manners and ready laugh, we can always use more helping hands!" Liz smiled at these words. Mr. and Mrs. Robinson wrote, "Liz, please let the other courageous young people in your underground group know that whatever happens there, they (and their families) will be welcomed here in Free America, if they're willing to work a little with their hands and go computerless."

It's much more than computers they'd have to do without, Liz thought. *But still, it's nice of them to remind me of it. I think I will pass this on tomorrow.*

So she did, at the start of their meeting up at the warehouse, which all of them had free access to by now.

"Thanks Liz," Anna said, "and I look forward to meeting your family there someday"—Liz smiled at her use of the word "family" to describe them—"but we're not gonna need to run anywhere. Not if we do things my way." Ana had found a loophole in the system. She went to school at a pager company, the largest in the Northeast. She found out how to send mass pages to Progeny Programs in a totally untraceable way. They had their safe means to communication, their route to disseminate. They just needed to wait for the rest of the group to come around now, and have a plan ready to implement when they did.

"Anna, you're a genius!" Liz exclaimed.

Anna merely beamed back at Liz. "It's gonna happen, Liz. We gotta be ready."

*****

The group had spent the next several hours discussing what the initial pager message should say, whether it should be directed to all students or just certain grades or certain companies, and whether they should try to select out readers. Not much resolution was found, but issues were explored, prodded, overturned, tossed around and generally manhandled. It was a good beginning.

That evening, when Liz delivered her customary hug and "I love you" to her mother, another beginning occurred. Mrs. Jones said quietly, "Me too." Liz, her back turned and already several feet away, stopped dead in her tracks. When she whipped around, losing all pretense of detachment, her mom was more engrossed in her computer monitor than Liz ever remembered seeing her. Liz smiled and left her mother's home office. It's true that she might have imagined what had just happened, that it might have been wishful thinking, but she didn't doubt that it was real, and that it would happen again.

That night as Liz laid in bed she let her mind walk backwards over the last many months, to the seed of an idea that had set off avalanches in her life. And now that the massive towers of snow had fallen, things were clear, and she could tell others what she saw. One thing she saw was herself, years from now, in the free states, helping people readjust from their decades of being playthings of the "bottom line." She would be like Harriet Tubman and the Underground Railroad that she'd read about. She saw her mother there, maybe her father; maybe even her grandparents if she could find them or anything about them. Another thing she saw was the play put on, she knew not where, striking people in their hearts, softening them, opening them, challenging them. Life wasn't easy but it was theirs, it could be theirs, again, if they only chose to want it to be. She saw herself watching a curtain fall at the end of the play, feeling a thing that moved through the audience like a tidal wave, huge and yearning for something above, something elemental and important as the moon. She saw herself smile with a happiness that was unpossessable because it wasn't hers alone, but that she would keep, forever.

Printed in the United States
22141LVS00004B/151-159

9 781413 732870